FROM MOUNTAINS OF ICE

Lorina Stephens

Best wishes.

Published by Five Rivers

Published by Five Rivers Chapmanry, 704 Queen Street, P.O. Box 293, Neustadt, ON N0G 2M0, Canada www.5rivers.org

From Mountains of Ice, Copyright © 2009 by Lorina Stephens

Cover Art & Design, Copyright © 2009 by Lorina Stephens

All rights reserved. Without limiting the rights under copyright reserved above, no part of this publication may be reproduced, stored in or introduced into a retrieval system, or transmitted in any form or by any means (electronic, mechanical, photocopying, recording or otherwise), without the prior written permission of both the copyright owner and the publisher of the book.

Publisher's note: This book is a work of fiction. Names, characters, places and incidents either are the products of the author's imagination or are used fictitiously, and any resemblance to actual persons living or dead, events, or locales is entirely coincidental.

Manufactured in the United States of America
Published in Canada

First Edition

Library & Archives Canada/Bibliothèque & Archives Canada Data Main entry under title:

From Mountains of Ice
Stephens, Lorina

ISBN 978-0-9739278-5-6

    1.   Title

Title and chapter headings set in Niagara Engraved
Footers and by-line set in Corbel
Text set in Book Antiqua

As always
For Gary

Genius Cucullatus, Genii Cucullati (pl.) [L genius, deity of generation or birth, guardian spirit; cucullus, hood fastened to cloak or coat].
A Dictionary of Celtic Mythology
James MacKillop

When the souls of the oppressed
Fight in the troubled air that rages, who can stand?
William Blake

PROLOGUE

He tried very hard to remain still, to be strong, project the image of the Royal Prince he was. That scream in his throat had a life of its own. He wanted to set it free, let it encompass the room.

How could she?

He allowed himself to scan the chamber – the afternoon sunlight so heavy where it poured through the open terrace door, the spiral of motes there, Prima Violina Pallavicini di Negli from Almarè where she stood murmuring in radiance with his father, Il Principe Aldo Valerio; the attendants padding about their business innocuously as possible; the ladies in waiting with faces of marble; the courtiers frozen like frescoes; the priest with his acolytes hovering behind the doctor where he sat on the edge of the Royal bed and held the withered, fragile wrist of his mother, La Principessa Viviana Pontiaro ni Valerio. And there, beyond them all, a lurid form in the shadows, the bone-speaker from the Temple of Nerezza, hooded, cloaked in red, silent as loneliness. Cucullatus. The one who would come before the priest to guide Carmelo's mother from life to death.

She seemed transparent to him now, gossamer and mist. She barely breathed, her face composed.

He felt the pressure of Sylvio di Danuto's hand on his shoulder. "You should speak with her now, Carmelo."

"I can't."

"If you don't you will regret it the rest of your life."

He felt Sylvio nudge his shoulder, urging him forward out of the shadows.

"Come with me." He winced at the plea.

"This is a moment you should have with her alone."

"Please. Don't leave me now." He wanted to turn toward his father's Minister of National Security, seek out the solace of their friendship. But the man taught him the mark of a good leader and statesman was his ability to refrain from self-indulgence.

His mother opened her eyes at that moment, turned her face toward him. Drawn, he found himself at her bedside, the marble hard under his knees where he knelt by her bed, his fingers lacing through hers – she was so cold –his tears hot and immediate despite every lesson and every self-imposed restriction.

"I have to go, Carmelo," she whispered.

He pressed the back of her hand to his mouth, trying hard not to sob, to be strong. But she was going. She was leaving. She wouldn't be back; the only remnant of her would be the bone effigy of her in the family shrine, this after her body was given to Nerezza, that greedy goddess of death that was his nation's patron.

He watched his mother's attention shift up and behind him. Sylvio was there he realized. Sylvio who had always been there guiding, teaching, offering friendship and advice beyond what was required of a Royal Minister, filling the gaps left by his father who was parent to a nation and not just a son.

"Watch over him, Sylvio," she said. He watched her pause. He couldn't tell if Sylvio made any gesture. "Promise me."

"I promise," he heard Sylvio whisper.

She smiled and her attention returned to him. "Remember who you are and what you have learned." He nodded, watched her relax. He heard the rustle of cloth, felt the presence of the bone-speaker next to him, the one named as cucullatus because of her ability to speak with the ancestors. A hand now upon his mother's shoulder, the hand of what should have been an ordinary woman, but for the red cloth that hung over her wrist. With all his heart he wanted to stop this, to keep his mother here in the now, not as a distant voice, but no, she closed her eyes and then lay utterly still.

"She has gone, mio Principe," he heard the doctor say.

His father gave a strangled groan, coughed. He could hear his father's footsteps, felt his hand upon his head. "I –" He coughed again, "I'll send for you in my chambers. I must address the people."

"Papa –"

And in the distance his mother's voice, disembodied, as gentle as morning.

"I will send for you. I promise." His father paused. "Sylvio –"

"At once, Principe."

He heard them leaving. All of them. His father. Sylvio. The courtiers, the dignitaries who had been close to her. They all left, even the cucullatus. He bent over her bed, inconsolable, alone with the voices of the dead.

CHAPTER 1

Sylvio knew he should be grateful. As far as he could see wealth lay upon the land, rich in this autumn haze. He should be thankful there was grain to harvest, that mares foaled and raced, even now as he watched, across the plains that faded to the purple rise of foothills and then mountains. On his ancestors' bones, he was grateful. It was just that a man could grow suspicious. A man could imagine. Given enough reason a man could think anything.

He unstrung the yew stave and left off tillering, his attention caught by his stallion, Ibacci. The chestnut horse sped arrow-swift across the meadows, in his wake a herd of mares and their foals. The stallion exemplified all the Simare horses represented – sturdy, hardy, quick and sure. The yearlings would fetch a good price at market in Reena. Shortly the drive would start. There would be brisk haggling for the finest horses on the continent. There would be grossi silver coins from Almarè merchants, and grossi would pay off the increasing weight of taxes and help compensate the trade restrictions imposed by Breena when again they sat to discuss the flow of goods. As surely they would discuss, even dictate.

Sylvio knew this. That grossi would be enough this time he doubted. Money went only so far when dealing with such people. And there was that new tax his prince levied. He didn't want to think of that now. Not now. Not when there was this hope, this promise after so much bitterness and betrayal.

Ten years!

Had it been so long? Ten years since Aldo's stroke and his son had come to power. Ten years since Sylvio left Reena amid rumour and rancour. And even after all this time he had no proof of his suspicions, nothing but the instinct of his gut and the caution of his wife's gift; Aldo had suffered more than a stroke. There was some sinister purpose behind Carmelo's ascendancy to the throne, and it was because of Sylvio's inquiries, his ever-so-diligent mind, that Carmelo reacted and banished Sylvio from court.

He could be wrong. There was always that hope.

He wished for hope as he watched his wife, Aletta, below him in the fields, watched as she tied sheaves with deft movements. She straightened from stooking the sheaf with others, her hands on her back, arching; likely she groaned from strain. Other figures were there with her, men and women of the village, all of them bent to the task of bringing in the barley. Like the horses they were a hardy lot, quick to fly, but never flee. They would never flee. Not these rough, vibrant people. Like his wife, these villagers did their share to ensure the well-being of each other. They spun together. They planted together. Whatever skills they had were shared with the village. There was no other way, and Sylvio could think of no other way. Time could do much to change a man's perspective.

Aletta raised her gaze, scanning the fields as he watched her, following a similar path his own had taken, and he wondered if her thoughts strayed in the same direction, if she, also, wrestled with a sense of foreboding despite the bounty upon the land. And as he had, she sought out the figure of her spouse. Across the distance he caught her gaze, held it, felt once more that ineffable bond with her. Air and earth. Stone and sky. Theirs was a song that carried over the fields and Sylvio felt its benediction, felt his apprehensions ease. Surely this beauty would not be blotted from the land. Surely, he thought, and he lifted his gaze to the landscape, to the rolling plains that stepped down and down to the sea beyond the horizon, to the villages dotted here and there, and then turned, slowly, so he could see the mountains at his back. Immense they were, purple above the tree-line and then capped with snow where they pierced a sky so clear and blue a man could fall into it. All that was his world sat in the shadow of the mountains that curved like a scythe from the south to the east. All was governed by them. Rain, trade, safety and communication. All depended on the mountains of ice. Without them Breena to the north would surely overrun Simare rather than dance in a carefully orchestrated economic manoeuvre designed for political ends.

At that he turned again to the possibility of trade talks, of the threat those Breenai still posed, out there beyond the mountains, plotting his ancestors knew what. Like the mountains themselves they were. An immensity instinctive in the bones and never really known. Despite the sanctions they imposed, aye, despite the sanctions, Sylvio was sure there was more to those Breenai than anyone imagined. Under the threat of increasing economic and political pressures there were some Simari who fled through those mountains, unable to afford passage around the isthmus and the continent to refuge in Almarè, the country to the west of the mountains that shared the peninsula with Simare, and the pressures from the north in Breena. He wished them well, those pilgrims to a new life. He wished them peace and prosperity.

Indeed the past years had been hard. There was reason enough to flee, but he stayed, Aletta and he. He was sure he would always stay. There was too much of this land in his heart for him to leave. It was there in the villagers bringing in the harvest. It was there in the stave of yew under his hand.

This stave of yew was something he knew. This he could coerce, cajole into something of beauty and value to his village and himself. Once he had encompassed more, shouldered more, had the weight of command and government and actions that dealt in very real human lives, and very real human deaths. Once. Not so long ago. With a different prince, in another life.

Again he returned to the stave, his fingers lingering over the pale slivers of bone he'd laminated between layers of yew. Not just any bone there. The tibia of Vincenze's sister. He felt like a ghoul, despite the respect he'd gained as one of the rare few bowyers who could make the legendary arcossi. This was a skill he didn't seek. It sought him. And still he didn't understand how it was the dead could whisper to him, sigh in the background of his mind like whispers lost in the chatter of fall leaves.

He traced the line of her bone, like a pale silver thread gleaming between layers of yew, feeling her spirit stir, aware of his reverence for the ancestors that watched over them all and hoping they knew it was out of love for them and this land that he plied his trade.

Beware!

He jerked his hand away, heart pounding. What was this? He glanced around, seeking the person who spoke. Alone. He was alone here in the bow-yard.

He shuddered, backed away from the unfinished bow, convinced he imagined the voice. Even at the best of times he didn't like working the arcossi. Now even less. This bow proved difficult, the laminations fussy, the bones of Vincenze's sister awakening sooner than the last time when he'd fashioned a bow for her brother. It had been at Vincenze's insistence her bones were dedicated to the bow-shop. The more who heard her voice the better, Vincenze said.

Gods! What had he become?

A ghoul indeed, he was sure, that he should handle the dead in this fashion, work their bones into deadly grace. He didn't like being what he was. This wasn't part of the order of the world, he was sure.

But still he had this boon. To him it seemed more a bane.

At least when Ministro of National Security he dealt with tangibles. This! This was close to abomination, he was sure. And he'd not asked for this ability. He'd not wanted it.

He rubbed his jaw, let go of a breath.

But a man had to do something with his life when he found it dissolving. Stripped of his position in government, stripped of title, land, he found himself in the embrace of the very villagers over whom he'd had governance. And they, in turn, found him a place. He was grateful. Indeed a man had to be grateful, for they risked much in accepting him into their fold. Il Principe Carmelo had not been impressed with Sylvio's inquiries. Ten years ago.

Carefully, he again touched the bow, lingering over the bone lamination.

Beware, Sylvio! The gods delight in play.

This is too soon, he thought. And he wondered at the warning. Wondered what it could mean. He'd done everything in his power to remain in the background, to draw no attention, to prove to his Prince he was of no danger. He should have been able to reason with Carmelo. He had been the boy's mentor.

Again he reached for the bow.

He's watching you.

He jerked back his hand, truly alarmed now. Who watched?

He glanced around.

Fool! Love can be hate!

Even across the small distance, without his contact, Vincenze's sister spoke, her bones vibrating so he thought the laminations would give way again. The bow settled. The voice gone.

He wiped the sweat suddenly beading his brow.

Carmelo? Is that who watches? What threat could he, Sylvio, pose to the Throne here in Danuto, without influence, without power?

Love can be hate? Indeed it could, but what reason had Carmelo to hate him? It had not always been so under the father, Aldo. There had been trust there. There had been friendship. He had been part of Aldo's extended family, a guide for the son, Carmelo. Carmelo, who had grieved silently, bitterly, for his dead mother. Who had been caught trying to sever a finger from her corpse with the jewelled dagger he always wore.

Peace, he thought, reaching out to the bow again. Be still.

He had the impression of ripples receding. A pool become placid.

What was a man to think? What was a man to do? Once he would have had no reason for caution. He would have known what to do. But, then, he'd been another man when he'd started his career in Reena, full of the confidence and arrogance only youth can truly enjoy. He'd sought glory, and thereby honour through the accolades proximity to privilege granted, before the weight of decisions and the repercussions of actions made a man cautious. Before honour became bitterest gall. Before he'd been banished by the son who had claimed the crown and since then found himself pursuing a simpler dream, a quieter life. Ten years ago, and to him still yesterday.

Again he lifted the obsidian scraper onto the heel of his hand, approached the stave carefully and shaved down the heartwood, delicately; it took only slight modifications at this point to tiller the bow into a weapon of perfection. He used to be a wielder of weapons. Now he was a maker. He used to be a maker of decisions. Now he was a deliberator. For a few moments he drew the black blade across the wood, stood back when one of his apprentices joined him in the open air. Sylvio looked over at the young lad, no more than fifteen years at best and already showing signs of being an adept.

"Well, boy?"

The lad all but twitched with excitement. "Vincenze's back."

Sylvio scanned the village, chiding himself that he had not seen Vincenze's approach. His shop had a clear vantage of tidy squares of homes that stepped down the hillside, all of them tiled and constructed of good Simare stone. Withy trellises bowed over the walkways, heavy with grapes. At the centre of the village was the well and the town square, around which grew a lattice work of gardens riotous with flowers. It seemed a frivolity but for the bees they attracted.

Throughout these trappings of the village were the people with whom he'd lived since finding himself distanced from the political centre of his country. Leonora there, broad and gentle, with her boys and one shining daughter, washing clothes at the stone tubs. There Tulio, the old patriarch where he sat in the shade of his orange tree, holding court with the young people and teaching sciences. And over the withy fence, in an arbour of wisteria Donato with that sloe-eyed Pina who was sure to be his undoing and joy. Beyond all this, set at a respectful distance, rose the modest temple to Nerezza, Her grove of trees and biers, ossuaries and silence enclosed in a brick wall.

But nowhere could he see Vincenze. Impatient, he asked, "Where? Is he well?"

"He's in the shop. He has sacks and sacks of spider silk. He's well, yes, Maestro Sylvio."

Sylvio set aside the scraper and hurried along the path to the shop, the boy in tow.

"He says it's good silk, Maestro. He says he found lots. That means we'll be able to make angeli strings again, eh, Maestro? Doesn't it? And it means the land's well, right? That must be right or else those spiders," the boy shuddered, "wouldn't be weaving such big webs, would they? They're awfully finicky, eh, Maestro? It must mean things are okay?"

Sylvio waved the boy to silence as he entered the door of the workshop, cursing his blindness after being in the bright sunlight. He could hear a babble of voices in front of him, discern bulky shapes.

"Oh, Vincenze, Vincenze, we're here," the boy shouted. "Maestro Sylvio's come!"

"Give over," Sylvio growled and the boy shut his mouth. To gentle his words he ruffled the boy's hair. "Go on. Go do something useful."

By now Sylvio's eyes adjusted to the change in light and he could see Vincenze surrounded by the other bowyers, in the centre of the commotion a ring of children tugging and pulling. The large workshop was filled near to overflowing. For a moment Sylvio feared this pandemonium might upset a table where one of his apprentices had left the work of laminating human bone to a maple core for an arcosso. That particular bowyer's husband died in a skirmish with the Breenai, a skirmish, which according to officials, never occurred. Such work was precious, sometimes years in the making. Thankfully, one of the crowd shooed people away from the table. Sylvio breathed a little easier, although he glanced rapidly over the walls where bows and staves were shelved, arrows bundled, and terra cotta funereal urns of bones sat on the floor.

Assured all was safe, his attention returned to the crowd. Vincenze un-slung his bow, a graceful arc of bone and sinew that had been made upon his sister's death. It had taken two years to fabricate, the first from her bones. Sylvio wondered how it fared in the field. Wondered what she said to her brother, if she spoke at all.

He caught Vincenze's attention and the man smiled grandly, white teeth in a broad, tanned face. His riding leathers were powdered with the dust of the road and the slack in his belt showed signs of haste and little time for meals. There were no new rents in his jupon, and for that, at least, Sylvio was grateful.

"Oh-ho, Maestro!" Vincenze said, "I've brought bounty!" He turned to the children. "Let me go now. I have to see that old brute over there."

The children giggled and parted, grinning up at Vincenze and then looking in Sylvio's direction. Their grins evaporated. Their laughter died.

"See what you've done, you old reprobate," Vincenze said, crossing to Sylvio and embracing him heartily. "It's good to see you."

"And you," Sylvio replied. He held Vincenze at arm's length, feeling the hardness of the man's arms. "You took your time."

"Oh, aye, Ministro, but I've news aplenty."

Sylvio flinched at the old use of title. "Then come. We'll go join Aletta for bread."

Vincenze raised a brow. "Don't trust what I have to say?"

"Always. But I want Aletta to hear your news."

"Ha. As I said. I'm to be brought before the village strega. She'll curse me if I lie." He grinned warmly, broadly, but Sylvio always knew when Vincenze attempted to spare him. People didn't live this closely and not know.

Together, they left the bow-shop for Sylvio's home where bread, wine and soft, new cheese were gathered, and from there headed down through the village. As they descended the streets people hailed, eager for gossip, eager for news. Despite his impatience Sylvio paused, passed pleasantries, watching as Vincenze deftly skirted revealing anything of import. At last they broke out onto the fields where Aletta and the others still laboured in the golden barley.

She stood, tying a sheaf tucked under her arm. Her red skirts shifted in the light breeze, stray wisps of dark hair fluttering over her tanned face. Still Sylvio was enchanted by her, still after all this time. She wasn't what could be called beautiful, but she was striking with those broad cheekbones and wide, carved lips. Her eyes were like obsidian they were so dark and could be as harsh at times when she flared to anger. Compact was how he thought of her, a neat, compact package. She had been treated with awe when he served as Minister of National Security in Reena. And it was because of her abilities he had been forewarned of the betrayal of his Prince.

Not for the first time he wondered what the children would have been like could she have had them. Sturdy, like her, all of them with that uncanny ability she had that was the very reason she remained barren. She tried to explain it to him once. He didn't understand, but he loved her all the same.

She looked up from her work, her voice cascading into laughter, husky and deep, when she saw them approach. "So my lover and his lackey come to ply me with drink, food and rustic manners." She set her hands on her hips. "Try, my sweet men, oh please do try." She pushed her forearm over her brow. "I hope you like the perfume of sweat."

Laughter ran through those within earshot.

Sylvio smiled and pecked her on the cheek. She looked at him archly, seized his face between her rough hands and kissed him soundly on the mouth. On his ancestors bones but she could fluster him. He took her hands in his and withdrew his lips from hers, albeit reluctantly, his blood singing as only she could make it sing, sweaty as she was. She smiled at him, one of her knowing, mysterious smiles and turned to Vincenze.

"And this bag of bones. Looks fit enough for the bow-shop,

what do you say, Innamorato? Look at the gleam in its eyes. A man lurks there? What say you, Sylvio, shall I test it?"

Vincenze set down the basket of breakfast and made a gesture for mercy.

"Coward," she said and embraced him warmly.

"You look well, Aletta."

"And you look like shit."

"Ever the diplomat."

"Would you have me any other way?"

"No."

Sylvio set out the food upon a linen cloth and with a gesture bade his wife and his friend join him. It was still soft upon the stubble, for which he was grateful. Watching Aletta he remembered many of the occasions that had caused him to suffer the stings of lying on dry stubble. And remembering that, he remembered also it had been two years since there had been stubble to abrade his skin. There had been no grain, no harvest, only fields left scorched under the retreating tide of Breenai. Breenai who hadn't raided. Not officially. But the evidence had been there in the skill with which those men moved. Common brigands didn't operate the way those raiders had. Only trained specialists operated as they did. Sylvio had good reason to know. He hadn't spent most of his life as Simare's head of national security for nothing.

"The harvest looks bountiful," Vincenze said around a mouthful of bread.

Aletta cast a glance over the fields, perched as they were on a small rise that overlooked the golden barley, the fields where hops wound round poles like gigantic pikes. "Bountiful, yes. The land has had an opportunity to rest, and all that firing did the earth good, despite our feelings on the matter."

"It would seem the same could be said for the spiders?" Sylvio said.

Vincenze nodded, swallowing. "The tree spiders are back, yes, spinning webs the likes of which I've not seen in many years."

"Big?"

"Big? There were some webs so large they spanned trees, some as big as two hundred metres."

"You exaggerate," Sylvio mumbled.

"He tells the truth," Aletta said, setting down the wine jug and watching Vincenze carefully. "Two hundred metres."

Sylvio kept his astonishment under control, wondering what it could mean that the spiders spun such large webs. "Well, at least we'll be able to make angeli strings."

Vincenze nodded. "I've a plentiful harvest. We'll be able to fit a large percentage of the bows for trade with angeli." He sipped from the wooden beaker of wine. "How look our goods for trade?"

"Good."

"Good goods," Aletta said. "Information, my love. It helps in conversation when you provide information."

Sylvio grunted. "I was getting to it."

Aletta let out a cluck of exasperation.

"We're going to have grain to trade," Sylvio said, throwing Aletta a frown. "That will be a first in two years. Should fetch a good price at market in Reena --"

"And horses," Aletta said. "The foals from last year are proving healthy yearlings."

"And horses," Sylvio agreed. "And it would appear we're also going to have a good selection of bows, many with angeli strings – some with angeli strings."

"Any decision on selling the arcossi?" Vincenze asked.

The arcossi. Debate among the bowyers and the villagers about selling the arcossi had been passionate and divided. There were some archers who swore there were voices in their heads when they used the bows Sylvio made, telling them how to draw, where to aim, when to loose. And pressed, Sylvio admitted there was something uncanny about them, of having images like memories swim through his head as he carefully sliced thin veneers from the bones, glued bone to wood, tillered and teased a laminated stick into a weapon of deadly, almost sentient, grace. It hadn't been until he'd worked with Vincenze's sister's bones that he could attest to hearing voices. Now today's occurrence. That disturbed him.

To offer the arcossi at market was to sell the bones of one's mother, or father, one's daughter or son. It was like peddling holy relics. Here, come own the finger-bone of the goddess Vitalia and protect yourself from infertility! Here, come buy this arcosso that was my brother and thwart your enemies!

"They've agreed," said Sylvio.

"But it was bitter," said Aletta.

"I can imagine," said Vincenze and he looked out across the fields.

Sylvio could speculate what the other man thought, the conflict of emotions and reasons. Vincenze himself used an arcosso. Sylvio made it for him from a prime yew stave he'd been saving and the bones of Vincenze's sister who had died resisting Breenai security measures. He had seen it all through her eyes as he'd made the bow, disturbing images, flights of darkest fantasy from his own overwrought mind, he was sure. It was what had made him a master bowyer and brought hopeful apprentices to his door. He very much suspected that which he couldn't explain with logic. And he was determined to find out why her bones affected him so profoundly.

She had run the local inn, brewed some of the finest beer that was even taken to trade in Reena. Exactly what security threat a brewer and innkeeper could pose Sylvio didn't know. All he knew was she had been targeted by the Breenai government, but he suspected she had only been an expendable gaming piece on a board filled with more valuable objectives. It was Sylvio's suspicion it had been a warning to him. Arrogance? He didn't think so. He'd been a vocal dissenting voice when in office against allowing Breena preferred trading rights, against harmonization of the two country's security systems to comply with the Breenai system. Such an action would have left Simare little more than an economic vassal. That a brewer and innkeeper had acted as a terrorist agent, especially one as non-political as Vincenze's sister had been, Sylvio doubted. It was a ploy. Nothing more.

Now Donato, her brother and Vincenze's, ran the inn, and likely soon Pina would join him. Donato still brewed beer. It was good beer, certainly fine beer, but somehow not the same as the thick, dark brew that had won so much acclaim.

"So that leaves the question of when do we leave for Reena?" Vincenze said.

Sylvio stroked his jaw, considering. "Likely a week, maybe two, three at the outside."

"Time to put together some angeli strings."

"And organize who's going and who's not," Aletta said. "There will have to be a village council. This concerns us all. We'll have to approach the Sindaco."

Sindaco Antonio Portelli was Simare's acting politico and landed aristocrat in the village of Danuto, generally an innocuous man, mostly ambivalent to the requirements of his office. For the most part he oversaw his woollen mills and left the governing of Danuto to the informal elected council, and skirted round the issue he'd been given Sylvio's confiscated station and holdings, and while doing so managed to keep the balance of harmony in the village. It had been at Portelli's insistence Sylvio take the Casa Portelli, while it had been at Carmelo's insistence Portelli take Sylvio's as required by Carmelo's edict.

"I'm sure we can pull him away from the mill for a short time, especially with the promise of coin for his cloth," Sylvio said.

Vincenze nodded. "And what about taxes for our beloved Prince?"

And there was the nut of the problem. Alleging increased costs for security, public works and administration, that beautiful boy of a prince, Carmelo III of Simare, had done everything he could to ensure his own silks were the best, his table bountiful, his private herd of deer stocked and lands secured. It was said even hoods of his hawks were cloth of gold. And this while the country sank under the depredations of raids and the slow decay caused by negligence. Many of the main roads were now so pitted it made transport by cart and wagon difficult, sometimes ruinous. Brigands raided along with the Breenai, leaving merchants little choice but to retain either their own protection or hire mercenaries, because hope of the well-trained policing units that had been prevalent under his father's reign, and Sylvio's authority, had all but evaporated. Transfer payments from the crown to the states had diminished to nearly nil, so that maintenance of public wells and sewers and baths had fallen down the list of priorities. Public servants had been cut and retired to the point any bureaucrats left were overworked and unlikely to be helpful to the very people who paid such exorbitant taxes to keep them employed.

And now there was the new tax. Nothing was exempt. Not food, not land, not even the wages a person made by the sweat of their own brow. Twenty percent. Twenty percent before you could even begin to calculate your cost of goods, your overhead, and cost of living. It was a ruinous tax, and Sylvio was now convinced if the Breenai didn't outright annex Simare, their own Crown Prince would bleed them dry and incite riot, perhaps civil war. And with the Senate nothing more than toadies to Carmelo's whims, there was little hope of meaningful opposition to a reign of ruin.

Sylvio nodded, considering. To meet with Sindaco Portelli

sooner would be better than later. There was much to organize, much to discuss, and the time they had left before Reena's annual market would be cutting things fine. "I'll go to him," he said, not relishing the prospect.

"You're sure?" Aletta asked.

He glanced over at her, aware she probably heard the reluctance in his voice, and not for the first time was disconcerted at the thought. "I'm sure. Better me."

"Then when?"

"Tomorrow morning."

She smiled. "Let the rest of today remain relatively unruffled."

"Can you blame me?"

She laughed, reaching over and squeezing his hand. "Innamorato, I can blame you for very little but the theft of my heart."

He grunted his embarrassment and avoided Vincenze's grin. "And what other news have you?"

Vincenze's grin evaporated. "Only observations." He looked back out across the fields. "It seems odd there are more incidents of brigand attacks near the Breena Pass than on the road."

"You ventured that far?"

Vincenze nodded. "The tree spiders tell you a lot if you pay attention to their clues."

"That's where you found the huge webs?"

Again Vincenze nodded. "They're laying traps where there's plentiful food supply because of corpses and movement of anything living."

"And you don't think the predations at the pass and of the road are from ordinary common criminals."

"Ordinary common criminals don't kill their victims and overlook jewellery and money pouches. And they certainly don't leave anyone living with any weapons."

"You're questioning their motives," Aletta said.

"I am. Why do this? Why this seemingly pointless exercise in destruction? Why not just invade?"

"Because," said Sylvio, "to invade would catalyze the support of Almarè, and that would mean not only land troops, but an excellent navy. Even now, even with our own security in disarray, enough time hasn't passed that troops and measures couldn't be mobilized and implemented. Breena would have a relatively even fight on their hands. But if they were to invade, with Almarè coming to our aid, Breena would face a war they couldn't win.

"So, better to undermine a politically weak country through economic and politic means. Tie them up in trade agreements that keep the flow of natural resources and finished goods moving north into Breena, at preferred rates, so that profits are reduced and thereby depleting the growth and prosperity of Simare. Less profits means less disposable income to the people who then become more and more reliant upon government subsidies. And government subsidies aren't going to happen because Breena is totally cognizant, as are we all, that the current government has relinquished all responsibility to the fiscal health of the country. So Breena, in a gesture gilded in terms of peace and cooperation, inveigle themselves into the very fabric of our security and economic systems."

"Conquest through economic and political invasion," Vincenze said.

"Exactly. And those brigand raids are part of it. How far south do they seem to have gone?"

"Imalfia."

That was a shock. Imalfia lay south of Danuto by another forty kilometres. "You saw them?"

Vincenze shook his head. "No. I had an interesting discussion with the innkeeper there. He showed me the arrows found in the bodies left behind by the brigands. Somebody made a tactical error."

"The arrows were fletched with vulture feathers."

Vincenze nodded.

"And the Breenai are known to fletch with vulture feathers. That *was* a tactical error." He considered. "Or maybe not. But I can't believe they'd be that arrogant. Not yet. They haven't secured their economic targets yet." He looked over to Aletta. "I think Danuto's trip to market this year is going to be very interesting."

"I think I should go with them," she said.

"I was hoping you'd say that. They could use your ears, Aletta."

She laughed. "But how ever will you survive without me?"

Sylvio flushed. "It's only a few weeks."

"There is more, Ministro," Vincenze said.

Sylvio raised his eyebrows, watching the unease on Vincenze's face.

"I wondered when you'd get to that," Aletta said.

Vincenze shot her a glance. "You knew?"

She smiled. "I *heard*."

Vincenze nodded. Sylvio watched as Vincenze drew a sealed canvas envelope from his vest, his calloused hand very dark against it.

"I met a courier from Reena on my way home to Danuto."

Sylvio stared at the seal upon the envelope, unwilling to accept what Vincenze offered. That seal was a funeral urn upon a blazing sun. None other than the Royal seal. He felt Aletta stiffen beside him.

"How is it you come by this packet?" Sylvio asked.

"It would seem even our Principe's messengers are easily frustrated and compromised. I offered to pay his considerable bar bill when our paths crossed at an inn."

Reluctantly Sylvio took the envelope, cracked open the seal and read the contents of the letter. The usual flourish of titles and greetings. Obviously written by Carmelo's scribe. A little further along he stopped reading, cold with the menace he knew lay in those words.

"What is it?" Aletta asked. "Sylvio, you've gone pale."

"I am summoned to Reena this year. Seems Il Principe regrets having stripped me of titles and lands and wishes to redress his actions."

He could feel the shock in his wife and his friend.

After all this time! Summoned to Reena. Alleged reparation.

When he'd been dismissed from office Carmelo had been incoherent with rage, then inconsolable in his grief, begging Sylvio not to leave him, not to abandon him, all the while his crippled father, Aldo, stood in the shadows behind the throne. The former Principe had leaned on the intricately carved staff that had become his trademark after he'd recovered from the stroke. He never spoke. He walked with a pronounced limp. Rarely did one ever see his face, robed and hooded as he remained since that fateful day. Sylvio remembered thinking how Aldo resembled one of the cucullati, the robed and hooded spirits that guided people from life to death, except that Aldo didn't wear the distinguishing red.

The day of Sylvio's banishment Carmelo said he needed fresher, un-jaded minds working around him, his grief forgotten. Sylvio made the mistake of speaking his opinion and finding himself exiled, without title, his family's lands confiscated by the Crown.

Now Carmelo wanted him back. That it was a true change of heart Sylvio doubted. There was more here. He didn't know what yet. But he would soon.

"You're not going to go," Aletta protested.

"I agree, Ministro," Vincenze said. "This doesn't sit right."

"I know it doesn't. But I am going." He looked up at them. "How can I not? If I don't that will cause more harm than good.

Who knows what Carmelo will do? He could send an armed guard for me and then all my ability to find out what he's up to will be thwarted."

"But, Sylvio –"

"I know. I know, Aletta. This could be a trap of some sort. But why? What possible threat can I be to him?"

"You are loved by the people, Sylvio, you –"

"And do you see me surrounded by an army? Threatening to overthrow him? Assassinate him? I've kept all the conditions of my banishment. I haven't been to Reena in ten years. I am not involved in any military activity –"

"We've done everything to be sure of that," Vincenze said. "Although you and I both know without your acumen I'd be lost organizing Danuto's retainers and patrols."

Sylvio dismissed that with a grunt. "I have no power. I have no lands. I have no capital to retain mercenaries. The closest I've come to anything military is to make bows."

"But rare bows, you have to concede that."

The arcossi. Indeed. Rare bows. Bows he did not wish to make, but felt compelled. The funeral urns which had been dedicated to the bow-shop sometimes vibrated with incoherent whispers as he passed. Whispers he knew only he and others like him could sense. He didn't like having this ability. He didn't want to be part of something that couldn't be explained, tracked, quantified.

And having that ability very much marked him as someone unusual.

Unusual enough to have Carmelo summon him?

He groaned in frustration, thrust the letter at Aletta. "Can you feel anything? Anything at all."

She took the paper and the canvas envelope, inhaled deeply, let her rough hands touch the words. He watched concentration set her features, watched the emotion slide away as she sank into her own gift. Then abruptly she refolded the letter, placed it back into the canvas envelope and handed it back to Sylvio.

"Well?"

She shook her head.

"No?"

"No. It's not that I can't read anything, hear anything. It's that there's something else there, some other.... I don't know. If I didn't know better I'd say there was power here. Power as I've never known before, heard before. But all that knowledge was outlawed and then destroyed long before our ancestors were born." She looked at him intently. He could tell how much this cost her to remain calm, to be the strega, not the wife. "And knowing there is something hidden here suggests dark dealings, suggests secrets and perhaps danger. Beyond that I unable to tell you anything of use."

"Then that settles matters. I'm going to Reena. We'll be sure to take our best retainers, spread our information net, but not leave Danuto unguarded. Whatever Carmelo wants of me, I'll not see innocent people put at risk."

And from there Sylvio led his friend and his wife into discussion of Vincenze's recent travels, of news, of matters of no import and general gossip. His attention was on little of it. His mind raced ahead to the sequence of events that might or might not unfold in the next few weeks and what lay down the road at market in Reena.

The porter at the gate of Portelli's home, once Sylvio's, immediately admitted his former employer, bowing, uttering greetings. The man rushed before Sylvio, letting fly commands to servants as he passed to have Sylvio taken to the Sindaco's study, to have refreshment brought. With as much grace as he could muster

Sylvio followed the servant he was handed off to, trying to alleviate the discomfort he knew these people felt on the rare occasion he entered his confiscated, reallocated, ancestral home.

Portelli kept everything as though he cared for a national treasure, with very little mark of his own. It was out of respect for Sylvio, he knew. That only added to his unease, and hence the reason he seldom attended upon Portelli here, and usually it was the annual journey to Reena that brought him.

Sylvio entered the study and crossed to the wall of glass doors, open to the gentle evening air, and looked out over the upper loggia to the inner courtyard where fig trees were pendulous with fruit. He remembered standing there as a boy with his father, biting into red-fleshed fruit as sweet as honey. And later, as a groom on his wedding night, standing there with Aletta. There had been rain. And figs as a blessing to their union, sweet as her mouth, sweet as the rain, and the thunder which might have been his heart or might have been the sky.

It was a pear melomel and a dish of figs one of the servants brought in, set on a side table; she curtseyed and left.

Sylvio turned back to the loggia, unsettled. He'd decided to meet with Portelli this evening rather than tomorrow. No point putting this off. No point hiding from what was going to happen.

He heard the door open again, Portelli say, "Ah, Maestro. I'm sorry to have kept you waiting. I just came back from the mills."

Sylvio turned again. Antonio Portelli was a large man in every sense, but most especially in character. He waved away Portelli's apology. "Are you pouring?"

Portelli grinned and handed Sylvio one of the beakers he'd filled. "To what shall we drink, my old friend?"

"To friendship."

Portelli nodded and drank, as did Sylvio. With a gesture Portelli invited Sylvio to make himself comfortable, and eased into one of the chairs with a back. There was a smear across Portelli's doublet, a tear in the sleeve of his linen shirt, all evidence he'd hurried directly here upon hearing he had a visitor. He looked down at his disarray, smiled apologetically at Sylvio and said, "I don't suppose I need to ask what brings you?"

"It's time, Antonio."

"I always delude myself into thinking one of these years I'll approach you about the annual market in Reena."

"You're busy." Sylvio set down his beaker. "But it's going to be different this year."

"Word travels fast, Sylvio. I've heard the news. It's why I was so long at the mill. People are worried about your summons to Reena."

"As am I."

"What could Il Principe mean by recalling you to the capitol?"

"Anything. Nothing. I don't know."

"I don't suppose you could even consider ignoring the summons?"

Sylvio laughed. "Are you a man bent on my destruction and that of this village?"

"It was a wish for your peace. That's all. If I could turn back time, Sylvio, I would; have you and Aletta return here to your home. Have all as it was. No, as it should be."

"I've done with wishes, Antonio. You know that. This home is yours, has been for ten years, and it is well cared for. I am content. And as for Nostro Principe, He calls and I respond. There can be no other way."

"But surely you don't believe you're safe?"

"Who said anything about believing I'm safe? I haven't been safe since the day he sent me into exile. Neither have any of you been safe for allowing me a place here. But it is done. And now I'll have to see what these next moves of his may mean. That means I recognize his summons. And I plan. You know this as well as I."

"Then I'll have Vincenze work on security, which, we both know, will mean you'll work on security for both our caravan and our village. I'll have word go out that we'll hold a public council tomorrow to discuss trade and who's going and who's not."

Sylvio drank the rest of the melomel. It was good. Dry, not too sweet, not cloying the way some vintners insisted making their honeyed wines. "There's just one more thing."

Portelli made a gesture to continue.

"I think Nina should stay here this year. And the children. I don't think it's safe to take your wife and family, not if I'm in the train of Danuto's merchants. Agreed they could be used against you just as easily here as in the capitol, but at least here would require some considerable effort on Carmelo's part if he's planning any harm. And I think she should know exactly why we're doing this, if at all possible."

"Why burden her with this?"

"If there is a possibility that Carmelo means me harm, he'll use all those around me as leverage. If Nina knows about these things, and matters go wrong for me, or us, in Reena, she can take the children, and those in Danuto who wish, into exile in Almarè." He lifted a finger to Portelli's protest. "It's a possibility we must consider. We can arrange for contingencies. We should."

He watched Portelli pale, considering the magnitude of what Sylvio suspected. After a moment Portelli nodded. "Of course." Good man. Portelli was no fool, despite what people often assumed because of his girth and his easy way with laughter. It was a mistake Sylvio had learned early not to make.

Sylvio rose. "Then if I have your leave, there's a great deal for me to do before our village meeting tomorrow."

"Of course." Portelli stood as well, rested his hand on Sylvio's shoulder. "This is going to sound very strange, my friend, but I almost wish you weren't such an honourable man."

Sylvio laughed. "What, you think I can't be ruthless?"

"I didn't say that. Only that you're bound by your honour. Nostro Principe is not. And he knows this about you, else he wouldn't have sent you that summons."

Sylvio felt the shock of that. He looked away, back to Portelli. "You may be right. But without my honour what am I?" He thumped Portelli's shoulder, managed a smile, turned and left.

All the way back home, winding his way through the darkened streets, past lanterns burning at the tavern, the gurgling of the piazza's fountain, cats sliding sleek as night along fences and alleys, he thought about his meeting with Portelli, about the long ride to Reena and how to prepare himself for the audience with Carmelo that would surely occur after his arrival.

When he entered his own gate the porter greeted him with a concerned look and lit his way across the modest courtyard.

"Are the dogs loose?" he asked.

The porter confirmed they were.

Sylvio nodded and stepped into the darkened halls of his borrowed home, stopping briefly at the small altar to light incense to the family's ancestors. As quietly as possible he padded his way to Aletta's chamber, lifted the latch and let himself in. He dropped his clothes at the foot of the bed. Her skin was warm and silky when he slid under the covers beside her, nesting at her back, and kissed the nape of her neck. She stirred and let go a sigh of pleasure, twining her fingers into his own.

It was a moonless night. He could see stars as cold as his dread in the night sky beyond the un-shuttered window.

"You went to see Antonio," Aletta said after a few moments.

"I thought you were asleep."

"No. Listening to you thinking."

"Loud, am I?"

"Thunderous. How is the Sindaco?"

"Unnerved."

"Like the rest of us."

"Mmm. It appears the whole village knows."

"Did you expect otherwise? Innamorato, they love you. They would follow you anywhere, do anything for you, have done anything for you."

"I know. And there's the danger."

"You think Carmelo would use them against you?"

"Without a pause."

She turned in his arms, lay the palm of her hand against his cheek. "You can only do what you can do, Innamorato, be what you are."

He looked down at her, kissed her brow, the lids of her eyes. She smelled of soap and the air after a storm, and home after a long journey away. Familiar and comforting, and, in the end, seductive. "And what am I, Aletta?"

"A man of integrity."

"Antonio just finished saying something similar to me. You're all making me into some sort of paragon."

She smiled. "Paragon? Hardly. We've all seen you in a temper. But your honour binds you. You can't deny this. Above all else, this is what you are. And I would have you no other way." She kissed him then, tenderly, intimately, the way only a woman could who has known the same lover for thirty years.

Not for the first time this morning Violina wished she could have just one more cup of coffee. Despite the beauty of this golden morning, and the pearly haze that lay out across the lagoon, she felt sluggish, creaky, irritated with the beginnings of a migraine and a craving for that warm, creamy third cup of coffee she couldn't have. It wasn't fair, she thought. It wasn't fair that when twenty and lithe and beautiful she could toss off an entire pot of the rich brew without suffering, but now, firmly entrenched in middle age, that invincible protection of youth abandoned her and left her rationed to a mere two cups of her one and only vice.

One and only? At that arrogance she smiled and rested her head back into the pillows of her chaise, closing her eyes to the soft light filling her loggia. "Well if I can't have coffee bring me orange juice, Julio," she said.

She heard her steward slide the tray with her empty coffee cup across the table at her elbow. "An excellent choice, Madonna."

"Don't' be impertinent."

"Never, Madonna." And heard him pad away into the interior of her apartments. She smiled.

Perhaps the orange juice would help sharpen her mind. She needed to be sharp today, free of the debilitating effects of a migraine and the constant pain of arthritis. The ambassador from Breena was to have private consultation with her today, before meeting with the Senate entire tomorrow. She didn't like granting that smooth, assured man any extra privilege. For that matter neither did the Senate. But he had been insistent he meet with her, not the Minister of Trade, nor the Minister of Foreign Affairs. No, only the Prima would do. And despite every attempt to tie him up in protocol and red tape he succeeded in gaining the very thing they all laboured to deny him. Of course, knowing the Breenai had been involved in two years of depredations and extortion across the mountains in Simare had helped to add caution, little say a measure of concern, to the actions of Almarè's government. Being a centre of trade as they were it was important to tread that very narrow and perilous path of diplomacy and compromise in order to assure the flow of goods and thereby wealth and thereby the very well-being of the people of Almarè.

Julio returned with not only the requested orange juice, but a plate with some of the harvest's first sweet grapes and soft new cheese. She arched a brow at him, glancing at the tray.

"You know how you neglect yourself when you're worried," he said. "And I've brought you a tea."

She peered over at the tray and the steaming cup of pale liquid, wrinkling her nose. "You know how I detest willow tea."

He levelled her with a stare for which any other servant or retainer would have been dismissed. "So which do you prefer, the percussion in your head, or a moment's epicurean displeasure?"

She let out an exasperated hiss and lifted the cup. "You dare too far, Julio."

He smiled. "I know. And it is for that reason I have been your steward all these years."

She rolled her eyes and resigned herself to sipping the tea.

"Shall I have your robes laid out, Madonna?"

She nodded. "I think the blue with the gold embroidered borders."

"Might I suggest the red?"

She tucked in her chin and looked up at him. "The red?"

"You are the Prima. To wear the red is to wear the colour of Almarè."

"And you have the most subtle mind of any servant I know."

He grinned. "Another reason you've kept me in your employ all these years."

At that she laughed. "Then the red, yes. Let's make this Breenai viper know we are aware of his and his country's machinations." She swallowed the last of the tea, wrinkling her nose, popped a few grapes in her mouth and pulled herself out of the chaise, leaning heavily on her canes. "And with that I suppose I should bathe and prepare for this distasteful meeting."

Julio retrieved the tray and followed her inside to a sumptuous suite of rooms within the Marè Palace. The floors she crossed were coveted white Almarè marble veined with gold, softened by priceless Breenai silk rugs and appointed with some of the finest cabinetry and woodwork from Simare. Paintings, sculpture, tapestries from the three countries graced plastered and frescoed walls and stone plinths, chased silver and wrought gold in bowls and hardware and bosses on doors. It occurred to her she had grown immune to this beauty, this gallery of art and history she called home. Which was perhaps as well, given the impression she wanted to leave with the Breenai ambassador.

Julio left her in her private chambers to the care of her maids and she acquiesced to their ministrations. The soft light, the lavender scented waters all did much to ease her head and soothe her limbs, while lilac and lavender oil massaged into her joints worked on the arthritis. Camica and stockings, stays and over-slip, gown, her hair pulled up into a severe but regal twist at the back of her head. She surveyed herself in the cheval glass, pleased with the decision to appear without ornament, with only the brilliantly scarlet robe of her office and the funny little mushroom cap perched jauntily atop her greying chestnut hair.

"You look very regal today, Madonna," one of her handmaids said.

Violina smiled. "Thank you, Tessa." She turned from the glass and limped out to her salon, ready with a command to have the Ambassador shown in when he arrived. To her surprise Julio stood there looking somewhat discomfited, an apology spoken before she could utter a word.

"What is it, Julio?" she asked.

"He is here already."

She looked around the room, back at Julio and gestured to the empty chairs, sofas.

"In the garden, Madonna."

"What? — "

"He arrived early, Madonna, and said he'd wait in the garden."

"And you let him?"

"It wasn't so much a question of *let*, Madonna."

"I'm all ears, Julio."

"He, well, he just took, well, he –"

"He flummoxed you." Which was a surprise if ever there were one. She had come to rely upon his judgment and good sense, his impeccable timing and propriety. She couldn't remember the last time she'd seen him like this, if ever.

Julio looked down at his red leather mules. "He did, Madonna."

"You, Julio? I'd have hardly credited it."

He looked back up at her, confusion plain on his patrician face. "He has a presence, Madonna."

She arched a brow at that, considering. "Plainly, to have unsettled you."

He gestured to the open glass doors to the garden. "Shall I have refreshments brought out? Or shall I have the Ambassador summoned here?"

"Yes. No." She frowned. "Yes, bring refreshments to the garden, but wait twenty minutes or so. This may suit our purposes better than I thought."

"Shall I announce you, Madonna?"

"No. I think not. Two can play at this game."

"I've prepared your chair."

She nodded, accepted Julio's assistance up the two steps to the doors, settled into the cane and elegantly carved wheelchair and wheeled herself into the gardens.

Late season lilies were still in bloom, filling the first beds with rich oranges, yellows and reds, behind them a dark green backdrop of manicured yews. The beds to her left and right were bifurcated by a flagstone path in which creeping thyme and a hybrid chamomile sprawled with wanton profusion, releasing perfume into the air. From here the pathway led her through a stone pergola from which hung the delicate blue and pink berries of porcelain vine. Roses grew to either side, red and heady with fragrance.

Where the pergola broke into a bisecting path she paused, looking off to her left where a sculpture of Leodorno, the god of love and gardens rose from a ring of silver-grey lavender, and from there the path continued in another series of spokes. To her right was a similar configuration but here Carolina reclined on frozen waves of marble while water cascaded over and around her in a sensual recreation of her birth from the lagoon of Almarè. She was the goddess of family and commerce. And it was here, perched upon the wide lip of the fountain, the Breenai Ambassador Maponos Ó Leannáin sat, long, musician's fingers trailing through the curtain of water, a red rose across the saffron folds of his leine which he wore belted over trewes of nut-brown worsted, ribboned up his calves with gorgeously finger-woven laces. At his throat was a heavy torque of ivory and gold, flashing with gems. His dark hair fell in oiled ringlets, sweeping back from a high forehead, dark, arched brows and lashes which were so thick she mistook them for kohl at first. An earring with a priceless baroque pearl hung from his earlobe. His facial features were sharp, although his mouth, framed in a meticulously trimmed moustache and goatee, when he turned his face toward her proved wide, full and sensual, revealing dazzlingly white teeth in a pale, porcelain face. He presented an image of contrasts, of harshness and sensuality, of studied poise and careless grace.

He rose and bowed deeply, hands clasped before his heart with the rose held there, and remained in an attitude of reverence until she said, "Ambassador Ó Leannáin, I believe." He straightened.

"Prima Violina Pallavicini di Negli. How good of you to allow me this meeting." His voice, although accented, was the voice of an accomplished singer. She could imagine what power he would have over people if that voice were combined with not only his hypnotic beauty, but his alleged intellectual acuity.

"Are you fatigued? Shall we stroll?" She gestured to the path to her left that ran along an avenue of climbing roses. He nodded and stepped beside her into curtains of sunlight. She caught the fragrance that swept with him, sandalwood and citrus, subtle and sensual. "The gardens are so lovely this time of day."

"I daresay the gardens are lovely any time of day, a place of refuge, for contemplation and relaxation." He laughed. "I speak in generalities, of course."

"Do you garden, Ambassador?"

"I do. I am afraid it is proving my undoing in middle-age, as more and more I prefer the company and solitude of my garden to the intrigues and frenzy of court."

"A problem for a man in your position."

"And a woman in yours."

"Ah, here look, we come upon Leodorno. This particular sculpture of the god was done nearly a millennium ago by the renowned artist Grazie. It was said –"

"–It was said he kept a steady stream of water running over the marble to prevent it from becoming brittle and to keep his tools cool, that he laboured so feverishly with his creation the water flowed pink from the cuts and abrasions of his hands, and that on the anniversary of Grazie's death Leodorno causes the lavender to bloom and the sculpture of his likeness to weep tears of blood." He looked over at her. "Is it true?"

"I have always found it prudent to neither corroborate nor abrogate such legends."

"And to allow the people their faiths."

She conceded him a nod of agreement. Damn but she wanted to

concede nothing to this man! Everything he represented was reprehensible. What on earth had Simare done to deserve such flagrant attempts at annexation that the Breenai government, his people, should attempt to swallow and scatter everything that tiny nation had achieved and given to the world? Their only fault lay in the fact they were sandwiched like bait between two powers and now faced compromise from within by their own head of state.

And there was to consider that if Breena were to gain control of Simare it would upset the balance of power. Simare was the keystone that kept both Almarè and Breena from crashing into one another and wreaking havoc across the known world. And it would happen. Sooner or later. But only if Simare could not, did not, hold.

"I think you had better tell me why you've caused such consternation to my ministers."

His eyes narrowed thoughtfully for a moment. "May we continue to walk?"

She nodded.

"Perhaps I lead you astray, Prima," he said, glancing around the gardens, "in causing you to believe I spend all my free time in my garden. Truth to tell I spend all my free time seeking out places of solitude, places I can be assured I am utterly alone. One of the difficulties of public office – one is never alone."

"A lamentable but obvious condition of public office."

"For which one should be prepared before accepting such responsibility."

She nodded.

"Even so, Prima, I think you will concede none of us are prepared for some of the surprises with which life, and indeed public office, tests us."

She frowned, sensing the mild undercurrent of his tension, the way he watched his perimeters carefully, casually, with the eye of a trained spy, or assassin. Was she in danger out here? But there were the guards. There were always the guards, hidden and unobtrusive, and there nonetheless. Peaceful Almarè might be, but still one always had to protect against fringe lunatics. And this man was free of safety checks because of diplomatic immunity, a perception of trust. But could she trust him? What did she truly know of him? Even her very best spies had been able to glean little about him other than his patent loyalty to his country, his absolute devotion to his chosen deity, that he remained unattached to any filial or romantic commitment. He lectured on political sciences and history at the University of Failc in Breena, apparently frequented opera and even sponsored a youth program for the study of voice where it was said he was known to sing from time to time. He also, apparently, painted, quite well so she'd been informed. There was a notable absence of information regarding family.

"Perhaps it is how we rise to the challenge that is the entire thrust of the challenge," she said, returning to his comment. "If one could concede we follow a pre-ordained path."

"And do we? Follow a pre-ordained path? Is this something you believe?"

"I believe we have choices, and therefore our paths are not fixed."

"Rather cast before us like the threads of a tapestry, but the tapestry is woven as we walk. And some of those paths we must walk alone by virtue of the enormity of our decisions."

There was a conversation here she should be hearing, she knew, but the implications of what lay beneath his words shocked her. Surely she was reading him incorrectly? Not for the first time she wished she had the services of one of Simare's strega.

She considered the risks if she were wrong. "Come," she said. "I believe refreshments are prepared for us." And she led him off to a small gazebo where she could see Julio stewarding servants in his usual casual efficiency. At her approach he waved off the servants, bowed and retreated to the side. She indicated one of the chairs to the Breenai ambassador. Julio stepped forward and poured green tea into bowls from a simply turned stoneware pot, all the work of the same artisan. Discreetly Julio poured a third cup, sipped, nodded to Violina and stepped back to the wall. She drank. It didn't pass her notice that Ó Leannáin didn't touch his. She arched a brow, to which he smiled.

"As I said, one is never alone."

And afraid for one's security? Was he that threatened by Almarè and what she represented? She gestured to Julio, who drank from Ó Leannáin's cup, wiped the rim daintily and set it once again before the Ambassador. He inclined his head to Julio, lifted the cup and said:

"You, for instance, Prima, are constantly surrounded by the appearance of security, and thereby ears which are privy to your most private conversations. So that even here, in this oasis of tranquility, only what you think is your own. What you speak is not."

Ah. That settled it. Without taking her gaze from Ó Leannáin she said, "Julio, have the guards moved out of range." That would send a clear signal she would grant him privacy, but not complete trust. Julio moved off and could be heard giving an order to another servant. When he returned she could feel him bristle with disapproval, but in character he kept his silence and his counsel.

Still Ó Leannáin sipped from his tea, watching Violina intently. When long moments stretched out into an uncomfortable silence she said, "Whatever you have to say can be said in the presence of my steward."

Ó Leannáin hesitated.

"He has my complete confidence," she said.

Still Ó Leannáin remained silent, watching her.

Unobtrusively Julio bent to pour her more tea, close enough to her ear to whisper, "I am willing to give him my guarantee, Madonna."

She nodded imperceptibly. Julio straightened.

"Ambassador," Julio said, "My life is forfeit should word of this meeting and its conversations escape this garden."

"Julio!" she said, rounding on him. This was excessive!

"It would seem the loyalty of your steward surprises even you, Prima." Ó Leannáin turned his attention to Julio. "I have a long memory."

"As do I, Ambassador."

Ó Leannáin nodded in acceptance. "Two days ago the Breenai government issued a proclamation declaring Simare under its protection. A tax has been levied of thirty percent on the gross income of every citizen and business in Simare, payable annually at the Reena market. As we speak ships are sailing into Reena harbour to collect this year's taxes."

The audacity of the action stunned her. "And if they refuse to comply?"

"Breena will close Simare's borders to trade. All her borders."

"You'll lay siege to her."

A smile flitted across his mouth. "I won't, no. Breena will, yes."

"And I can only assume you're telling me this out of…."

"An attempt to threaten?" He truly smiled then but there was no humour in it. "No, Prima. It is not my intention to threaten." He set down his cup. "It is my intention to give you advance warning."

"Why warn Almarè?"

He didn't answer for a moment and looked away out into the garden, toying with the rose he still held in his hand. "Because there are times a man must weigh where his loyalties lie and from where honour springs."

"Your government doesn't know you carry this warning?"

He shook his head slowly.

Of course! This was the reason for his need for privacy. The game he played was dangerous indeed.

"Are you asking for asylum?"

"Asylum?" He looked over at her. "No. Not asylum. I will carry out my formal mission to the Almarè Senate and return home with my ship. I believe I can do more good within Breena than fleeing as a refugee. And there are other considerations."

"Such as?"

"A niece."

"But –"

"Your reports indicated I had no filial obligations?" He laughed again and she wondered if ever this man had an opportunity to exercise that beautiful voice for joy. "Some things are best left unacknowledged. My niece has no idea I am her uncle. She is well cared for by a family in my employ. Given my background and occupation I thought it prudent when it was she came to be my ward that I keep her distanced from my life. Loved ones often become hostage to influence."

"You risk much in telling me."

He nodded.

"A guarantee."

Again he nodded.

"And what will be your presentation to the Senate tomorrow?"

"To begin negotiations for a bilateral trade agreement excluding Simare. The forms must be met. This drama must unfold. But those of us who are forewarned can now set into motion actions to undermine any agreement."

"And why oppose such an agreement? Certainly together Almarè and Breena could offer a powerful trading force to those who lie east and west of us. New shipping lanes could be opened."

"Have I misread you, Prima?"

"Not at all. I no more wish to see a bilateral agreement than you, especially in light of what will be happening to Simare. Sooner or later Breena will press for harmonization of security forces with Almarè, economic standards, on and on, just as she is doing with Simare. But I suspect any harmonization that would be undertaken would be to make the world Breena, rather than incorporating the best of each system and allowing for cultural differences and sovereign nations.

"Having said that, I know what some of our Senators will think, especially in light of the fact they will be forming opinions without the information you and I have to hand."

He watched her intently once more, and she withstood his scrutiny. It wasn't the first time she'd undergone that sort of silent interrogation. At first it was because of her youth and beauty. Men generally didn't expect there to be sharp intelligence behind the face of a goddess. Now she was often discounted because she was a widow, middle-aged, and therefore assumed to be without juice.

"I came to you, specifically, Prima," he said slowly, "because I have believed you to be a force of reason despite all obstacles. You govern in a country dominated by essentially a patriarchal system; you hold lands; run businesses. You have had to reason through obstacles many would have found daunting, male or female.

"It is my belief you wish to see people living autonomously, able to make decisions about their own destinies; that you esteem, above all things, the variety of cultures, beliefs and skills there are in the world. You believe in that most rare and elusive of political ends – peace."

"Very flattering words, Ambassador."

A flash of frustration crossed his features, there and gone. "No flattery, Prima. The urgency of my mission compels me to speak my heart."

She shrugged an apology. "Then assuming the Senate will refuse Breena's proposal, how can that counter what is about to happen in Simare?"

"It leaves Almarè, and more specifically you, free to prevent an assassination attempt."

That left her utterly shocked. Assassination? They would dare? Of the Simare Crown Prince? To what end?

"No, Prima, not Prince Carmelo," he said, almost as though reading her thoughts. "The Prince is already Breena's puppet. Unlike his father he is a libertine. He has not the wisdom to see the crown he wears is not a right, but a responsibility.

"No, Prima, there is but one person in Simare who could raise an army, a loyal one, and with intimate knowledge of all Simare's security and political systems, a person who believes in the higher ideals of responsible government."

"Sylvio di Danuto."

He nodded. "The man who has retired to the life of a bowyer."

"He is not Simare's only salvation."

"Agreed. There could be others. But, Prima, memory is fresh in Simare."

"Even after a decade," she said by way of agreement. "Certainly it was a surprising move when the Prince took power." Her husband had been alive then. News of the Prince's dismissal of di Danuto had caused him to forget his usual impartiality to Violina's position. He, like so many of the Senate, predicted nothing but disaster and the decay of Simare's eminence in the world.

"Even after a decade," Ó Leannáin said. "And if di Danuto is removed from influence, permanently, it would greatly affect the morale of the people, and it is my belief, as it is plainly the belief of Breena, the stability of the country."

"On the other hand it could make him a martyr to a cause."

"I will concede that. It is possible. There are a few of his people who could organize opposition to the Crown and my country's hopes, but it is my conviction that opposition would lack the strength and cutting intelligence it could have under the guidance of Sylvio di Danuto." He leaned across the table and placed the rose across the brim of her empty cup. "Will you go to the Grand Market in Reena this year, Prima?"

She glanced down at the rose, at the hope that lay in that gesture, back up at him. He looked burdened, concerned with matters beyond the scope and requirement of his office. It had taken courage, and no little conviction, to meet with her today.

"Maponos Ó Leannáin, what will they do to you if you are revealed as a spy and a traitor?"

His brows lifted slightly. He retreated across the table and leaned back into his chair, assessing her again. She realized this was a man who made decisions based upon the precise gathering of information, that the diplomatic dance he trod was mined with peril. "We believe a person should wear this dishonour and guilt. That is the greatest punishment of all: to be refused the sanctuary and absolution of anonymity and death. So it is we tattoo a person–"

"– From head to toe," she finished. "But that has not been done for some time in Breena."

"If you knew, why ask?"

"Like you I'm searching for the inner workings of my company's mind." She picked up the rose. "I know you only by reputation, Maponos."

The familiar use of his name clearly startled him. She knew he caught the implication in that. "You seem confident they would do this to you, despite the fact this punishment has not been used in hundreds of years."

"There has never been such treachery for hundreds of years." He nodded. "I am cognizant of the gravity of what I do. And yes, if the counsellors and King were to discover what I have done, what I plan to do, I will be stripped naked before witnesses and tattooed with my guilt, left to find my own way in a society which will call me pariah and refuse to offer succour.

"It is as good as a sentence of death. And it is more."

She took the rose into her fingers and inhaled its fragrance. "Then we shall have to ensure this end does not come to be. We have an accord, Ambassador Ó Leannáin."

He let go a breath, and it was only then she had an indication of just how tense he had been, how unsure of the outcome of this meeting. "I thank you for your confidence, Prima."

"We should then perhaps discuss how it is we are to thwart this assassination attempt, and how we are to ensure the safety not only of Sylvio di Danuto, but of his country." She turned to Julio. "I do believe coffee is in order, Julio."

"With all haste, Madonna."

It had taken force of will and Sylvio's gentle bullying to get the caravan and traders from Danuto on the road in any semblance of timeliness little say order. Gods but it could frustrate a man. Were it not for Vincenze and Aletta he was sure he would have lost his temper more than once. But with them to bear the brunt of his frustration he'd managed to bite his sharp tongue and convince Portelli and the others that half of their usual household staff was more than any of them need bring. Truth of the matter was Sylvio would have preferred two, perhaps three staff in Portelli's entourage, rather than the ten to which he'd had to agree. But what was a man to do? Given the alternative of facing a journey more like a processional, Sylvio in the end saw the prudence of Portelli's plan.

Who was at this moment ordering his steward to break for lunch.

"Lunch?" Sylvio barked, ready to turn his horse back to Portelli and tell him exactly what he thought about breaking for lunch after only two hours in the saddle and a late start at that.

Aletta stayed him with a touch to his arm. He glared at her. "Let him be," she said.

"Aletta, let him be –"

"You'll catch more flies with honey."

"I'll keep him to a brief lunch," Vincenze said.

"We do have to be sure our Sindaco is contented," Aletta said. "He does, after all, personally host the Danuto village trade caravan every year in Reena."

Recognizing his defeat, Sylvio waved Vincenze to go and have a word with Portelli. Indeed he and the entire village owed considerable gratitude to Sindaco Portelli. Were it not for his largess every year, from the moment he was appointed mayor, the village of Danuto would have faced even greater losses because of the expense of renting quarters in Reena. As it was, the entire cost of feeding and housing the Danuto traders, along with the cost of feting dignitaries and prospective buyers, all came directly from Portelli's private coffers. He brooked no recompense. He firmly believed this was part of his duty to his village. And for that, at least, Sylvio was immensely grateful, if not for his lack of organization and predisposition to excess.

"It's going to be chaos," Sylvio said, turning back in the saddle toward Aletta.

"You'll sort it all out."

"By all the gods, would it be asking so very much to have a smooth, ordered expedition?"

"You wouldn't know what to do with yourself," Aletta answered and slid down out of the saddle. "Come, Innamorato, and have some bread and cheese. You might as well chew on something other than your frustration."

With a growl Sylvio dismounted and set to hobbling their horses off the road while Aletta turned to the saddlebags for provisions. Vincenze returned with the news Portelli wished the entire caravan to join him for a celebratory drink. Sylvio threw up his hands and laughed, shaking his head.

"I admit defeat," he said. "What's the point?" He nodded to Vincenze. "Would you do me the courtesy of making sure our escort, at least, have picquets set?"

"Of course, Ministro –"

"And don't call me Ministro! That position was taken from me long ago!" Sylvio flung the hobbles off Ibacci, threw himself over the saddle and kneed the stallion into a trot to where Portelli stood atop Donato's lead wagon of beer barrels.

Immediately he felt guilty. Vincenze didn't deserve the brunt of his frustration. In fact Vincenze deserved a great deal more from him, given the man had resigned his position in protest and followed him to Danuto when Carmelo dismissed Sylvio. Indeed Vincenze deserved more. He deserved to be happy. He deserved a life of his own. And most of all he deserved to be free of the shadow of Sylvio's failure.

He felt as though the day was miring in debts he owed. Debt to Portelli for his part in the welfare of the village. Debt to Vincenze for his loyalty. And were he to admit it, debt to Aletta for not only fulfilling her obligation as strega, truthsayer of the village, but for her considerable patience with him. She had offers aplenty, both romantic and business. To wife, or employ, a strega was highly desirable, and why she had chosen him still was a matter of bafflement. She could have had so much more than he had to offer.

By the time he reined in Ibacci, a ring had formed around the wagon where Portelli stood astride Donato's beer casks, in full song and drawing screams of laughter from the village traders. Every verse he sung increased not only in volubility but lewdness, embellishing an old folk song about the marriage bed. By the last stanza he sweated profusely, his broad, round face flushed. With a flourish of his overfull beer mug he came to a crashing finale, beer slopping over the crowd. He slumped to the barrel, took a great gulp of beer and grinned like an idiot.

Sylvio watched the traders around him, watched the way they laughed, dabbed at their eyes, saw their tensions and apprehensions ease if only for a short time. He looked back up at Portelli who watched him closely, still grinning. Sylvio nodded his gratitude. Portelli shrugged as if to say, it's nothing.

He heard Aletta shift in her saddle beside him.

"I don't give him enough credit," he said.

"I know," she answered. "But he understands."

He looked over at her. "Does he now?"

"Well of course he does. We don't follow him as Sindaco because of his beauty."

He nodded to that, conceding the point.

Portelli, with surprising grace, descended the wagon, shouted for his steward to be sure everyone had enough food and drink, and strode his way through the crowd, exchanging pleasantries as he made his way slowly, inexorably, toward Sylvio. Portelli's groom arrived with a horse. All in the same effortless way he had descended the wagon and threaded his way through the crowd, Portelli mounted his horse, and turned toward Aletta.

"Would you join your husband and me for a small ride?"

"A pleasure as always, Sindaco."

"You know better than that, Aletta. We come together as friends."

She inclined her head. "Antonio, then."

With a click of his tongue he urged his horse out to the road. When they were well out of earshot of the traders he turned to look at Sylvio as they rode.

"I owe you an apology."

Sylvio arched an eyebrow at that.

"I've done everything to frustrate you, yet again, for our journey to market, and, as always, you've taken it in your stride. I thank you for that."

"It's nothing."

"On the contrary it's very much something, which is why I've asked Aletta to join us. I want her to hear so you'll know I'm speaking the truth."

Sylvio frowned. "Really, there's no need for this –"

"It's not about my delays or my entourage I wish to speak. I've used them as a means to an end, Sylvio, and we must have this conversation in haste."

Sylvio moved to rein in Ibacci.

"Don't," Portelli warned. "It's important everyone think we're simply discussing the caravan. Wave your arm as though you're arguing with me."

Hesitantly, Sylvio did as Portelli wished. He felt Aletta tense beside him, felt her concentration. What was going on here?

"It would seem the integrity of my household in Reena is compromised. There is a spy for the Prince." Portelli made a placating gesture to interrupt Sylvio. "I don't know, yet, who that person is. We hire extra staff every year for the market, as you know. I have a trusted retainer working on an answer for me.

"This, of course, begs the question: Why does Carmelo want a spy in my household? And, of course, I think we all three know the answer to that."

"I am a thorn in his side," Sylvio said. "But I have done everything to remain non-political all these years. What threat can I possibly be as some back-country bowyer?"

"If anyone can fathom the answer to that I think you can. You were his mentor. Now yell at me, something suitably florid, and I'll return to the caravan and sheepishly get them underway with Vincenze's help."

His thoughts elsewhere, Sylvio threw a string of inventive invectives at Portelli, even shrugging off a restraining hand from Aletta for added drama. Portelli trotted back to the caravan looking reasonably abashed and kept his word.

"What am I to make of this?" Sylvio said, turning toward Aletta.

"He's concerned, not just for the safety of the traders, but for you. He's having every person in his employ monitored. The expense is going to rob him of any profit this year."

"You heard this?"

She nodded.

Gods! What was going on? He felt stripped of the network of information upon which he used to rely. That Carmelo put a spy in Portelli's household could mean anything. Carmelo could be suspicious of Portelli. He might have a spy in every trading compound, trying to prevent any skimming of taxes. He might be in league with Breena.

Or he might want me, came the next thought. Aletta had said: He's concerned, not just for the safety of the traders, but for you. She heard that.

Nonsense. Why him?

Or was it nonsense?

Too well he knew how Carmelo detested being alone. He had come to hysteria when La Principessa, his mother, died. And then when his father, Il Principe Aldo, had taken a stroke and stepped down from office, again Carmelo revealed just how terrified he was of being alone. That scene of bitter rebuke and irrational anger was one Sylvio would never forget.

But then why dismiss him?

Reject before being rejected?

And for the first time in his life Sylvio didn't know what to do.

"I need more information," he said.

"I know. But that's not going to happen till we get to Reena."

He grunted an acknowledgement and turned Ibacci back toward the caravan that was underway. To his credit, Portelli kept a chorus of songs sweeping up and down the caravan, brisk songs, Sylvio noted. Marching songs, one might be tempted to say.

By late afternoon they'd picked up two other caravans, all heading for Reena. Sylvio grew concerned about security, and Vincenze, in his quiet, efficient manner made a circuit of their escort, passing the word to increase their vigilance. At least there was safety in numbers, and the escort took care of dissuading any would-be brigands from trying their hand at a surprise road tax.

By now terraced fields of grain gave way to olive groves and vineyards, the famed Imalfia region known for its pale green oil and dark purple wine. The westering sun burnished tree and vine, rick and cot, blazing a golden road that wound in graceful curves down to the town of Imalfia. From here the white stone buildings shone like gilded masonry, the red roof tiles like carnelian. The air was aromatic with oil and wine, roses and lavender, and as he scanned this bucolic scene bees and insects eddied like gold-dust in a lazy current. It was a scene to calm the nerves, to whisper a person's paranoia into slumber.

They'd make good time so that the gates would still be open and afford them passage through and beyond to the western gates where they'd emerge and camp up against the walls.

When stopped at the excise gate for their papers Sylvio chatted up the official on duty, gathering gossip, of which there was very little. Another caravan had passed through today, an amalgam of traders from several hamlets and farmsteads, carrying a small assortment of goods – leather, embroidery, produce and grain. The usual complaints about taxes, brigands on the road, that sort of thing. But nothing for which Sylvio was unprepared.

He thanked the clerk, palming him extra coin for his trouble, and gave the order for the caravan to exit. They camped that night off the road near a stream where a small copse afforded shelter, grazing for the horses along the wide verge where the ostlers set their withy corrals and watches. There were stone cucullati on the bank, crusted with lichen, ancient by the look of them. Sylvio wondered who had carved these hooded, robed figures, who had decided to place them by the stream, and what spirits lingered here waiting for passage from life to death. Not far from there was a rude wooden shrine to Nerezza where some of Danuto's people lit incense and knelt in prayer.

Drizzle set in before dawn and continued in a fine, grey mist as they broke camp and continued to Reena.

Throughout the day and the drizzle Sylvio gauged his sense of a gathering storm, the human kind, not the environmental, cursing over and over again his lack of information. All he had were a few bald facts which alone could mean anything from a paranoid boy to a deeper, political problem. Why put a spy in Portelli's home? Why now? For what purpose?

By now the caravan had grown to huge proportions so that even Vincenze expressed his concern. While there was safety in numbers, this was unwieldy, and what was unwieldy was likely unpredictable.

"Our retainers are stretched too thinly," Vincenze said, rubbing his forearm over his brow to mop away the rain.

Sylvio turned in the saddle as he rode, feeling Ibacci's heat and soaked coat under his hand. The stallion would earn a good currying tonight.

Behind him the caravan stretched as far as he could see, filling the road and spilling over onto the sides. With but thirty of their own retainers there was no hope of containing any problem, scattered as they were. Vincenze was right.

"Bring them in. Pass the word among our people to stay close, keep formation. Impress upon them the importance of remaining a tight group when we reach toll booths."

Vincenze nodded and turned away.

"If you thought any louder you'd be shouting," Aletta said.

He smiled. "Only you would notice."

"So tell me. Maybe it will help."

"From where have they all come?" He waved behind him at the caravan. "Not since I was Ministro – not since I left office can I remember so many traders coming to the fall market."

"We have had lean years."

"And bounty this year, yes. But, Aletta, look at them."

"I have. Tell me what you see."

"See? I see desperation. I see people trying to hide their fear. I see a disaster waiting to happen."

"You are such an optimistic man."

He turned to her, ready to fire an angry retort, only to be confronted with her gentle face and her smile. "I am an optimistic man, Aletta. But I have had cause to suspect a great deal, you must admit, in the past decade."

"I know. Which is why I'm trying to get you to articulate what it is you see with that oh-so adroit mind of yours."

"I see people so starved for any profit and business they're ready to turn on each other. And that is not the way of things in Simare. We are a nation of artisans and people schooled in land-husbandry. We cooperate. We work through consensus. We work through sharing our strengths and thereby overcoming our weaknesses. Not to say we don't squabble and enjoy a good debate. But we also love harmony and work toward it. We work very hard toward it. And what other nation can say they have a reverence and harmony with their ancestors as we?

"In one short decade Carmelo has managed to destroy a

legacy."

"But how do you see that manifesting itself, now, here?"

"Just look at how they've arrayed their own retainers."

Aletta turned in the saddle, studied the caravan behind them for some time. When she turned back to face him she was grave, a frown on her brow. "I see."

"I knew the moment the first caravan joined us. Other years retainers were pooled; caravans camped as a mixed group. Shared gossip and stories and developed bargaining platforms for when they'd meet with the major buyers from Almarè and Breena. That's what I remember before I was exiled. That's what Portelli and Vincenze have told me since. There has been none of that this year. They're all turning turtle."

"And so we'll be fighting ourselves."

"Exactly. And I cannot help but wonder if this isn't part of a larger plan, Aletta. Maybe the raids have only been the very first attacks on our crumbling walls." He rubbed his jaw. "And here am I a back-country bowyer, completely impotent to do anything to help."

At that he fell silent. And was grateful Aletta had the grace to leave it there. If a man were to be honest with himself, he might admit he was loathe to accept that old responsibility, to shoulder the weight of decisions that affected so many lives, even nations. If a man were to be honest with himself, he would admit he enjoyed the quietude of life in Danuto, of working with wood and fabricating bows. Of discovering there was so much dimension in the minutia of life. So much satisfaction. He felt he had only just begun to live. And for that, if a man were to be honest, he felt guilty, because he had held high office, he had been responsible, and once responsible it was difficult to acknowledge the responsibility was no longer his.

To allow himself to be free.

Even thinking such a thing made him wince.

The subject was not broached again.

When the caravan shambled off the road for the day the people were grim. Sylvio found himself studying them, gathering information, realizing old ways never really left him. He was who he was. When he ducked under the rough lean-to Vincenze had thrown up for Aletta and Sylvio, he was grateful.

"You're like an old dog," Aletta groaned from somewhere under a mound of blankets and oilskins.

"Fine thing to say to your husband."

"I'm cold. Come under the covers."

He smiled and shook out of his doublet and boots, kissed the pouch that carried the icons of his ancestors, those rattling bone effigies. As always he heard a whisper of voices, his father among them, no more than a susurration beneath the rain, and then he was under the covers, gathering Aletta to himself as he spooned against her back. The smell of her filled him, warm, earthy, like a garden. As only could happen when alone with her, he felt himself still, as though coming to anchor in a safe harbour. How many years now had they lain thus in the dark? Safe. United.

"I wish you weren't coming this year," she said softly, like the rain on the tarp over their heads.

"Oh, strega mia."

"I am afraid, Sylvio."

He closed his eyes. "You? The witch who scorned the status afforded by her Prince?"

"I am afraid for you."

"I know."

"Don't go."

"I must."

"We could flee through the mountains."

"And be tracked."

"Not before we reached safety. He won't know you're not coming."

"Think, Aletta. He'll know." He bent and kissed her neck, closing his eyes against the throb in his chest, the fear in his heart. "And how could I face you if I ran away? Mia strega. Mi'amore. How?"

She turned in his arms then. He felt her fingers on his face, felt them tremble. "I don't want to lose you, Sylvio."

"Hush. You won't lose me." And because he needed to as much as she, he kissed her and from there made love with familiarity and freedom that only comes from old intimacy.

Rain gave way to brilliant blue skies, the air vibrant with autumn warmth. Sylvio and the Danuto caravan continued to make their way toward Reena. Day followed day. As always they camped outside the villages and towns they passed, Sylvio ever keen to glean any kernel of information from officials, townsfolk, whomever they met.

By now it seemed to be the general opinion market this year was to be huge. There was talk of high officials coming from Almarè and Breena, even rumour of the Prima Violina attending, as well as the famed singer and politician from Breena, His Excellency the Ambassador Maponos Ó Leannáin.

By the time the white walls and red tile roofs of the capitol of Reena came into view, Sylvio bristled with the tension around him. The caravan had grown to huge proportions, some several hundreds of traders, retainers, servants, clerks, animals and wagons in a rumbling, jostling, colourful cacophony. Danuto's own retainers dressed this morning in their fine livery, red and gold, blazoned with their crest of: Gules, a horse rampant Or, and on a chief

Or a longbow Gules, string to chief. It once had been Sylvio's arms, but the right to bear them was no longer his.

The procession slowed now as each group of traders cleared through the toll-gates of the grand capital, Reena. Sylvio watched the pale cerulean of a dawn sky deepen to azure. Shopkeepers and innkeepers from establishments outside Reena's gates opened their courtyards and their doors, watching the traders that should translate to coin in their coffers. Flagstone terraces were swept. Dust swirled like mist and settled as movement through the gates came to a near standstill. Sweeping turned to watering orange trees and wisteria. An enterprising baker sent a saucy, rosy-cheeked girl with a pannier of fresh sweet rolls to sway along the procession.

Shadows shortened. The procession inched its way along. The girl from the bakery was stopped by city retainers from the closed gates. Plainly upset she returned to the bakery. Morning patience gave way to murmuring irritation. Sylvio's sense of unease stirred. Portelli shifted on his mount, Aletta and Vincenze unconsciously mimicking him. He'd suggested Vincenze give orders for their caravan to stay mounted; better to be prepared than caught off-guard.

"You have the documents?" Sylvio asked Portelli.

"Of course."

"In the right order."

"Yes, yes."

Sylvio grunted an acknowledgement, his attention drawn by a growing disturbance ahead. There was a shout. Then a growl of dissent rumbling back through the procession. After a moment he said, "Vincenze, send one of the retainers ahead."

"Maestro?"

"Find out what's going on up there."

Vincenze reined aside. In a moment Sylvio could see one of the men riding ahead, pausing, chatting, riding forward again until he was lost from view.

"I should go," Aletta said.

"You will not." He knew she bristled at his tone.

"I will hear things that retainer won't."

"I know. I don't want you up there."

"Oh for the love of peace, Sylvio, I can certainly handle myself among a bunch of traders."

He turned toward her, watched the anger on her face, her eyes like obsidian. "I have every faith in you, Aletta. But I don't want you up there."

Understanding flooded her features. "Gods, Sylvio! You don't really think—"

He waved her to silence. "I do. Listen to me, Aletta." With all his will he wanted her to hear what he did not say in those words, that ahead he was sure disaster waited for every group of traders.

It took near an hour but the retainer returned. Sylvio watched as the man leaned toward Vincenze, watched the tension on their faces. Vincenze rubbed his jaw, gestured to the man to follow him and together they returned to where Sylvio leaned over the pommel of his saddle, stroking Ibacci's neck to ease his mount's displeasure. Sylvio nodded to Aletta, who turned her full attention to the retainer.

"Speak, but do so quietly," Sylvio said to the man.

"Only one group of traders is being allowed through at a time. The gates are closed while they're being cleared."

He felt exposed here, despite the crowd sweating in the increasing heat and glare. "I want you to take another retainer up there with you. Lose the livery. Wait for us. If anything unusual happens one of you come back to find us."

The man nodded, turned his mount around and melded into their traders. When again Sylvio saw him emerge, another retainer – a woman – by his side, Sylvio approved of the man's clever disguise. Who would suspect a man and his wife? She had slung pack baskets across the rump of her mount, her hair suitably bound in linen as would any labouring woman on the road. The man had a wine skin hanging from his shoulder and had slopped a quantity down his doublet.

Sylvio watched them ride easily into the crowds ahead, using their skill to thread their way around others, skirting wagons, all of it done in a shambling, idle manner that would draw no attention. Soon they were lost in the crowd.

Morning grew to noon. Movement along the road ground to a near standstill. Lunches appeared. Sylvio chewed on cheese and bread without tasting it, scanning his surroundings, listening to conversations.

He made note of the innkeepers glaring from their doorways, of the lack of trade strolling the avenue outside the gates.

Portelli long since turned back to Danuto's own people, keeping them entertained by sharing stories and songs. By mid-afternoon even that fell silent. Children fretted. Horses stamped. The huge caravan moved forward again. Stopped. A shout of outrage rose. Ebbed. Time was marked. And the process repeated.

He watched a scuffle at the gates of an inn, watched as a group of traders were turned away. He couldn't hear what was said. But it was plain the inn wasn't open for business.

Not open for business?

"Why would they close for business?" he said, turning his attention to Aletta who had been watching the exchange.

"They're afraid," she said. "The innkeepers are afraid."

"Of what?"

"I don't' know."

At last Sylvio could actually see the city retainers at the gates. The caravan ahead of them would be next. In the shadow of a shrine to some god or other sat the two retainers Sylvio sent forward earlier in the day. Casually they rose, packed away their lunch, their actions somehow making it seem they had far more to accomplish than fact.

When at last the pair rejoined the caravan, they melded into the heart of activities and only returned to Sylvio when once more liveried. A simple change of clothes, hidden among the press of people, would do much to disguise who they were and their movements from unwanted eyes.

"Well?" Sylvio said.

"I have nothing concrete to tell you, Maestro," the man said.

"Only observations," added the woman. "Reena's retainers are careful to allow one and only one caravan through the gates at a time. Once the gates are closed there has been only one common occurrence all day –"

"Shouting," finished the man. "There has been shouting."

"About?" Sylvio asked.

"We were unable to discover, Maestro."

"All we do know, Maestro," the woman said, "is that every caravan allowed through has been outraged by some news or action."

Sylvio rubbed his jaw, looked up to the gates, back to the retainers. "What are they doing up there?"

"I don't know, Maestro."

Sylvio nodded. "You did well. Join the others."

They reined around and took up positions around the caravan.

"What do you make of this?" Vincenze asked.

"I don't know." He turned to Aletta. "Anything?"

She shook her head, her attention on those beautiful, massive gates of Reena. Sylvio watched her face, turned his gaze to the gates. Cast of bronze by ancient masters of the city, the gates were reliefs of two funereal urns of Simare on blazing suns, the country's emblem. It occurred to him this was a grim icon for a country of such life-loving people, that he and his countrymen had a preoccupation with the rites of death.

Across the castellated battlements guards looked down at the river of merchants. A decade prior there would have been banners and buntings shifting in the dust-filled air, greetings, camaraderie. Now there was only the glaring sun on stone, the glitter and bristle of armour and weapons.

"I think I should be with Portelli when we are cleared through the gates," Aletta said after a moment.

Sylvio nodded. "If you're sure."

She turned toward him, laying her hand on his forearm and that brought his attention back to her. "I am sure. Do not be concerned. I need to do my duty as strega."

He nodded to that, unwilling to allow her to put herself in harm's way. But what harm could there be? It was standard procedure to be cleared for trade through the gates. Or at least it should have been standard procedure. What was going on up there, however, seemed anything but standard.

Patience, he told himself. He should listen to his wife.

The gates opened and the next caravan shambled forward, Reena's retainers filing back along the procession to where it became obvious Danuto's caravan began.

"Get Portelli," Sylvio said to Vincenze, and the man kneed his mount around to notify their Sindaco. As Portelli arrived at Sylvio's side the Reena retainers came abreast, looking harried.

Sylvio watched the scene through the open gates, how the caravan's officials were pulled aside by the warden of the toll booth, the way the remainder of the caravan were hemmed in by Reena's retainers.

The gates were closing.

"Public or private?" one of the retainers asked, halting any forward movement of the Danuto caravan.

"Private," replied Portelli, who also watched the closing scene through the gates.

The retainer scribbled a note on the documents he carried. "Region?"

The gates shut with a resounding boom. A shout of outrage went up beyond the gates, just as Sylvio's own people had described.

"Danuto," Portelli answered.

"Gods!" Aletta whispered.

Another scribble on that official sheaf of documents. "Wait here."

Sylvio tore his attention away from the gates, from the official. Aletta's face had paled, her fingers to her breast.

The retainer walked away toward the sally port.

"What is it, Aletta?" Sylvio asked.

"I cannot have heard right."

"What?"

She turned toward him, her usual reserve gone, her eyes wide with disbelief. "There is a tax."

Sylvio laughed at the irony of it. "And this is news?"

"It is a ruinous tax, Sylvio. I could not hear more, but it is ruinous."

"Damn him," Portelli growled.

Sylvio shot Portelli a glance, concerned that the usually unflappable Sindaco should have revealed so much even to someone like Sylvio who had none of Aletta's skill. He wanted to be able to say something that would make a difference, to say he would right all the wrongs that had been done in the last ten years. In truth if he knew what to do he swore he would do it. But short of deposing Carmelo, which was unthinkable, he had no idea what to do. Even to consider such a thought was so beyond Sylvio's code of ethics as to be foreign. Whatever Carmelo's faults he was still, by law, Principe, and therefore sovereign ruler of this land Sylvio so loved.

And so there was yet another tax. A tax on what? And how much? Payable by when and to whom?

He turned his attention to the shopkeepers along the avenue, the way staff or the owners themselves lingered in doorways, at the open gates of courtyards. He should have noticed earlier. He should have realized they should have been plying their wares and services all up and down the jammed street of traders all day, doing everything to keep what should have been a windfall of business flowing to their establishments. Many of them looked away when he caught their attention.

What was going on here?

He cast another glance around, drawing on long-unused skills he had honed when in government.

Where was the general business of the city? Where were the people doing their daily marketing? Lounging in the courtyards of inns? Sipping strong coffee and dunking biscotti under the awnings of bistros? The bone-speaker's shop should have had clients seeking the advice of their ancestors, but instead the red door was closed, the windows shuttered.

He reached over and gripped Aletta's wrist, still watching the environment of the street. "I've been a neglectful husband. Allow me to buy you a drink."

He heard her quick intake of breath, knew he had delivered his message to her. With a murmured note of caution to Vincenze he dismounted, took Aletta by the elbow and steered her through the crowd to the sign of a bakery where he had seen that saucy girl with her basket of goods earlier in the day.

At the door he met the baker, a young man dusted with flour and a flinty-eyed stare. The baker made no attempt to allow Sylvio and Aletta into the shop.

"Closing?" Sylvio asked when the baker simply stared.

The baker shook his head.

Sylvio glanced through the windows at the racks full of bread, biscuits, pastries. There were festival panettoni like fruit-embedded puff-balls stacked on shelves, delicate marzipans painted like fruit. Goods aplenty. No customers.

"Trade's been poor today?" he asked.

The baker shrugged.

Sylvio gestured around him. "Don't seem to be many people buying today."

Again the baker shook his head.

"Would it be possible to buy a cup of coffee and a biscotti? Something fresh after the rigours of the road would be welcome."

The baker glanced up to the gates, back down the road. "You'd best return to your caravan, Ministro."

Titles? "Have we met?"

"You once helped my father. "

Sylvio raised his eyebrows.

"He worked on your staff, wanted to retire after Il Principe came to power. You helped him obtain permits to open a bakery." The young man glanced around. "I'm not supposed to be speaking with you, Ministro. It could cost me my livelihood."

"By whose order?"

"Please, Ministro –"

"I apologize. Give my regards to your father."

Sylvio turned, confused, outraged.

What was going on here?

Before they reached the caravan, Aletta said, "There's been an order from the Castello. No trade is to be conducted with any of the merchants coming to Reena before they've cleared the gates. No discussion is to take place. Fines and penalties, I don't know to what extent, are to be levied. His name is Giacomo Vitali. His father is Paulo."

Sylvio felt as though Aletta had just plunged him into an icy stream where the temperature and the flow were almost more than he could bear. "I remember Paulo Vitali."

"As do I."

"Good man."

"Loyal to Il Principe's father."

"And to me." He turned his attention to her, seeing the strain on her face, the concern. "What more?"

"I wanted to touch him, Sylvio. I wanted to put him under the power of the strega, gods help me, but I dared not. He was terrified. There was so much more he could have told us were he allowed. As it is he risked much." She squeezed his arm. "I am afraid, Sylvio."

That chilled him further. He wanted to take her in his arms, comfort her, Aletta, the woman who was strong and sure and not given to alarm. But they had reached Vincenze and Portelli now. He mounted, as did Aletta. The gates opened, ponderously, inexorably. Retainers filed down the sides of their caravan, for all intents and purposes escorting them forward.

Disaster, Sylvio was sure, waited for them when finally they crossed into the city of Reena.

CHAPTER 2

"Reason for caravan?"

Sylvio watched the excise officer from where he stood in the doorway. The man looked worn, avoided eye contact and kept his attention firmly on his board of papers. The office would have been spacious but for the shelves of paperwork, ledgers, what appeared to be confiscated goods piled in disarray around, on and under desks and tables instead of stored in warehouses run and controlled by the government. It all had the look of too much work, not enough time or staff.

Besides three other people, the only added manpower he could see was in the form of brawn – two heavily-armed retainers at the back of the office, standing in front of an enormous bronze chest. Presumably it was locked, if the hardware on it were any indication.

"Reena Grand Market," Portelli answered, standing further into the office with the official.

"Public or private?"

"I told your man there—"

"Public or private?"

Portelli sighed. "Private."

Sylvio felt Aletta's hand on his arm. He glanced at her, saw her nod toward the scene outside the open door of the excise office where retainers harried Danuto's traders. "He's stalling for time," she whispered.

"Sponsor?" the official asked.

"Sindaco Antonio Portelli," Portelli answered.

"And he is where?"

"Gods, man, I see you every year. Right in front of you."

Sylvio saw the excise officer look up at Portelli briefly, glance at the doorway, back down, scribble something. "Duration of stay?"

"The duration of the market, give or take a few days."

Voices rose in the piazza, traders plainly indignant with their treatment. Gone was the grand procession Sylvio remembered. Banners waving. Cheers. Trumpets and tambourines, heralds and ribbons whirling in the hands of dancers. Calls from people familiar with this or that merchant. Grim was how it seemed now.

"How many is a few?" the official asked.

"I don't know!" Portelli said. "A few. However long it takes us to pack up and head back to Danuto. I might wish to stay in residence a little longer."

"We require specifics."

Sylvio watched their caravan being herded through the gates, watched the way Reena's retainers ringed them like an armed guard. As if they feared unrest, even riot.

"Gods!" Portelli said. "Say three days after the close of market."

"Where is the caravan billeted?"

"Casa Portelli, Piazza da Luna."

"Papers?"

Portelli shoved them at the official. Sylvio felt he didn't have enough eyes to take in everything, to note everything he should.

"Manifest?" the officer asked.

"At the back."

The officer flipped through pages, nodded, flipped through a few more. "There's no complete retail total here."

"It's never been required before. We're a conglomeration from Danuto village."

"Doesn't matter. Need a total." The official tossed the sheaf of papers to the woman at the desk, her fingers flicking over an abacus as she wrote.

"What for?" Portelli asked.

Sylvio could feel Portelli lose patience. He glanced over to the piazza where Vincenze tried to keep their retainers in a protective ring around Danuto's traders and goods. They were almost through the gates. Other retainers from Reena had formed a line just outside the gates, the way they had when the Danuto caravan waited their turn.

"To assess the Security Measures Tax," the official said.

Here it comes, Sylvio thought.

"Security Measures Tax?" Portelli asked.

"New law."

"Why weren't we notified?"

The official looked up then. Sylvio caught the man's frustration. He looked familiar. "I'm only doing my job."

"I know. Why weren't we notified?"

"You'd have to ask Il Principe about that."

Sylvio listened to the clickety-clatter of the abacus, to the whicker of horses, the traders' voices rising, grumbling. Dust swirled in the piazza.

"He's afraid," Aletta whispered.

Sylvio noted the lack of townsfolk in the piazza, the way they hovered furtively at doorways and balconies. The last time he'd seen this piazza it had been a hanging garden, balconies riotous

From Mountains of Ice   67

with flowers, potted trees outside gates, vines and scents creeping over wall and window. What he saw now was existence. All beauty chipped away. Ten years. So much had changed.

And seeing this, Sylvio realized there were times a man wished for a simpler life, wished for simple truths and simple dealings. He wanted to see flowers in the piazza. He wanted to hear laughter, good-natured bickering. He wanted to see those banners and buntings he remembered. Ten years ago. That longing weighed upon him. Everything had a price.

"Sylvio, no," Aletta whispered.

Despite her warning, despite what he knew she saw in him, he moved into the office, away from the door toward the official.

"We're asking you why the people weren't informed," he said, "as you are Il Principe's voice here."

The excise officer paled. "Ah, Ministro – Ah, em, Maestro. Yes. It has been a long time since we've seen you in Reena. Welcome back. Ah, yes, I'm supposed to deliver a message for you." He turned to the desk where the woman tallied figures, pulled a sealed canvas envelope from the top of a pile of papers and handed it to Sylvio.

"Seems I'm getting a lot of messages from the Castello these days," He looked back up at the officer. "Thank you. Now, perhaps you would inform us of what, exactly, this new tax entails, and why?" He could hear the rumble of the gates closing, watched as the other two officials in the office took portions of the Danuto manifest and walked toward the caravan, clearly intent upon taking inventory.

"Breena has placed Simare under protection," the man said. "As a means to compensate for added security we are required to levy a thirty percent tax on all goods for sale."

"Thirty percent!" Portelli roared. "Why that –"

Sylvio put his hand on Portelli's arm. "Sindaco, aspetta – wait."

Portelli rounded on him, shuddering with outrage. "Do you know what this means?"

"Better than you realize, Sindaco. Please, allow me to do this. It's long overdue." He glanced at Aletta, saw her struggle to remain the strega, not the wife. Only he would have known, because he was the one privileged enough to be allowed inside the strega's code of non-partiality. He found he had the grace to give her a smile, and in that gesture attempt to assure her all was well; he knew he shouldered responsibility he wasn't required to accept, not by anyone's standards but his own.

If a man were honest with himself he would admit he didn't wish this burden. Not again. If a man were honest with himself he'd admit he'd been content as a back-country bowyer. There was peace in simplicity.

"Security against what?" Sylvio asked.

"I don't know. I'm just following orders."

"He doesn't know," Aletta said, her voice flat.

Sylvio watched recognition cross the man's face. Saw him remember Sylvio's witch-wife, the woman who had refused to act as strega for either prince.

"Of course you are," Sylvio said. "My apologies. When is the tax payable?" He watched the man, the way his face was lined with stress, the way he avoided eye contact as though ashamed or nervous of what he had to do. Aletta said he was afraid. Sylvio was sure he knew this man. Ten years.

"Immediately, Maestro. The tax is payable immediately."

"And if all the goods aren't sold?"

"Then the village can apply for a refund."

"You have the paperwork for that?"

"You'll have to pick it up at the Minister of Trade's office."

"And how long would a refund take?"

"I'm not sure, Maestro."

"As a citizen, not a public servant – Frederico, isn't it? – any idea how long a refund might take?"

The man let go of a breath, evidence of his tension, looked up at Sylvio. There was desperation on the man's face. "Weeks, I'd expect, Maestro. There aren't many of us left attending the country's business."

"I can see that." There were shouts now in the piazza. He felt more than heard the gates of Reena close, felt the rumble of it through the soles of his feet. Like earth-tremors, the shudders before the quake. This news was what had caused the shouting he'd heard when waiting to enter. He'd expected it. He just hadn't expected the news to be as crushing as it was. There would be traders who would go home bankrupt this season. There would be desperation. Reason enough for added security. The whole thing seemed so ridiculously defeatist and circular. There were voices in his head, a weight at his hip where the pouch of his ancestors' effigies hung.

Carmelo, what have you done?

"Will you take my surety until we can settle at Casa Portelli?"

"I'm sorry, Maestro, no, we –"

"Prince Carmelo wants his tax."

"The Breenai ships are in harbour to take the Security Measures Tax back with them."

Sylvio laughed then, the sound of it bitter to his ears. "Of course they are." He turned then, strode to the doorway, feeling the despair rise in him like darkness. "Vincenze!" he called. He watched as Vincenze wheeled around from a heated discussion with one of Reena's retainers. "Bring my personal coffer." He watched Vincenze turn away from the retainer and stride off toward one of the wagons.

It took a few moments but at length Vincenze came to where Sylvio stood, his face full of anger and question. "Give it to the good Senore there," Sylvio said.

"This will ruin you," Aletta said, her voice hoarse with emotion.

Sylvio shrugged and turned back to the excise officer. "This is my personal coffer. It is all I have with me. When your team out there have finished, I'll give you the keys to that coffer and you can take the tax from that. I'll want a receipt." He glanced around at the others, Portelli, Aletta, Vincenze. "This is my responsibility. The villagers are not to know. Is this understood?"

One by one, they gave their agreement, reluctantly, but they did.

He strode away from them all, out into the dust and despair of the piazza. He didn't want to see their faces. Didn't want to see the thoughts there for anyone to read, plain enough for even an ordinary person. Bad enough there were whispers in his head, louder than ever he'd experienced, the dead clamouring at a distance, like a wind rising. There were bonds here tightening around him, ties he couldn't sever. Never really had. Never really able. Strip a man of title, of trappings, and still there was this responsibility rooted in him he could no more deny than his name. Or his face. Or those voices that followed him and were the mark of a bone-speaker.

And what was it now Carmelo wanted of him? Why did he ransom a nation? What need was there so great to sacrifice home and hearth?

Or was it arrogance on his part to think Carmelo went to such lengths to bring him back into Royal service?

He felt the grit on his face, sticking to his eyelids. Felt the weariness in his limbs, no longer young. Not old, but not the body of a man convinced of invincibility. He looked around at the traders of his village, the wives, the husbands, the lovers and friends, the staff from Portelli's household. Good people. Not perfect. Fallible. Human. Wonderfully, colourfully human. Friends and acquaintances. The fabric of his village. The cloth of the life he'd tried to wear for ten years.

"Listen to me," he said, careful to keep his voice at a normal pitch. A conversational voice. He was to have an ordinary conversation with the traders of Danuto. The words may be cause for alarm, but his tone should not. Silence settled, slowly, like the dust of the piazza. "I want you to assist these servants of Il Principe. They are only doing their jobs. I promise you I will explain once we reach Casa Portelli. Let us be efficient about this, eh?"

He turned to one of the officials who stood by the archery cart. "Let me help you with this. There may be a few details with which you are unfamiliar."

And so it went. Driven by his example the remainder of the traders followed his lead, biting back their outrage, their questions, trusting Sylvio's word.

They finished within the hour. Paperwork signed. Copies distributed. The levy paid, receipt issued. By the time they clattered into Portelli's courtyard shadows were long and tempers given to resignation.

Sylvio said little, letting Portelli do his job as Sindaco and host. What occupied Sylvio was what he'd seen while riding through Reena's streets. There had been a few buntings draped carelessly across the main thoroughfare. But beyond that he'd seen the same decay as in the piazza. Backstreets and alleys that ran off Via Major were thick with refuse. The air was rank. Buildings in disrepair, stucco flaking away leaving white scabs against pink and ochre, madder and blue. Commercial areas displayed more boarded windows than establishments thriving with trade. Many artisan shops remained dark, quiet. The only thing he'd seen in abundance had been the stray dogs and cats, foraging. And the poor. They begged at every corner, trotted beside the caravans.

Sylvio could only feel relief when he slid from Ibacci's back and released him into the care of Portelli's ostlers. He stood for a moment watching his companions, Portelli's servants, Portelli's courtyard. The triple orange trees and fountain were still the centerpiece of the courtyard, the trees larger, the patina of years on the fountain, all of it once his, stripped and given to Portelli. He noted the good repair of the cobbles, of the buildings, the plain but tidy garments of Portelli's staff. What the upkeep of this estate must cost would be enough to beggar the man, Sylvio thought. Especially in light of the lean years they'd just endured. And now this secondary new tax. It would mean fifty percent of all income skimmed. Inflation was bound to follow, the destabilization of Simare's currency.

He walked to Aletta's side, draped his arm around her shoulders and whispered in her ear, "I love you, witch-wife."

She looked up at him sharply. He saw her take in his mood, reading his voice, and then her features soften. She said nothing, only pressed the palm of her hand to his cheek, as if to say, I know.

And for him, at that moment, the courtyard, the tension and uncertainty fell away and there was only this understanding between a man and a woman who had grown familiar and easy.

Piazza da Luna was a large market square serving the out-of-town traders, and this early in the morning it vibrated with voices haggling, carts rumbling, birds squabbling. Somewhere in that multi-coloured mass a minstrel played a vielle à roué, which sounded for all the world like stringed bagpipes. Certainly the singer was an improvement to the overall whine and thump of the instrument.

A gentle rain in the night settled the dust of the piazza, and at least the traders there, hawking everything from cabbages to cooled milk, made an attempt to clear the refuse of the previous day. Still, the scene before Sylvio was nothing the way he remembered. It all looked tired, shabby, worn by Carmelo's years of misrule. Portelli's steward complained this morning of that very lack of quality, apologizing for the fare spread for the breakfast board. Certainly there was nothing wrong with the food, just that staff paid premium prices for less than premium goods.

Hanging from balconies around the piazza were the woven banners of some of Simare's traders, advertisements they were in residence and open to trade. Danuto's cascaded from the large main balcony on this, the second floor, heavy with gold threads and fine wools from Portelli's own looms. Sylvio's banner should have hung from the balcony where he stood, as it did the last time he had been in Reena, but the titles and position that gave him the right to display arms were no longer his, and to have defied Carmelo would only invite disaster for all those who depended on him.

He turned away from the morning market toward the cheval glass, having dismissed the servant assigned him, and jammed a green, double-cut velvet hat onto his grey-streaked head, tilting the plate-like thing in an attempt to make himself look more like a man of substance than a back-country artisan. Aletta insisted he wear a single jewel pinned to it with a spray of cock's feathers, as she had insisted on the matching green velvet, sleeveless surcoat lined with ordinary squirrel fur. Under this he sported a russet silk jacquard doublet, sleeves plain but tied with points of silk ribbon that ended in gold filigree aiglets, breeches cut of the same cloth, and sensible white silk hose. His shoes were of fine Almarè leather with discreet buckles of gold. His purse was of plain leather with only a simple gold latch. He eschewed any rings. Not too opulent. Understated. Respectable.

He would do, he supposed, for what was to be a day of carefully navigated negotiations, meetings and social landmines, a repeat of his days since arriving for the Grand Market. This evening, however, was the grand fete they were to attend at the Castello, part of the Festa da Nerezza. Sylvio specifically was to attend.

He lifted the invitation, delivered at Reena's gates when he'd arrived, from the dresser, the seals all now broken, unfolded it again: a florid list of titles and salutations, professions of greatest love and longing, veiled accusations of betrayal through Sylvio's absence, enforced though it might have been, earnest wishes to redress absence. Just the fact Carmelo singled him out was fraught with potential, none of it with any hope. Sylvio set the invitation back onto the dresser. He let go a breath.

There already had been another message delivered from the Castello, essentially a reiteration of the invitation, this time in Carmelo's own hand. Apparently Sylvio was very much desired in the Royal Presence.

Sylvio crossed the room to the small shrine, fingered the bone effigies of his ancestors, murmured a wish of hope, heard what could have been a cry from the piazza or a cry from another distance.

He withdrew his hand. Now was not a time to lose himself in this growing ability. Not now. In a few moments the buyers from Breena, Almarè and the rest of Simare would begin an endless stream into Portelli's warehouses that would, hopefully, result in endless purchases, that would in turn, hopefully, fill Danuto's traders' coffers. Or so it should be.

Void of hope, and late, Sylvio racketed down the wide, marble stairs to the main floor, out into the gentle, morning sunlight of the courtyard and across to the stables and warehouses where the rest of Danuto's traders supervised the display of wares. Two of Danuto's junior notaries, who had traveled with them, fussed over tables set up to tally accounting and prepare lists, dour in their black gowns and caps. One of Reena's officials bent over a set of scales, inspecting them for approval. Portelli's liveried servants were ubiquitous, there to move bales, untie cording, run errands.

The real business of Reena's annual market took place not here in the warehouses with the notaries set out for display, but later when buyers retired to the salons of the traders where un-watered wine and spiced edibles were served around a dance of conversation that wove in and out of the hard negotiations of price, quantity, supply, delivery and terms of payment.

He strolled through the preparations, listening in on conversations and instructions between Danuto's traders and Portelli's staff, and eventually found Portelli amid his bales of fine woollen cloth, hands punctuating his orders. Portelli's gaze shifted to Sylvio. He nodded, gave a final word to his staff and turned away to join Sylvio, draping his arm around Sylvio's shoulders.

"Come, my friend. It's time we joined the others in the salon. I've received word the Breenai trading agent is to attend upon us this morning."

"Oh?"

"It is what we're here for."

"It rankles."

"I know. But we need their coin, and that's the brunt of it."

"And I don't know this?"

Portelli dropped his arm from Sylvio's shoulders and waved him inside. "Of course you know, better than many of us."

The loggia here let into the grand foyer that opened again onto an atrium, two staircases spanning either side like stone wings. Fragrant myrtle spilled along the edges of the stone pool in the atrium where lilies floated and delicate birds fluttered and piped. Here the pillars were black marble, none of this trompe l'oiel. An artist's hand had its place, but Sylvio felt it was meaningless attempting to disguise one thing for another. He was glad to see

Portelli agreed. A gallery ran around the pool from the second floor, picketed with marble balusters also in black and ornamented in gilt.

Beyond, the atrium let into a grand salon Sylvio remembered from years past. He remembered the lacquered chests and inlaid tables, the large, long windows that looked out to the north and the gardens and let in light and airiness to counterpoint the heaviness of walls laden with paintings of ancestors, historic events, allegories and scenes from Simare's mythology. He knew it all because it once had been his, confiscated and gifted to Portelli when Sylvio fell from grace.

A servant offered wine when Sylvio entered the salon, which he declined with a gesture and instead poured water from a painted stoneware ewer into a chased silver cup.

Portelli laughed. "Don't trust yourself?"

"It's your wine I don't trust." He turned to the doorway at the far end of the room. Aletta chatted with one of the other traders as she entered. Today she eschewed the stiff, formal gowns and wired headdresses of voile that were so fashionable among the rarefied, and opted instead for a simple chiton of shot plum-grey silk, heavily embroidered with gold sheaves of wheat at the selvage and secured across the top of the arms with gold brooches of the same design. From bust to waist the same plum-grey silk ribboned her torso, gathering the chiton into gentle, hissing folds. Her sandals were gilt leather, and upon her head she wore a small diadem of trembling gold sheaves that cascaded into face jewellery of gold and moonstones. Gold dust powdered her lids and cheeks, khol outlining her dark eyes.

Immediately he knew why she dressed this way. She was a strega. A witch. A diviner of truth. All of her presentation did everything to emphasize what she was, and give notice to anyone she met there were no secrets from her. Truth to tell, he knew she could only sense the truth of someone's statements. She could not tell what they hid. Still, it was enough. And best cultivate the myths about the stregare.

She meandered the room, nodding to those who were gathered here, overlooking the small desk set discreetly in a corner where one of the notaries sat. There was to be a business-like distance between them today, he knew, but how he longed to bend to her ear, whisper his adoration and respect for and of her.

"So," Portelli said, reeling in Sylvio's thoughts. "You still haven't said how you plan to proceed with negotiations for your arcossi."

Ah, so they came back to this. "No."

"Given the Breenai representative will be here shortly, I think it would be wise to discuss how we're going to handle that."

What was to consider? Selling weapons like the arcossi to a people who very likely would use those weapons against you was nothing short of lunacy, little say suicide, profits be damned. He didn't care what the Breenai offered and damned if he'd give them that kind of advantage. "I don't like it."

"I know you don't. But what trading policy are you going to present? You're the only part of Danuto's team that hasn't decided, and other merchants that have presented themselves have placed inquiries as well."

"How can I sell the arcossi to Breena? Tell me, Antonio."

"That's fine. All of us concur."

"Oh, so you've all discussed this without me?" He was being obstructive. He knew it. It's just that he felt himself standing at the mouth of a trap now he was in Reena and also knew he had to walk into it before he could figure out how to escape from it.

Portelli simply shook his head and smiled, as if to say, what else? And indeed what else were they to do but discuss every aspect of their trade team and policy? That they'd found it necessary to hold council in his absence spoke too clearly of their concern for him and any action he might take.

Sylvio rubbed his jaw. "I am all at odds, Antonio. Forgive me."

Portelli clapped him on the back and laughed. "You're not alone, Sylvio. You know this."

Sylvio nodded, his thoughts in complete disagreement with the gesture. Of course he was alone. Whatever Carmelo's current concern with him it had nothing to do with the rest of Danuto. Oh, yes, Carmelo might use Sylvio's associations. But that was just business. Sylvio should know. He taught Carmelo to use the tools at hand. Little had he thought the boy would so ill-use those tools.

Portelli's steward entered and aimed a straight line toward them, his face grave. "Padrone, the Breenai Ambassador Maponos Ó Leannáin is here with the trade envoy from Breena."

Portelli threw Sylvio a glance. "Have they been to the warehouses?"

"They have, Padrone."

"They wasted no time." Portelli gestured as if to say, what to do? "Then show them in. And let's be smart about it. Can't have them thinking we're dullards."

They arranged themselves in the room as if preparing for the curtain, set places on a set stage. Portelli's steward announced the Breenai trade envoy by precedence, with, of course, Ó Leannáin being the foremost among them. Ó Leannáin's doublet of rich brown silk was minutely highlighted with a woven gold thread, under that the traditional saffron leine, but his of silk. Over this a black and brown brocade surcoat hung in carelessly elegant folds from shoulders Sylvio was certain were no stranger to the demands of pulling a bow of considerable weight. Ó Leannáin, although he had no need, genuflected before his hosts, which, after a moment's hesitation, brought similar if stiffer response from the remainder of his entourage, five in total, men and women in excellent imported wools and silks fashioned in the Breenai style. Portelli returned the honour, followed by the Danuto host, and then a booming welcome from Portelli himself, and introductions.

When Sylvio was introduced, Ó Leannáin responded with a wide grin. "Ah, the Maestro Sylvio di Danuto. Are the fine arcossi in the warehouses the result of your hand?"

Sylvio stiffened. "I made them, yes."

Ó Leannáin's eyes glittered. "Five hundred arcossi?"

Sylvio thought of all the dead who found their voices in those bows of laminated bone, wood and sinew. "I've had time to fill."

"Perhaps you will do me the honour of later discussing their art?" He smiled around at the traders in the room. "Of course, after we have settled other matters of trade this morning. I know there are those with me who are very interested in the fine woollens from Danuto's mills and that remarkable beer. And let us not forget your horses."

What was he to answer to that? Tell the man to piss off and take his trade envoy skulking back to Breena? No. He glanced at the tense faces of the other traders, of the hooded eyes of his wife, the strega, whose face was an iconic mask and a signal of danger. He smiled, all teeth. "It would be my pleasure, Ambassador. Perhaps when you have finished here you and I can return to the warehouse? It's easier to explain construction of the arcossi if I have them to hand."

Ó Leannáin leaned close when he sketched a bow, whispering, "Perhaps your esteemed wife would join us?"

Aletta? Sylvio shot her a glance, back to Ó Leannáin. He must surely know she was a strega. What portend this that he should wish their conversation witnessed by a truthsayer? Sylvio nodded. Ó Leannáin passed on, exchanging pleasantries while the rest of his envoy fanned out and began the hard negotiations that were expected of this morning.

He watched as groups formed, unformed, voices rising and falling, sometimes bantering, sometimes bickering. Danuto's senior notary sat at the desk in the fine, gilded chair, comparing exchange rates, the abacus clacking, his ascetic face framed by the lappets of his black cap. A junior clerk bent over a small board at the notary's back, double-checking figures and terms. The wine flowed. Tongues loosened, voices slurred. Through the windows facing the front of the casa Sylvio could hear the riot of a tarantella playing in the piazza, the insistent shiver of a tambourine. He watched Ó Leannáin who wove through the discussions as though dancing a pavane. It surprised Sylvio how little comment Ó Leannáin offered, and how Ó Leannáin's cup remained full without refilling despite his continual sipping.

A careful man, Sylvio thought. He glanced at his own cup. Like himself. He set down his water and turned his back to the room, unsure of what he was about to do, unsure of this whole series of events. Lost, he slipped out to the atrium where the sounds of the fountain and birds drifted by, out to the courtyard and the dust and noise and heat of a stunning autumn day where the servants and escort of the Breenai mingled with the staff from both Danuto and Portelli's household, and from there into the gloom of the warehouses where his arcossi were stored.

Here there were no people. Here all was quiet, but for the faint whisper of sound only he could hear.

Hush, he thought to himself. Be still. And ran the palm of his hand across the lid of the top box of arcossi.

How could he put such a boon into the hands of a nation bent on subverting his people?

Gods, help me, he thought.

He heard whispers, dry and chittering, looked up sharply into the dust and gloom of the warehouse. Only the scuttle of a mouse. In the distance a horse whickered, followed by the firm but gentle command of an ostler. A burst of laughter then, plainly from the traders viewing Danuto's horses. Whispers again beneath his hand, fading like a breeze lost in leaves. A swallow swooped along the vaulted ceiling, blade-like wings almost silent. Almost. Like the voices in the boxes beneath his hand.

"Guide me," he whispered into the gloom and looked up again as footsteps echoed off the stone. His vision was blinded by the light behind the figures that approached, something for which he cursed himself as foolish and poor planning.

You're getting soft, he thought, to let yourself be caught like this.

Even so, he could tell from the outline and grace of movement one of the people who approached was his own Aletta, and given the flowing surcoat fluttering around the other, taller figure, he surmised Ó Leannáin walked with her, which suited him well enough. Better that Ó Leannáin should come to him. It set the tone of what was to follow. Or at least so he thought.

The moment Ó Leannáin drew abreast, the Ambassador placed himself with his back to the light so that his features were shadowed.

"Ministro, I wish you to hear the truth of what I speak," he said without preamble. "And I have little time." He glanced to Aletta, who nodded, her face inscrutable. Sylvio felt the shock of Ó Leannáin's use of his obsolete title, the implications around that. "Watch for anyone who approaches. It is imperative I'm not overheard."

Sylvio made a gesture for silence, turned and inspected the boxes and bales, the passages between them, to be sure there were no hidden eavesdroppers, returned and stood facing Ó Leannáin and the entrance to the warehouse. "Go on."

"You will come to the Breenai flagship this afternoon to finalize the sale to us of all your arcossi." He held up a hand to the protest

Sylvio was about to utter. "Please, this is of utmost importance. Surely you must by now realize the arcossi will guide those who use them to protect the homes and hearths they remember. You're going to ask yourself how I know this. Suffice it that I, too, study the mysteries of life, and of death. No harm will come to your people. If you don't know this, you will soon.

"Once aboard my ship you will find Prima Violina of Almarè aboard. She and her retainers will arrange a suitable decoy and subterfuge that will have you and your esteemed wife aboard the Almarè flagship before the festival this evening where you are expected, and where it is planned you are to meet your demise.

"How I know these things is not important at the moment. That I do know these things should be your only concern." He turned to Aletta. "Do I speak the truth?"

She nodded. "Without let or hindrance. Although I would know why it is you warn us in this manner. You would have us believe you are on a path of treason to your own country."

"It is so. The present course of our collective governments' actions will benefit no one in the long run. There are times men of conscience must act, whatever the cost." He smiled. "As a gesture of good faith, let Portelli know the spy he has in his household is none other than his own faithful and trusted steward. It was of import that I should have someone of unimpeachable character work for us both and fabricate a fantasy for your Principe. Between us all, we may be able to avoid an annexation and invasion. I have lingered overlong. You and I will haggle about price as we return to the salon and settle the terms of our sale. I will expect you aboard ship no later than dusk. It is imperative you are not late."

"There is no lie in what he says," Aletta said.

Gods, Sylvio thought. Why assassinate him?

It was then he inwardly cursed himself for a fool. Indeed why not assassinate him? Despite all he had done over the past decade,

Sylvio now realized he was very much a threat to Carmelo's control of the country. Isolated as he'd been, he'd not realized until recently how the people remembered him, how they still held him in high esteem, esteem for which he felt unworthy simply because he'd done nothing in all those years to earn their regard. He'd sat with Carmelo's banishment on his shoulders as effective as the bars of a prison, allowing himself to find refuge, disturbing as it was, in the mysteries of being a bowyer of the arcane. And all the while the people remembered a time of tolerance, of prosperity, of a man who had worked beside the retired Principe for the good of them all. And, it would appear, they felt his dismissal and banishment as keenly as if Carmelo had dismissed and banished them all. His fall from grace had been a national affront. He'd been too blinded by betrayal to see it.

Now, with Breena squeezing Simare until it would bleed, the people were ready to accept whatever faint hope there might be. His recall to court could only be seen by the people as that hope. And Carmelo, being the bright if misguided boy he'd tutored, would use that hope and crush it in order to retain his tenuous control of a crumbling country.

"And what when I go into exile in Almarè?" Sylvio asked. "What then?"

"I cannot advise you in that regard, but only to say that as do I, so must you – follow your conscience. We buy you time, and protection. Without either, any hope you may conceive will be lost."

Sylvio looked over to Aletta, back to Ó Leannáin. "Then let it be so."

It was all too much of a shock. He needed time to think and

collect information. Most specifically he needed information from one woman alone, and she could not come to him. He would have to go to her.

After returning to the salon and operating like an automaton through the rest of the trade talks, he slipped away into Reena's streets and wandered. Afternoon waned, the light gold where it touched the cobbles, the leprous stucco of houses. By now the piazza held only the echoes of market, with a few stalls offering snacks, hoping to catch the last sales that might be gleaned from departing traders. Pigeons clattered into the air and brushed wide, swooping arcs, the sound of their wings harsh in the emptying space. There were a few gates open around the circle, final exchanges and pleasantries, many traders with armed escorts, some with palanquins or litters, most on horseback. He kept his head down to avoid recognition, aware he likely should have brought his own escort, not given in to impulse. But he'd be damned if he'd go back now. Besides, where he wanted to go he wanted no witnesses, and what he had to ask needed no other ears. What Ó Leannáin intimated about his dark art unsettled him as much as the threat of assassination, and there was one voice he wanted to summon before he walked any further into the trap Carmelo set for him.

He took the street that rose up the hill where temples of gaudily painted marble rose to serve those who could afford to worship in comfort and glory, unlike those who scraped their knees on dirt floors before wooden shrines. The smell of roasting lamb drifted through the traffic he traversed, heavy with garlic and rosemary and the earthy aroma of cumin. He realized he'd not eaten all day, tossed a coin to the operator of the kiosk and bit into the skewer of meat. Juice dribbled over his chin. He palmed it away, continued to climb the long, steady ascent. Acolytes danced before the temple of Vitalia, lost in their supplications to bring life back to the people of Reena, their cymbals shivering like rain on water and ribbons streaming as the dancers whirled. Down the adjacent alley a whore, her gown cut to cup her breasts, had her back to the wall, her patron lost in his own rhythm which, in itself, was an affirmation of life. She caught Sylvio's eye.

"Just a few minutes and I'll be glad to service you," she said, and laughed.

He turned away and continued to climb, past oracles prophesying into clouds of hallucinogenic smoke, zealots lost in a miasma of self-flagellation, grizzled madmen growling out damnation and doom. Among them were the beggars of Reena, those who were disenfranchised, dispossessed, those who had drowned under a sea of taxes and neglect. A girl, a child of no more than six, tugged at his surcoat, her eyes enormous with want.

"Signor, only a grosso and I can give you an hour."

Gods! Surely this child didn't mean that?

"I can do with my mouth what she can do," the girl said, pointing to a whore barking her wares near an impromptu Punchinello show.

It was appalling to accept what the girl said in her soft-palate lisp, appalling to believe a child knew of such things, spoke of them with such candour. She was a baby, on his ancestors' bones, she was just a child. He handed her the skewer of lamb, two grossi from his purse and said, "Do you know where the Piazza da Luna is?"

She nodded. "Sure."

"You know the Casa Portelli?"

"Everyone does. It used to be Casa di Danuto."

She hadn't even been born when he'd been banished. How was it the people kept this history alive? Had they made him a martyr?

"Good," he said. "I want you to go there fast as you can. Tell the porter you come from the husband of the strega there. Her name is Aletta. Tell Dona Aletta I want her to find you a place in our household."

From Mountains of Ice

The child's eyes narrowed with suspicion. "You're buying me?"

"I don't buy people, especially not little girls. But I do need a bright girl to help with our household." He nodded over-shoulder to the whore. "And you won't have to do anything like she does."

She glanced over at the whore who rubbed her palm over the cod-piece of a prospective client, back up at Sylvio, flashed him a smile and darted off through the crowd, hummingbird swift and for a moment just as bright. He hoped she would make it. He hoped her life would change.

Sylvio moved on, shouldering his way through clots of people, passing on with his head down through open spaces until at length he came to the temple of Nerezza, patroness of Simare. Here the buildings seemed to give way for the temple of death, built at a distance so that space opened out around the enormous edifice. He stood before its red marble portico, the stairs of dull terra cotta, the cucullati carved in the columns. A wall of red brick enclosed the groves of Nerezza, and beyond that the ossuary where the bones of Reena's elite were shelved in terra cotta jars amid the cool dust of domed red brick houses. Here there were no street vendors selling savoury pastries, skewered meats and roasted nuts. No catamites and whores sought coin from people seeking a moment's diversion and relief. No acolytes whirled, voices proclaimed. It was as if the city parted here, creating an island of stillness.

He walked up the steps, unsure of what he did, knowing he needed an answer to this question that drove him beyond common sense. He should have brought a guard. Carmelo had plans for his life. What more perfect ending than to have him followed and brought to his end in the house of Nerezza, goddess of death?

Before stepping into the dim light of the temple he glanced down into the square where the late afternoon sun shone across the sparsely populated cobbles. As much as Nerezza was Simare's patroness, people gave her temple a wide berth. No point drawing her attention. No point joining her sooner than need be.

He turned and entered Nerezza's house.

While the noise of the city had been muffled in the square, in here Reena may have disappeared for all the sound that intruded. An enormous rectangle rising into a vaulted dome, the temple expanded around him. Dust eddied on the tiles of the terra cotta floor. He walked toward the altar at the far end, his image rippling over the polished red marble of the walls, a ghost of himself appearing and disappearing in the red marble columns that rose to the golden dome. Over the altar stood the figure of Nerezza, huge, overwhelming as you drew nearer because of the black stone from which she was carved, hard as basalt, and the height which at a distance seemed proportional, but once close was designed to render a supplicant insignificant. At her bare feet the red marble altar shimmered in the flame of hundreds of candles, the smell of oranges and pomegranates, rosemary and lavender as heavy as a shroud. He could feel the heat of the candles on his face.

He looked up into those blank, hollow eyes. Candle-flame reflected there, wavered on her broad cheekbones. He felt she stared down at him, impassive, immovable. What did his life matter in the face of eternity?

He found his fingers had a tremble when he dropped coins into the alms box. He bowed and stepped away, moving to one side of the altar where sunlight filled the doorway that led out to the gardens and the ossuaries of Reena's privileged.

The last time he'd walked out to these groves he'd come in the train of La Principessa's funeral procession. There had been rain fine and spectre-soft, ghosts of mist drifting through the trees of this wooded space where biers rose on tall stilts and offered the dead to the vultures that were sacred to this place. Their feathers rustled now in the late sunlight, their glassy eyes watching. Today there were no dead awaiting their final rest in jars of terra cotta and a shelf in the brick domes that hunkered like mushrooms amid the trees. Today there were leaves falling red and gold in a zephyr of a breeze, hissing over the cobbled path. Dark feathers from cinnamon ferns chattered against each other. From the earth rose the smell of decay, sweet and pungent.

Sylvio paused, thinking he heard footsteps under the hissing of the leaves. No. The breeze stirred. A cold touch to his cheek. He continued along the path to the central ossuary, watching the round hole of the doorway gape like a mouth. His feet scuffed through the leaves. He stepped into the coolness of the ossuary, watched leaves scatter on the floor, felt the pinch of dryness in his nose. Gooseflesh rose on his arms. A sudden gust drove the leaves chattering across the floor. Dust-motes spun like stars in the shafts of sunlight from the dome.

That sound again. He paused, straining to hear. The leaves hissed. There, under that sound, whispering. He was sure. He walked toward the shelf where he knew her funeral urn stood, he remembered, she who had died and left a son shattered by grief. The whispers swelled beneath the hissing leaves. Again Sylvio paused, straining to hear the voices he was sure were there.

Everything had fallen apart after she died. Aldo suffered a stroke not long after. Carmelo rose to the throne, unsure and unnerved, grieving for both his parents who were lost to him, his mother to death, his father to the silence that had taken his voice and his wit with the stroke. And somehow Sylvio was sure there was more to Aldo's situation, but he'd never been allowed a moment to speak with his former prince, his friend.

Sylvio ...

He stared at her funeral urn, reached out to touch the red clay, to find the voice he now knew was there. I'm here, he thought, afraid of his gift and afraid what might result because of his silent declaration. Viviana, I'm here. Guide me.

Voices shrieked around him, calling for justice, calling for audience, as real and pressing as if he stood in the forum of the Senate and faced an inquisition. He clapped his hands over his ears, whirling. Leaves scattered. He was alone. But for the voices, those insistent voices that were legion. He touched her urn and felt the shock of her presence.

"Viviana!" He gasped, stepping back from her urn, lifting his fingers from the cool clay. His breath steamed and evaporated into the dimness. All the royal line of Simare called to him in sibilant whispers, hissing with the leaves stirring at his feet. They wailed their outrage. They wailed their helplessness. He backed and sank to his knees amid the dust and the duff, his head bowed under the weight of their demands, sunlight a pool of hope in the darkness.

"Please, Viviana...." He thought of Vincenze's sister, how through her bones she breached the barrier of death and offered him warning. *Love can be hate. He's watching you.* "I beseech the wisdom of Reena's ancestors. I beg you, guide me."

And then clearly, above the shift and sigh of the others: *You should have harkened what she said. My son watches you, and he loves you as much as he hates you.*

Gods, what was he to do? He knew how to set defences, networks of spies, but had little knowledge how to deal with this growing simpatico with the dead.

He will kill you and raise you again into an abomination as he has done with my beloved. As he tried to do to me.

Aldo? An abomination? "I don't understand."

The key is Aldo's crutch. It will be a direct link to him. My finger was to be my doom.

"You speak in riddles."

It's too late, Sylvio. You should have brought an escort.

Gods! He rose to his feet, aware he had only the small knife at his belt. With a shrug he slipped out of his surcoat, wrapped it around one wrist and loosed the knife from its sheath, as he did so stepping out of the sunlight and into the sepia shadows where the voices lurked.

When all hope is gone, remember the dead of Reena. The dead you have allowed to become weapons.

Wind skirled leaves through the ossuary. Footsteps. He heard them. There. And there. And then Vincenze was with him in the gloom, his sword a cold gleam, his face shadowed.

"Six of them," he said. "I tracked you. They did as well. I couldn't warn you."

And then there was no time left for talk. His assassins burst through the doorways, fanning out with precision. Sylvio laid about him as best he could, using his surcoat as a blind, diving in and slashing, tumbling over the sweep of a sword and skidding across the stone and leaves. He heard Vincenze covering him, his sword screaming along the edge of another. He was good. To hold off so many he had to be. Sylvio slashed out and took out the hamstring of one of the men. With a curse and a howl the man went down, the crash and splash of an urn hitting the floor. Vincenze parried and whirled, drew blood on the sword arm of another, took a hard down-stroke from yet another, saw it barely in time and stepped away but not before the blade cut through jupon and left a gout of blood as the steel rose and switched direction for another blow. Sylvio slid in under the assassin's guard and plunged his knife up under the man's arm, twisted the blade and raked down, severing muscle and sinew. And then Vincenze went down. Three of them were upon him, kicking and hacking. With a roar Sylvio crashed into them, sliced open a man's face from hairline to lip. Then the air went from his lungs as he took a blinding blow to the groin. The last thing he remembered was covering his head and curling into a ball, the voices of the dead taking him down into darkness.

"What do you mean he's gone?" Aletta said. "You were supposed to be watching him." She knew her voice was strident. But damn them she didn't care. This was her husband they'd let slip away, unarmed, unescorted, with that beautiful but deadly boy of a prince determined to steal Sylvio's life from her.

Portelli turned to his steward, issuing an order to put together a search party.

"Not him,' Aletta said. "He's working for several masters. Lock him away until I can deal with him."

Portelli looked at her, frowning, turned back to his steward who had served him and his family before him, a short, slight man gone to bones and age, bird-bright eyes sharp with intelligence. "Is this true, Calvino?"

The man sank to his knees, bowed his head. "My life is yours to do with as you would, Padrone. Only know that what I've done, I've done out of love for you and Simare."

Portelli let out a strangled sound, barked an order to one of the servants to have a retainer secure Calvino is his quarters and to be sure no one was allowed entry except for himself and Aletta. He passed a hand over his face, let go of a breath.

"Who last saw the Maestro?" he asked, looking around at the rest of Danuto's entourage who had been involved with this day of trading. They glanced from one to the other, naming moments, exchanges, which seemed few enough, dissolving into conjecture and argument. That Sylvio, you know, he could just disappear when he wanted. How were any of them to know where he was? They'd been trying to put a little coin in their pockets, didn't you know, trying to save their village from starvation and dissolution. Not to be ungrateful, but they'd been about their business, assuming he was doing the same. And besides, wasn't he the former Ministro of Security? If he decided he needed some air after being summoned back to Reena, well, by all the gods he deserved to take some air.

Aletta watched them, noting who was here, who was not, filtering their talk and asked, "Where's Vincenze?"

"I'm here," he answered, striding into the room. "I've questioned the porter."

Thank the gods, Aletta thought. The years away from court and political navigation left her out of trim, she realized. Like a novice she found herself reviewing a calming mantra. Relax the mind to sharpen the senses. She saw Vincenze's agitation, followed signals and realized he was casting about the room for clues.

He turned his attention back to her. "The porter saw the Maestro heading across the piazza up the Via di Dios. I'm going after him." To Portelli: "Send retainers to follow. There's no time for me to wait." He turned briskly from the room. She could hear his footsteps retreating, the sound of orders rattling about as retainers made ready to follow.

"I'm going with him," she said.

Portelli restrained her arm. "Aletta, no."

"He may need me, Antonio."

"He'll be fine. Vincenze's good at his business. Besides, Sylvio likely needed to clear his head." How to tell him they'd been warned without giving away Ó Leannáin? "Let Vincenze and the others do their work. They know what they're about. You'd only get in the way."

That brought her rising panic to a halt, although she'd been careful to school her features, to moderate her voice. She let go a breath, inhaled another. She was a strega. "Yes. Of course." Ó Leannáin. She glanced out the window, determining the hour. There was still the rendezvous to take place aboard the Breenai flagship. That might be where Sylvio had gone, attempting to gain further information before the grand festival at the Castello tonight, before their planned escape into exile.

Another servant bustled into the room as Danuto's traders dispersed in knots of conversation, delivering an urgently whispered message. She watched Portelli's features, heard him say, "Bring the child here." He turned to her. "It would appear you have street urchins calling on you."

She heard the surprise in his voice, said, "Perhaps this child brings a message from Sylvio," and brought her attention to the girl escorted into the light and fragrance of the atrium. The linen shift the girl wore was a virtual rag, held to her shoulders by bone brooches which, as the girl came nearer, appeared to be little more than sawn roundels, the pins slivers whittled smooth. Her feet were unshod, mottled with filth, wild hair dark, eyes like flint. Under the grime Aletta could see fine features, too spare for a child her age, a mouth that was a full bow and like ripe fruit.

"What do they call you?" Aletta asked.

"Passerapina." She cocked her head to the side. "You're Dona Aletta. You're a strega."

Little sparrow. Indeed she was that. Impertinent, clearly a survivor. Aletta narrowed her eyes, studying the child who was plainly more than she seemed. "Why have you come calling on me?"

"Maestro Sylvio di Danuto sent me." She lifted her open palm to Aletta, showing her the gold grossi. "He gave me this. He said I was to find you, and that you would put me in your household."

There was absolute truth in what she spoke. "And where did you meet the Maestro?"

"On the Via di Dios. Why don't you ask me what you're really thinking?"

Aletta raised a brow to that, studying the girl carefully, aware the girl gave back as good as she got. "Do you know where he was heading?"

"No. I think he was going up the road. He was thinking hard."

Aletta curled the girl's fingers around the gold grossi. "You're going to need a purse to put that in." And she was going to need a bath, and clothes. So little time.

"May I have a small escort for myself, Antonio?" she said. "Someone has to go to the Breenai flagship to finalize the paperwork in Sylvio's absence." She gestured to Passerapina. "And can we have our little bird bathed and dressed?" She turned back to the girl. "That would suit you? You would like to make a small journey with me?"

The girl nodded, eyes wide.

"Of course." Portelli answered. "Do you wish me to go with you?"

"No." She touched Portelli's arm to gentle her response. "No, Antonio. Someone needs to be here when," Gods, if! "Vincenze and Sylvio return. You'll know where I am. I'll have an escort. I can send a messenger if needed, as can you. We have to proceed as though everything is normal. Do me the courtesy of sending a messenger to Ambassador Ó Leannáin to let him know I shall call on him shortly. And in the meantime, before I go, I need to have a talk with your steward."

He took her hand and squeezed it. "Go get ready and I'll assemble an escort for you and take care of what needs to be taken care of." He signalled to one of the servants, gave hurried instructions, and had a retainer follow Aletta to his steward's quarters.

She turned away, thinking of contingencies, thinking of possibilities, trying to reassure herself all would be well, that Sylvio had simply gone out for a walk to clear his head and would be back shortly. They would discuss the day. Prepare for peregrination to the Temple of Nerezza where Carmelo would once again present himself to Simare's patron goddess, then the festa this evening. Prepare to flee.

Her immediate destination lay to the back of the house over which she had once been mistress, past the gardens and over to a quadrangle of pale stone buildings that served as quarters for staff, bake-house, ale-house, drying sheds, granaries and more. Chickens squabbled and clattered, doves cooing from the red-tiled roofs, a cat skulking nearby in hopes of an easy catch. Over near the bake-house she watched as women bent over pink granite querns, their arms circling in perpetual motion as conversation followed their movements, a dog curled into sleep nearby. The smell of barley was nutlike and moistened her mouth, the querns rasping as rough flour spilled into wooden trays.

Servants dipped in obeisance as she went.

A small stone cottage lay tucked into late roses when she rounded the corner of a long series of row-houses for staff. The cottage was a privilege of the steward of this household, and at the moment a temporary prison. She nodded to the two retainers who stood at the cottage's neatly painted blue door. They gave a slight bow in deference to the *strega*.

"Our captive?" she asked.

"Quiet, Madonna."

"Then let's be done with this," she said, set her hand to the latch and stepped into the late afternoon light of the simple domicile. Calvino, Portelli's steward, sat composed at the rustic wooden table that served for dining and preparation surface. She noted how he didn't sit in the only chair with a back at the head of the table, rather one of the two benches that ran down each side, facing the door, his hands before him, his face composed.

He made to rise. She waved him to remain, sat across from him. He made no offer of refreshment. She asked for none. He knew why she had come. There was no room for pleasantries.

"I'm interested to know why you chose to serve several masters," she said, schooling herself to settle into the regimen of the strega.

"Believe me, Madonna, I had only the best interests of my country and my padrone in mind."

She heard him hedging. "I'm listening."

He passed a hand over his face, his first sign of discomposure. "I've watched for ten years our country decay. Being situated as I am, I'm privy to gossip from the great houses, an indiscreet word here and there, an unhappy servant. I heard rumour the Ministro would be recalled to Reena."

"He has not been Ministro for a long time."

"He will always been Ministro to us," he said. "We remember."

She heard the passion and loss in his voice. She gestured for him to continue.

"I decided I might be of use to the Sindaco and the Ministro. So I let it be known I was dissatisfied with my station, and as I hoped word passed from servant to steward to the Castello. I was visited by Il Principe's security. They made it clear any information I could feed them would be rewarded, and so I began fabricating a series of tales that would withstand scrutiny without harming those I serve. Eventually I was brought before Il Principe himself. That's when I met the Ambassador." He looked away for a moment. "I don't know who I'm more afraid of, Il Principe or the Ambassador."

"Tell me about this." To her surprise there was no falsehood in anything Calvino said. His fear, however, was rising.

"Il Principe – there is something not quite right there. He is always shadowed by his father, who says nothing, only leans on his staff, his face always hidden by the cowl he wears. The way Il Principe looks at him. And he speaks to his father all the time, breaks off a conversation to say something to his father, who never answers, but Il Principe acts as though he had. And then carries on with whomever he was speaking, always glancing over at his father. It's eerie."

"And the Ambassador?" she asked, hearing the discomfort in Calvino's voice His comment about Carmelo was something she understood. It was what alarmed her a decade ago and gave her reason to warn Sylvio to tread lightly.

"He's so smooth. Il Principe seems to trust him. But on the other hand the Ambassador assured me he wanted information about the Ministro because he wished to ensure his safety when Breena assumes governance of Simare. His reasoning is impeccable. Try as I might I can find no flaw in it, and yet every ounce of common sense says I shouldn't trust him. He is the enemy. And so I've been careful about what information I've fed him. And now, I am completely undone. I've succeeded only in the betrayal of all I love."

She let silence hang between them a few moments, considering all he said, the undertones in what he hadn't.

"Perhaps you're not completely undone yet, Calvino," she said at length. "I'm not sure how you're going to convince the Sindaco you're worthy of his trust, but you're going to have to try, and the very fact I'm going to allow you to walk out of here a free man, without any recriminations, hopefully will speak loudly to your padrone."

"You believe me?"

"Of course. Had you been withholding anything, I would know. But you speak only the truth, Calvino." She stood. He scrambled to his feet, bowing deeply. "But I warn you, Calvino, it's going to be hard for you to continue in your roll unless you're very careful. Il Principe is sensitive to change, this I know from experience. And it is imperative you continue to feed him information about my husband's dealings. Do I make myself clear?"

He nodded.

Satisfied, she turned for the door and returned to the house and preparation for her excursion to the Breenai flagship. Once in her room, she suffered her handmaid to check her cosmetics, draped a silk scarf over her head and shoulders. A knock came to her door. She spoke. One of the notaries stepped in, a satchel tucked under his arm. She waved off the handmaid's attention.

"I've taken the liberty of compiling all the necessary paperwork, Madonna," the notary said. "The arcossi are loaded, your litter prepared. A messenger was sent to the Ambassador and has returned with a note." She nodded and accepted the sealed envelope, quickly broke it open, read its contents and tucked it into the purse at her belt, then turned from the room and stepped out onto an uncertain course of action.

In the courtyard her escort was turned out in suitably smart array, the child Passerapina, clean and dressed in a fresh linen robe, waiting with ill-concealed excitement by the carved and gilt litter. Aletta noted the bone pins that had been transferred to the shoulders of the girl's robe. She waved the girl to ride in the litter with her, watched as the child folded herself at Aletta's feet, back straight, her face alert.

Gauze curtains closed on the litter, the escort a shield around her, Aletta fretted away the time it took to move from the Piazza da Luna to the docks where the Breenai flagship would have been warped and secured. She passed gates that led to the compounds of the visiting merchants and envoys, noted the presence of heightened security everywhere. No one rode or walked or sat within a conveyance without a perimeter of brawn and steel. Pennants proclaimed regions, guilds, mercantile families, precaution against mistaken identity and possible difficulty with Reena's roaming security that seemed little more than hired thugs.

Beggars and the dispossessed thronged among the superficial

glitter. Their calls for help and obvious destitution were a wound. What had happened to the social security nets upon which Simare built their egalitarian society? What had Carmelo done but reduce them all to this bitter, vulnerable state?

She glanced at Passerapina. That a society should shelter a system that could leave a child in such desperate want. Where was her family, her family's guild?

By now Aletta's journey had taken her down through warehouses and government buildings, the streets steep and rough, congested with traffic that flowed to and from the harbour. Brine and tar, fish and tobacco, the fetid waves of humanity and commerce washed over her as they emerged on to the broad pavement of the harbour and the quays. Between the curtains she could see other ships anchored in the roads, spars shrouded with furled sails. While there were ships from visiting countries, replete with trading envoys and private traders, it was plain Breena had sent a fleet large enough to impress and to threaten. Its flagship, the *Devlin*, was festooned with streamers and bunting, the smell of paint still fresh from her preparations to enter harbour smartly turned out. Her figurehead was a young man who held in his outstretched hands the sun, all of it heavy with gilt as was the fretwork of the *Devlin's* stern where glass glinted red in the late afternoon light.

Passerapina remained quiet throughout the journey, remarkably disciplined, although her eyes were wide and darting. Aletta noted how the child observed everything, watched conclusions and questions flicker over her face like sun and shadow. What was this child Sylvio had sent her and why?

"You are about to meet some very important people," Aletta said. The girl's attention snapped to her. "You are to do as I say, remain silent. Can you do this?" The girl nodded. "You are to speak to no one of what you see or hear. It is very important. Are you good at keeping secrets?" Again the girl nodded. "Good. And are you good at being ignored? Can you pretend you aren't real?" Another nod. "Molto buono."

As was proper, Ó Leannáin had a welcoming party arrayed at the gangway. Aletta heard the call of her arrival travel up to the ship, the stamp of feet, a trumpet bray. Her own escort, glittering in polished armour and shields, stomped to a halt, her herald proclaiming her presence. She unfurled from the litter as Ó Leannáin approached, a broad smile on his face, his dark eyes flashing warnings. Behind her she felt Passerapina slide quietly from the cushions to stand behind her.

"I have light refreshment for us," Ó Leannáin said, tucking her arm under his, "while we wait for the goods to be loaded and accounted. Our notaries can take care of the details,"

She could feel his tension, hear the underscore in his voice. When they arrived at his cabin he gestured for her to enter. She noted the guards he had posted outside, the way they made allowance for her own that inserted themselves seamlessly. Just as instructed, the girl followed her and stood nearby, schooling herself to be still. The door closed. In this day bursting with tension and surprise she withheld her shock once more.

A woman sat in the shadows, middle-aged and trim, her gown discreet but plainly of excellent cloth and cut, her hair bound with pearls and voile. Sunlight streamed at her feet from the windows at the stern. The woman rose, leaning on canes of chased silver.

Aletta did everything she could to settle her pulse, to keep the shock from her voice. "Prima Violina Pallavicini di Negli. It is good to see you again." She honestly had not thought Ó Leannáin would follow through with his promise, despite what she'd heard when he addressed them earlier, but here was some indication of the integrity of the man.

The Prima of Almarè embraced Aletta in a formal greeting,

stood back. "I am only sorry this couldn't have been under happier circumstances."

Ó Leannáin waved Aletta to a bench, placed unwatered wine beside her. "Is your esteemed husband to join you presently?"

"I hope so. He's missing. I'm sure he's just gone out to clear his head, but we're concerned. We understand he headed up the Via di Dios."

Ó Leannáin and the Prima exchanged glances.

"You were right to come alone," Ó Leannáin said. "I received a message just before you arrived. That you come alone lends credence to what we've learned."

She let the wine touch her lips but not her tongue. "You have news of the Maestro." Maestro! Gods, this was her husband she discussed so coolly. She clasped her hands in her lap to still the tremble she could feel beginning.

"With regret, yes," said Ó Leannáin. "Il Principe had him escorted to the Castello, albeit under duress. He and your retainer, Vincenze, are being detained for their own safety."

"And you don't entirely believe the report."

"Would you?"

She shook her head, continued to stare at him. "Was this a verbal or written message?"

He smiled, looked down. "Neither. And I know you can hear the reluctance in my voice when I say that." He took a drink of his own wine. "You must trust me when I say I have talents not dissimilar to your husband's." His fingers strayed to the torque he wore at his throat, carved and delicate like old ivory, and it was then understanding hit Aletta like a blast of frigid air.

Ó Leannáin was a bone-speaker like her Sylvio. And that meant there was someone, or something, inside Carmelo's holdings that betrayed him.

"Are you sure of the integrity of your source?"

"Utterly. But I am restricted from telling you more else all communication will cease."

"Are you able to ascertain if Sylvio is alive?" What it took for her to ask that, but it came out calmly, despite the hammer-blows of her heart.

"He is. He's unconscious, but not dying."

She realized her hands ached from clenching. She inhaled deeply, let it go. "And so what do you propose?"

It was Prima Violina who answered: "You and I are going to spirit away to my ship and take sail with the tide. There is another ship from Almarè in the roads with my trusted steward aboard. He is under orders to await word from Ambassador Ó Leannáin, and hopefully be joined by the Maestro, then to make all haste for the open sea."

"Prima Violina," said Ó Leannáin, "will incur Carmelo's anger, but it won't be the first time, and he is too eager to placate me, my entourage and my country to fuss over recriminations against Almarè and this perceived slight.

"I, on the other hand, will attend upon Il Principe this evening and attempt to retrieve your husband during the Festa da Nerezza."

"You don't hold out much hope," Aletta said.

Ó Leannáin shook his head. "Carmelo grows more and more paranoid and unpredictable. None of us can determine what course his actions may take at this point. And I, for one, prefer to cling to planning and the surety of known facts. There is too much at stake here."

"You will forgive me for asking," Aletta said, "but why go to all this trouble for us? You are surely treading a treasonous path."

"I will tell you what I told Prima Violina. I, as do you, your husband, and my esteemed colleague, believe in that most rare and elusive of political ends – peace. Were my country to succeed in its political ends, there will be no peace, not for many years. The world we know will become Breena, and all differences melted into the pot of Breena's choosing, and there brews a very unsavoury broth of discontent."

"How do you propose to free Sylvio? You're not going to try to tell me you control Carmelo's palace."

"Indeed I do not. But coin placed in sympathetic hands does not go amiss. And my informer knows where best to spend my trust."

"And then what of all these arcossi?"

"The transaction will be completed. And when my country invades, as they will, those bows will serve Simare well. You don't for a moment believe the bones of your ancestors will betray the living?"

"It hadn't occurred to me."

He smiled briefly. "Something to think on then, during your journey." He rose and bowed to her. "I wish you peace. It is my sincerest hope." He turned toward the door. "And now, if you will excuse me, I must take my leave and oversee the transfer of cargo. The good Prima will fill you in regarding the remaining details."

When the door closed on him she wanted to find some fault in what he'd said, some clue in his tone and inflection that would betray him. There was only truth there, and his reluctance when it came to speaking of his contact within the Castello. She could find no fault. She could find nothing on which to hang her concerns.

She turned to the Prima, feeling very much like a character in Commedia dell'arte. "And so?"

"And so now we begin a very elaborate ruse. My handmaid will join us presently. You and she will exchange clothing. She will travel back with your maid to the Casa Portelli. You, disguised as my maid, will accompany me back to my ship. By the time Carmelo discovers you are gone we will be well out to sea."

"My maid goes with us. That is not negotiable."

"You present me with an interesting problem."

Aletta turned to Passerapina. "Can you be brave and allow yourself to be boxed and loaded aboard another ship? I will have you released as quickly as I can. It will only be for a very little while. You have my word." Passerapina's eyes widened for a moment and then she nodded. "Good girl." Aletta turned back to the Prima. "Solution presented. She goes as one of your coffers."

True to her word Violina's maid entered within moments, curtseyed and without a word stripped, carefully laying aside her garments within Aletta's reach. Taking her cue, Aletta also stripped, exchanging costumes. She took a moment to arrange the hair and face jewellery on the maid, draping the fine silk shawl around the maid's head in such a manner as to disguise her features from unwanted spectators. Violina left while this exchange occurred, returning some while later to announce that she'd purchased some of Breena's silks which she was having brought up to the cabin to show Aletta. When the bale arrived Passerapina was wrapped like fine porcelain into the silks and wrappings, a discreet tube secured for air. The girl made no protest. She watched Aletta throughout with frank openness. Given what was likely the girl's background Aletta felt stunned by her trust.

Porters arrived to take away the bale and other goods the Prima purchased. Ó Leannáin swept in, all business, took his leave with suitable aplomb. The maid dressed as Aletta left in the company of the guards. Moments after that Aletta disembarked with Prima Violina and settled herself amidship where any handmaid of worth would place herself. Hair covered in linen napkins, her gown of good but serviceable cloth, she was careful to keep her face down under cover of the large-brimmed straw hat pinned in place.

By now the sun was sinking into the harbour, shards of amber and crimson glittering across the water. From somewhere a sailor called the turn of the glass. A bell tolled from the temple of

Nerezza, a call to the dead, a call to oblivion. Tonight, she remembered, would be of greater significance. Tonight Simare would light candles for the dead and set them adrift on boats of paper into the streams and rivers and lakes. The harbour would fill with passing lights, lights of the dead, a river of dead, a river of mourning. A tribute to those who would not be forgotten.

A touch to her arm brought her out of her thoughts and to the realization they had arrived at the Almare flagship. She allowed herself to be trussed into the bosun's chair and hauled aboard like baggage, where she waited demurely at Violina's side until dismissed.

To her relief the bundle that was Passerapina was carried to the main cabin where she followed, and with her own hands peeled away the layers of cloth to find the girl unharmed, if a little shaken.

"Are you fine?" she asked the girl.

Passerapina nodded. "I have to pee."

Aletta laughed, looked up at the steward who was in the room. He was well-made, patrician nose, beautiful eyes, broad brow, long-fingered hands that would do well on a lute or a lover. "There is a water closet in the corner, Madonna. I am sorry we could not have met again under better circumstances."

"Thank you, Julio." She gestured Passerapina to the screened area Julio indicated. "You'll be leaving soon?"

"Immediately, Madonna. I was to be sure you and the child were safe. I must caution you before I go to stay away from the stern windows until we are at sea. There must be no surprises."

"Of course," she said, and watched him bow and leave.

When Passerapina rounded the screen, dabbled her hands in a bowl of water and towelled them dry, Aletta sank into a large chair, listening to the stamp of feet overhead, the call of orders. The child came to her side. Aletta lifted the girl to her lap, folded her arms around the girl's thin shoulders and watched the harbour. She felt the first tug of the warping lines, measured off the length of ships they passed, heard the first sheets thunder down as men fisted them into order, trimmed lines.

The skyline of Reena was now in view, the roads like black spires. Lights garlanded the harbour walls, ran like ribbons through the stratas and vias. There was the spire of the Gigantico, the beacon that signalled to all the world Simare's glory and wonder. There the extravagant sweep of the Castello's water-steps that descended from the heights to the private mooring below. There where her husband now languished in who knew what delirium, what pain, what danger?

Sylvio, Innamorato.

A flotilla of lights filled the harbour, sinuous rivers of amber flowing out and around the ships, engulfing all of them in memory. Carried by the outgoing tide they'd be swept out to sea, just as she.

"See," said Passerapina. "The dead come to guide us."

Sylvio tried for a deep breath and flinched. Best not do that again too soon.

Gods, let Aletta be safe.

He fingered his chest, found the bandages they'd wrapped around him. They were just a little too tight to be of any use other than to remind him he was here at Carmelo's mercy, damn him. Likely he had a broken rib or two, judging by the flame in his side. Why they'd beaten him was not immediately obvious, unless you knew Carmelo as Sylvio knew him. This was a tantrum. A very adult and potentially deadly tantrum, agreed, but a tantrum nonetheless. Plainly Carmelo wished to take up his pique where he'd left off ten years ago. Only now Sylvio knew there was a threat of assassination behind all this, and so the beating, he knew, was simply an overture of what was to come. Foreplay, one might say. If one were a sadistic bastard. Which Carmelo was. But now he'd graduated from torturing cats to people.

Taking a slow, careful breath, Sylvio sat up from where he lay; he found he was in the bed-chamber of his old apartment in the Castello, everything where he'd left it: the coffers, the chests, and the writing desk. All the locks had been hacked from the wooden surfaces, and likely the contents confiscated, but otherwise it was a time-capsule. He remembered the haste with which he and Aletta left a decade ago, hounded into exile by Carmelo's sycophantic staff. So much had been left behind. He remembered comforting Aletta in the hush of the night at the first inn they'd hired, telling her what they'd left behind were only things. Just things. They still had each other. Carmelo couldn't take that.

He realized now he'd lied to her and her gift as strega either failed her or she refused to listen. Carmelo could take them from one another. He could exact this one last brutal price from Sylvio in payment of a debt about which Sylvio remained ignorant, even now, ten years later.

He took another slow, painful breath, and eased his legs over the side of the bed. Gods but there wasn't a part of him that didn't hurt, and right now it was his back and bladder that hurt the most.

Someone had made up the fire, dispelling the pervasive chill that went with living in a huge stone building. Out the window the clouds ran amber and crimson, as though the sky reflected the hearth. Bells tolled, clear and full, resounding and insistent, calling the worshipful to prayer at the temple of Nerezza, calling the living to reverence the dead, the hopeful to acknowledge the wise. Festa da Nerezza. A river of lights. Above the bells, sweet and pure, a young voice soared in a requiem, Pie Nerezza, Merciful Nerezza.

Carefully he lifted himself from the edge of the bed and handed himself along the mattress, from there to the wall, the hearth, shuffling toward the privy. He thought he'd faint by the time he got there, leaned heavily against the white marble wall. Gods! He decided to sit rather than stand. What should have been simple proved difficult. As he suspected there was blood. The bastards had kicked him in the kidneys. He wondered how much damage there was. He wondered how close they came to finishing him off. Beaten not dead.

When he washed his hands he splashed water over his face to clear the sweat and his head, turned and began the arduous trek back to the bed-chamber. He decided he'd catch his breath and then reconnoitre to see about clothes and which doors were open to him, and which were closed.

He was saved the effort when Carmelo's physician entered the room, two assistants with him. The man made to bow, caught himself. Sylvio remembered him, remembered how he'd nursed Viviana in her last days. Unsure how to proceed, Sylvio gave the first move to the physician, who gestured to the assistants. They helped him back to the bed, set about checking his wounds, applying salve and unguents. The bandages around his ribs were undone, fingers probing, gently. The physician made a moue, nodded, wrapped new linen strips around Sylvio's ribs. When Sylvio complained, the physician said, "They have to be tight to minimize movement. Nothing is broken, but badly bruised, yes."

Sylvio grunted an acknowledgement.

"There is blood in the urine?" the physician asked and straightened, indicating for his attendants to continue.

Sylvio nodded an acknowledgement to the query.

"I don't suppose you thought to use the sample flask I left for you?"

Sylvio wanted to laugh but checked. "My apologies."

"No matter. Is there a great deal of blood?"

"Enough that I think they rearranged by heart and my

kidneys."

"And the pain?"

"Which one exactly?"

Annoyance flickered across the physician's face. "I'm trying to help you."

"Then get me out of here."

"You know I can't."

"Anything is possible. I know you won't." Sylvio batted away the attendants. "And now?"

"I'm going to give you something to ease the pain. Il Principe wants you suitably attired to attend the festival."

Of course! This would be funny if he weren't in such pain and such a fool. "Am I allowed to send a message to my wife?"

"I regret."

"I'm sure you do. And you will forgive me if I refuse to take any of your medications." Plain stubbornness was what it was, Sylvio knew, but let it stand. If Carmelo wanted him dead he would have done so long before. There was to be some further entertainment, he was sure. Why else have him beaten and then give him the best care possible? Give hope to your victim. Snatch it away. Do that enough and you render the victim yours.

Just one problem. Sylvio knew this. He taught Carmelo all the best and worst of statesmanship. And so Carmelo, being no fool, could only be doing this for play.

The physician shrugged off Sylvio's refusal of care and sent one of his attendants to fetch a valet. Within moments the attendant was back with said valet, clothes on a rolling rack pushed by a lackey. He wondered if it was worth the effort to put up a struggle, decided against it. He could still gather information, see if there were any allies, a way to shift the course of events to his own advantage. He needed to find out where was Vincenze, if he was still alive.

Let him be alive. Sylvio didn't want Vincenze's death on his head. Bad enough he'd been a fool to think he could wander on his own, to think Carmelo wouldn't close the net as soon as his prey was there for the taking. Fool.

"Be careful, man," Sylvio hissed, almost overcome just from the tension of the waistband on his breeches. "Loosen off the laces."

Altogether the ensemble into which they trussed him was far too elaborate for his taste. Silver-gilt thread and pearls, polychrome embroidery. He felt like a cushion. They gave him a staff, a thing of bone and mother-of-pearl, gilding and ornament. No human bone this; no voices stirred. He didn't know whether to feel relieved or disappointed.

They escorted him from the bed-chamber out to the hallway where guest-rooms ran, through the main salon to the atrium and the foyer – all as he remembered – and from there to the grand and labyrinthine corridors of the Castello. Anyone they passed avoided his gaze. Not that he would have been capable of any decent acknowledgement. He had to pause several times, seek out rest on a bench, and breathe in careful gulps. Once the doctor passed a vial of what he assumed was ammonium carbonate under his nose. That brought him sharply back to consciousness and a fit of coughing that threatened to tear apart his insides.

"You need to let me give you some relief from the pain."

"No." He levered himself up onto the staff and stubbornly continued on, not knowing if he headed in the right direction, but assuming they wanted him to go to the Sala Pubblico where traditionally the royal celebration of the Festa da Nerezza began and ended. They made no attempt to correct his course.

He made several more pauses to rest, husbanding his strength as best he could. And then the bronze doors with Simare's royal crest were before him, opening like wings, a herald booming notice of his arrival to the court. No titles. Sylvio di Danuto.

The scene before him was macabre in its proportions. Most of the court was dressed in red to mark the festival, most of them masked. There were fantastical animals, white faces with glittering tears, feathers and lace, gold and jewels, all against a backdrop of white marble columns and gilded capitals, painted frescos of myths and the Simare Royal House above the wainscoting. For a moment the music faltered. Conversation died. It was like a frozen tableau.

The tableau parted like earth furrowed by a plough, the point Carmelo and his armed entourage. Aldo walked in his train, cloaked and silent, as still as a cucullatus, beside him the immaculate Ó Leannáin. Carmelo himself had filled out into a muscular, powerful figure, the soft lines of adolescence sharpened into the planes and angles of a man, cleverly accentuated by the cut of his clothes. Sylvio thought of a stalking cat. As befitted a prince, Carmelo was dressed in silk and velvet, his buttons faceted diamonds and filigree gold, the diamond bezels in the band of his beret the ransom of a nation. And then unbefitting a prince, Carmelo increased his pace, his composure flickering. That mouth of painted, sculpted lips broke into a grin as innocent and bright as a child's, his attention all for Sylvio.

Pride as much as pain prevented Sylvio from making the proper obeisance. He nodded. Carmelo's black eyes glittered, the faintest crease on his brow. He paused in front of Sylvio, the pulse of a heart, touched Sylvio's cheek, his long fingers lingering, and then he glided past without any further acknowledgement. It was plain he'd timed his exit for Sylvio's entrance. The armed escort absorbed Sylvio into their train.

Now began the journey to the Temple of Nerezza where Il Principe would prostrate himself before Simare's patron goddess, binding himself once again to the power of their ancestors.

By the time they reached the main entrance to the Castello, where people thronged in a yelling, massive crowd, Sylvio regretted his stubbornness and wished he had something to take the sharpness of the pain, something to keep him focused. He wasn't quite sure how he'd make the arduous peregrination to the Temple of Nerezza. Near to delirium, he watched as Carmelo made the appropriate gestures to the crowd, and folded himself into the ornately carved litter that awaited him.

The doctor touched Sylvio's arm, gestured to a litter. "Il Principe wishes you to follow in comfort."

Sylvio wanted to laugh. Beat him and then show him every blessing. Oh, the boy had style. He had to give him that.

He nodded and pulled himself onto the litter. Someone in the crowd shouted out, "Danuto! Speak for us!" The cry was followed by a wave of pleas that was quickly silenced by ubiquitous armed guards, guards that hadn't been there a decade ago. Shaken, Sylvio looked around for the source of that cry. There was only an ugly knot of men, plainly Carmelo's under-cover, wrestling away the protestors. The faces he saw there were ones of anger and desperation, a mob waiting for the right fuel to set them alight.

"Where's Vincenze?" he asked the doctor.

"Alive. He will join you once we return to the Castello."

"Is he conscious?"

He saw the doctor measure the acuity of Sylvio's understanding. "He is. He's hurt, but in no worse shape than you."

Well that was both saying something and not. Think, man, he told himself. You have to find a way out of this. But that escape wasn't going to be easy with guards bristling around him and Vincenze held hostage in the Castello. Carmelo knew him too well. There wasn't a hope Sylvio would leave a friend to face what Carmelo might contemplate.

All the long procession Sylvio tried to keep his wits about him, to deny that a decade had taken the edge off his ability and his endurance.

Long before the temple came into view he could hear the

antiphony sung by Nerezza's acolytes. It could reduce a cynic to tears. He shut his mind to the music. Concentrate on the pain. Concentrate on escape. The litter swayed, descended. There were hands to help him to his feet, to place the staff under his arm. Voices and bells rose and fell against each other, call and response, and still there was that one pure voice soaring above them all.

There were others. Sylvio heard them as a sibilant whisper. The chatter of leaves. The dead. More insistent than ever he remembered. He inhaled sharply, caught his breath on a crescendo of pain. Carmelo stood above him at the height of the stairs, his eyes closed, his face tight as though concentrating and preoccupied, which Sylvio was sure Carmelo was. The boy was juggling too many players. Carmelo's understanding of political theory was good, but without experience or the foresight and craftsmanship that comes from time and self-control. Beside him were Ó Leannáin and Aldo, both of them watching the prince and then together turned their attention to Sylvio.

What was this? Did he imagine their scrutiny? Or was there something there? For more reasons than his heart he wished Aletta were here.

With a groan Carmelo opened his eyes, raised his arms to the crowd in benediction, turned and entered the temple. The court followed, as did Sylvio.

Only hours before he'd been here, watching his reflection in the red marble. The temple had been deserted then, silent of any living thing. No one intruded upon the dead until a body was brought to the temple, or until this day of reverence. The only exceptions were those who came to honour their ancestors, and those who came to commune; the latter were rare. Even among the chosen of the temple, few were bone-speakers. He was one of those rarities, he realized, albeit unwilling. And now the dead slid into his thoughts, an undercurrent to the song of supplication, whispering but audible as they'd not been when he used to come to the temple as Ministro. So much had changed.

Carmelo now stood before the gargantuan figure of Nerezza, stripped to his loincloth, while the priestesses anointed him with myrrh. By the light of hundreds of candles Carmelo seemed transported, a face and a figure that could capture and break the heart. He was Nerezza's messenger wreathed in incense. Decani and cantoris of the music called and answered in the cavernous space, voices rising to the golden dome.

Carmelo turned to face the goddess, performed the three obeisances as ritual required and then prostrated himself upon the grit and the cold of the terra cotta floor. The singers reached the main theme of the piece, half-tones and complex harmonies creating a sense of urgency.

Sylvio found himself separated from his guards and caregivers, flanked on one side by Ó Leannáin, on the other by Aldo. At the moment the choir reached the height of the piece, Sylvio felt Aldo's hand upon his, his fingers working Sylvio's around the staff Aldo held. And as Sylvio felt the shaft touch him he was aware that not only had Aldo taken Sylvio's staff in turn, but that Aldo's voice was in his head, demanding, powerful.

Say nothing. Do nothing. I must be quick while Nerezza has Carmelo in thrall.

Sylvio found it hard to control his shock. The quality of Aldo's voice was familiar, although disembodied, as though coming from a distance.

I am what Viviana told you. Abomination. But I can be of assistance. Ó Leannáin has arranged to have you taken to the mountains with Vincenze. The harbour's now being watched; it is suspected Aletta has escaped. Trust your guards. They are Ó Leannáin's. Trust the staff I have given you. It is me, and my link to this half-life I must live until I bring my son to enlightenment and judgement. Take refuge in Almarè and there begin your work to return and fulfill your duty as Simare's son. I will keep you apprised of Ó Leannáin's progress. He, like you, is capable of hearing what the ancestors say. Do not fail us, Sylvio.

A tremor passed over him, his heart thudding painfully. I won't fail you, he thought. Gods help me!

Aldo and Ó Leannáin stepped away, melting back into the court and the crowd, the guards moving back into place. The choir began the long descent into quietude and simplicity. Carmelo arose from the floor, attendants helping him into a robe of silk, heavy with gold and pearls that were symbols of wisdom and tears. Upon his head they placed the crown of bone from which descended garlands of pearls and fine, filigree plaques of gold. Carmelo turned to the host. He looked like an icon, a figure the people of Simare could worship and love instead of fear and loathe.

Officially reconciled with Simare's ancestors, Carmelo crossed the floor to where Sylvio stood and embraced him, his dark eyes glittering. "We welcome you home, Sylvio di Danuto." And kissed him on each cheek, the sweet fragrance of myrrh heavy around him. "We will speak this evening regarding your future here." And then in a whisper, "I have missed you so!"

Sylvio said nothing. He inclined his head. Carmelo withdrew, tears glistening on his cheeks. He turned away, passed on, the entourage around him like a living cloak.

Not a little shaken, Sylvio watched Carmelo retreat.

Missed him? Good the gods, but why send him away in the first place? Why try to take his life? But then perhaps the tears, the words, the entire elaborate display was all for show. What other explanation could there be?

The heart could be such a deceiver. He wanted to look into that face glistening with tears and bright with beauty, and believe the good-natured, easy-to-love boy was still there. Could be there still. Surely that boy wasn't silenced by the complex, cruel, clever man evidence of the past ten years said Carmelo had become.

It was some moments before Sylvio's escort led him through the temple and down the stairs to his litter, well behind the bulk of the court. As they went, his escort and bearers fell back further without apparent notice. A detour was made down one of the lesser side streets, switching again to an alley. Without fuss Sylvio was assisted to a covered carriage that waited. He raised a question, baulking.

"Move, man!" the physician hissed. "We haven't much time!"

"Not till I know where you're taking me."

"Out. Away. This is your escape. It's all been arranged."

How Aldo had arranged this he didn't know. As he ascended into the carriage he noted someone climbing onto the litter in his place, the physician beside the fellow. And then his attention was all for the interior of the carriage where he found Vincenze sitting stiffly in a corner, the window shuttered, a man in physician's robes leaning over him.

He heard people speaking outside. Sylvio slumped to the seat. The carriage lurched forward.

"I didn't think I'd see you again," Sylvio said, watching emotion play across Vincenze's face.

"I didn't believe them when they told me you were alive," Vincenze answered.

"How bad is it?"

"Likely as bad as you look."

"And this is?" Sylvio gestured to the physician.

The man straightened from Vincenze, tucked the wooden tube he'd held to Vincenze's chest into a leather satchel on the seat beside him. "I am one of Ambassador Ó Leannáin's men. You may call me Pisano. I am to make sure you arrive safely in Almarè." Pisano lit the interior lantern and pulled the other shade down. "There are travelling clothes in the valise under your seat. I can assist you if you wish."

Sylvio shifted to the other bench, leaned forward to lift the seat. A lurch of the carriage sent him groaning back to the deep cushions. Pisano retrieved the valise for him, and without fuss set about helping him out of breeches, doublet, hose, replacing each article of clothing with serviceable linen and woollens, well-made but without mark or ornament to indicate any social status. These were the garments of any ordinary artisan.

Pisano held up a small white tin and rattled it. "For the pain, whenever you require. No more than two, four hours apart. They will make you drowsy, so use them with caution. And they can be addictive, so –"

"– use with caution," Sylvio finished.

"Yes. Pain is an alert there is something wrong. But you will need rest, and there will be little opportunity. I trust to your discretion." He rattled another tin, this one painted green. "One a day of these, to prevent infection. You shouldn't be travelling, but these are extenuating circumstances, and we have to thank your tormentors for breaking no bones."

Pisano pulled another satchel from the bench. "Hard rations in case things go awry and you need to make your way overland on your own. There are water purification tablets. Boil your water if you can, then add the tablets. Wait thirty minutes before drinking.

"I have weapons here of the type any traveller would carry, short sword and dagger each. And we managed two bows, your own arcossi, although I doubt either of you will be capable of pulling anything for some time, and a quiver of arrows each."

"And we're headed for?"

"The border outpost in the Simare Pass. Ambassador Ó Leannáin has made an arrangement with the captain there. He believes the captain is to be trusted." Pisano shrugged. "Of course, everything is subject to change, so we must proceed with haste and caution. Your prince is intelligent, despite what he's doing to your country. We're not sure how long our agreements with operatives will last." He dumped the satchel back into the bench and let the seat fall into place. "We're riding straight through to the last friendly home before the mountains. Fresh mounts have been arranged at farmsteads along the way. I have provisions for the road. All of it is detailed here." He withdrew a booklet from the purse at his belt. "In case anything should happen to me. Pray the gods nothing does, because in that event it means the Ambassador is discovered and has to flee."

Sylvio looked over to Vincenze who, despite obvious physical distress, had absorbed all information. He nodded to Sylvio. "I have the same provision pack as you. I can do this." And then to Pisano. "And the traders from Danuto?"

"They know nothing of this. And we have done everything to keep them free from implication."

"That won't stop Carmelo from having them questioned," Sylvio said.

"We are aware of this. But we have done all we can. They will understand the necessity of getting you out of the country."

Sylvio couldn't argue with that. It just galled that people he held dear might come to harm because of him. Then with practical need, he bent forward, found the valise and the small white tin, tossed two tablets to the back of his throat and swallowed relief and the hope of sleep.

He looked Pisano in the eye. "I'm trusting you to keep watch while Vincenze and I attempt to sleep." With that he braced himself into the corner to keep his body straight, and closed his eyes.

The hours and days that followed were a fog of half-sleep and necessities. They were not pursued. That was a concern. The silent and disturbing communications that occurred with Aldo through the staff indicated Carmelo knew very well they had escaped. But

From Mountains of Ice

whether pursuit had been dispatched was uncertain. Ó Leannáin remained at court. Aldo could add nothing to their knowledge.

What the landscape they travelled through was like Sylvio had no idea, shuttered in the gloom of the carriage as they were. On brief occasions, when horses were changed at farmsteads, they were offered a few moments walk around the carriage, a quick bowl of pasta fagiolo or polenta and tomatoes, washed down with fresh milk and honey as they were restricted from the rough, hearty wine of the country-folk. There was no conversation. Usually contact was minimal, one person delegated liaison. He knew they sped along back-roads, hazarding the main highway that bisected Simare only when necessary, following routes recommended by the last farmstead.

The pain he and Vincenze suffered was considerable, exacerbated by the jouncing, shattering movement of the carriage. He was glad neither of them had broken ribs, otherwise this flight and hazard would be impossible. It would have taken weeks for bones to knit, even months before they would have been capable of the rigours of the road, and while neither of them was capable of a marathon, they might, with blessings, do well enough.

Out of those brief stops Sylvio began to formulate an understanding of a resistance growing, of operatives risking life and livelihood to free Simare of this oppressive regime. He felt no little guilt and frustration that he ran from this resistance. What he should be doing is staying, helping these people to achieve their ends instead of seeking refuge and asylum in Almarè. And just what he was going to do once he arrived in Almarè he had no idea. Raise an army? Invade? And what then of the army that might support him? Only reasonable the government that aided him in his coup d'état would want some sort of military or political concessions. Only the edge of a slippery slope, one Carmelo had walked in his own way and landed them in the mess they were in.

Or perhaps a more prudent route was to lobby sympathetic governments to impose economic blockades. But that path lead only to further privations for people already taxed and burdened almost beyond all means.

And then there was the matter that Carmelo, whatever else, was the rightful crowned head of the country. He was the first in that long, unbroken line to have betrayed his people. But he was there by birthright. And so how to depose someone who was the legitimate ruler, without recourse to an heir?

These questions plagued Sylvio still when they made another stop. By his reckoning they'd been ten days in flight. They paused at a cottage which, although well-maintained, showed signs of want, a common and familiar sight to him now. Fresh horses were put into the traces, bred more for the plough than the demands of a hard run. The pair of mares that were taken away, heaving and lathered, would take time to recover and likely welcome the work of a farm-horse over the marathon they'd just run.

It was a sweet evening, the faintest of breezes coming down off the foothills. All day he was sure they were close to the mountains, judging from the incline of the carriage and the increased use of the whip on mounts already taxed for endurance. He finished a bowl of minestrone and crusty bread that he ripped off in chunks and dipped in the season's pale green, peppery olive oil. They ate while standing. No discourse.

The buildings of the farmstead were few and built of stone and tile, evidence of earlier wealth, although in a simple style that spoke of attention to serviceability rather than beauty. The house itself was two storeys, larger windows in the lee of the mountains. A barn, another building that was likely an olive press judging by the orchards, and another that appeared to be a granary. The usual chickens and ducks squabbled in the garden, and beyond in a stone enclosure a sow wallowed with what were likely her litter. Wild roses bloomed in a show of late colour over stone walls. He watched the mountains looming over them, black and bleak, even more imposing at this proximity than lost in the purple haze of distance.

Vincenze elbowed him lightly, raised a finger, his attention on the rise of the mountains. One day? Sylvio nodded. Yes. One day, if they kept to this pace, they'd be into the mountains and headed for the pass. No deviation then from the main road, unless they were to abandon the carriage for mounts and travel the lesser known tracks of goat and shepherds.

They were back on the road with haste. The look on Pisano's face was enough to cause Sylvio to say, "I gather there's been bad news."

"Possibly. We've lost contact with the outpost. We're not sure what that means."

"It means Carmelo knows where we are."

"We can't be certain," Pisano said.

"It's a fairly educated guess if you know Carmelo," Vincenze said. "He hasn't pursued us. There's been no evidence of any of his people. Which can only mean –"

"–Carmelo knows we're heading for the outpost," Sylvio finished. And while he and Vincenze were making good recovery from their wounds, they certainly weren't what he would call fit specimens to be testing themselves against the mountains or another attack. But what to do? Vincenze uttered that very question.

"I don't know," Sylvio answered. "You can bet Carmelo has the road behind us watched. There's no turning back. Best we can hope for is trade the carriage for horses and make for the pass, hoping haste and blind luck will see us through."

"Those aren't favourable odds," Pisano said.

"I'm afraid they're the only odds we have." He looked at

Vincenze. "Can you ride?"

He watched the man consider the question, saw his jaw set. "Yes."

He turned back to Pisano. "Turn us around quickly."

Pisano rapped on the carriage wall, called out, "Back to the farmstead. Quick about it."

It took some careful manoeuvring to turn them around. The road was not well-maintained nor wide, not much more than cart-tracks bordered by orchards. But they were soon face-about and heading back to the farmstead, urgency hot on Sylvio's mind.

He broke with the protocol they'd set when they began, entered the cottage and took over discussion with the farmer who seemed a stalwart sort, not given to panic, as did his wife whose only outward sign of her distress was the wringing of her hands and crease of her brow. Sylvio couldn't blame her. They risked everything.

His discussion yielded that there were no other horses to be had, just the two that were blown, carriage in lieu of payment or no. This was going to require some creativity. He assessed the exits, inquired about the lay of the land. This might work. Might.

Sylvio ordered Pisano to stay behind. One riding pillion would only slow them, and Pisano knew too much to risk capture and torture.

"I'll have to get a message out," Pisano said.

"Tomorrow, when the horses are better rested, take the carriage south and head for one of the fishing villages. Make no stops. Do whatever you have to do to hire a boat and make for Almarè."

"Why don't we all do this?"

"Because I'm going to use you as bait, my friend. If there are any spies watching the farmstead, and you can be assured there are, they're going to see three people enter the carriage tomorrow morning." He looked at the farmer. "I'm asking a lot of you and your family, I know."

"Just get to Almarè and bring us some hope," the man said, his wife agreeing behind him.

Sylvio nodded. "Vincenze and I are going to slip out under cover of darkness tonight. With a little luck we'll be well-away before you head out in the morning. And let's hope whoever is watching believes the ruse."

To reinforce the plan they carried out a careful charade that day to indicate one of them had a relapse. Pisano went out of doors and washed after having quickly and quietly slaughtered a chicken in the kitchen, allowing it to liberally splash his apron; to his credit he'd added a number of screams and groans, in case their watchers were closer than they thought. The whole sham had the four children of the farm laughing behind their hands. Even the driver and the two guards, who were given lodging in the stone stables, created tableaus of serious discussion with much grave nodding of heads and rubbing of jaws.

By nightfall they'd set their watch. Sylvio allowed himself the first decent rest he'd had in days.

It was Pisano who woke him with a double dose of espresso, which Sylvio welcomed with a grin. "I'm given reprieve?"

"You're going to need that," Pisano answered. "I'm not sure you're exactly capable of what you're about to ask of yourself."

Sylvio tossed off the last of the coffee. "When are we ever ready?"

Pisano smiled. It was the first time Sylvio could remember the man doing that. "Here, I need to check your ribs."

With gentle precision the bandages were unwrapped, Sylvio's torso probed, his heart and lungs monitored. "You're doing remarkably well for a man your age."

"What do you mean, *a man my age*?"

"Well, you're not old, not by any means, but most men at

middle-age let themselves go. I've treated men half your age I wish had your physique."

"I'm going to take that as a compliment."

Pisano wrapped fresh linen around Sylvio's ribs, explaining it was more for support now than anything. "Just don't go doing anything heroic. Or at least try not to. Just get to Almarè. I wish I was going with you."

"Better this way." He gestured to where Vincenze stood by the hearth. "And him?"

"He'll do. He took a greater beating than you did, although he's mending well." Pisano straightened. "I've taken the liberty of checking your bags and have put some extra medications in there for both of you. If things go wrong, and you have no hope left, the red tin will remove you from the equation. I sincerely hope it doesn't come to that."

Sylvio studied him a long moment, and then, "Thank you."

Pisano nodded.

Leave-takings were done quietly and with dispatch. There was heavy dew in the grove when Sylvio and Vincenze slipped away, a cool breeze off the mountains pungent with the scent of olives. They each wore a belt with a gladius and dagger, oiled leather packs on their backs, arcossi in linen bags over their shoulders and quiver of arrows each neatly separated by a round leather disk and bound in another linen bag for carrying.

There was no moon, which made for dark travels, but he had a compass and the North Star to guide him. The farmer told him to make straight from the back door up into the hills, to keep the sound of the river to his right. A goat-track could be picked up if they were lucky enough to find it, and from there lead them by relatively passable routes into the mountains.

By dawn they'd left all sign of cultivation behind and were into the low mountain meadows favoured by the goats and sheep that were infrequently herded. It was a fine morning. Jewels of dew flashed. Spider webs hung like pearls over the meadows. The sky was clear and cobalt, and Sylvio remember one such morning not so long ago when he'd stood in his bow-yard and contemplated the complexities of his country and his situation. Aletta had been working in the barley harvest.

Gods, let her be safe.

They followed the animal trails, hoping their passage would be taken for mountain sheep or goats. It was a brisk pace they set, wanting to push distance between them and the farmstead while husbanding their strength as best they could. Sylvio, like Vincenze, eschewed the pain-killers but remembered to take the antibiotic Pisano provided. Neither felt comfortable about the open landscape. One more reason to make for the dense forest that rose above them.

All that day they climbed higher, until around mid-afternoon they came upon the first out-riding trees. Here there were dense carpets of myrtle in the shade, fragrantly sweet. They took a brief pause and chewed on thin slices of prosciutto and hard cheese, facing away from each other to keep alert for signs of pursuit.

Within minutes they were on their feet again. Sylvio found himself leaning upon the staff more and more, aware always of Aldo's presence, periodically his voice. There was no news, which was news in itself. Carmelo clearly trusted no one, not even the father he'd murdered and brought back to a corruption of life.

By nightfall they were well into the cover of forest. Camp was made within the dense cover of ferns and hawthorn. The thorns of the younger branches would serve as some protection, and certainly the haws, although wretchedly sour, provided them with some augmentation to their spare meal of bread and cheese. They eschewed a fire, not wanting to leave any more sign than possible.

Wrapped in oilskin cloaks, they caught what sleep they could, turn about, which was made miserable by the steady drizzle that set in. Vincenze shook Sylvio awake in the half-light of dawn. They swallowed pills and bread with water from their skins and set off once more. It continued to rain. They climbed over deadfall and meadows of bracken, outcrops that grew more and more frequent as they passed through the tree-line. Soon they left all sign of trees behind where the air thinned and the mountains exposed themselves for what they were.

Harsh and black the stone created a hard foundation for this canvas of unforgiving beauty, a wind that could strip the moisture from your mouth and your skin, and was unrelenting in its power. Above fell a sky more indigo than azure, a stream of cloud cascading endlessly from the summits. There was no grace here. There was only power, absolute, immense, implacable. It was not the first time Sylvio thought of the mountains as indifferent gods. And now he knew many of Simare's people had fled through these rough trails. That had been made manifest during his race to this point, and hence the reason for the safe houses along the way. While he'd been sequestered in the back-country as a bowyer, the remainder of the country reacted to Carmelo's rule of oppression.

How ironic, he realized, that his survival now depended upon these very mountains of ice and stone. He glanced over to Vincenze who laboured to keep up, nursing his side with shallow gulps of air that was getting thinner as they made their way further and further toward the pass. The staff under Sylvio's hand remained quiescent, which was both a relief and an irritation. He wondered where was Aletta, if she was well, if she was safe. He wondered about the traders that had journeyed from Danuto to the fair.

Vincenze, pale, grasped a shallow breath. "For the love of peace, let me rest."

An interminable trek through the mountains was something Vincenze would have done without question or difficulty at any other time. Sylvio studied Vincenze's lean face, saw the extremity there, the glitter in the man's eyes that spoke of too many painkillers. Rest, yes, Vincenze needed to rest.

If he was honest with himself he'd concede they both needed shelter out of this hellishly biting wind. Black and hard, this granite provided little. There was no room here for weakness. And seeing Vincenze's extremity he knew he would have to use some of his famous ingenuity if he were to bring them to sanctuary.

He looked up to the sky, watching as that stream of cloud off the peaks lowered, darkening. Portend of snow there. Winter came early to the mountains.

Ahead an outcrop of rock seemed a likely place to find a little respite. Above that the way was smooth and steep, a black plain of rock with pockets of pale, blue ice in fissures, acid green lichens like webs where the sun and wind hadn't scoured everything clean. Above that the snow began. From there to the outpost would be the real trial.

He knew Vincenze could go no further. The man needed rest. They needed to eat, to drink. Sylvio found himself short of air.

"Just up to that outcrop," he said, his voice sounding gruffer than he would have liked. Certainly Vincenze deserved more than book and rule, but just how to go about indicating the deep concern he had for the man was something Sylvio still found difficult. Even now he could hear Aletta's gentle admonition: *It is hard I know, Innamorato, but sometimes even warriors need to hear they're esteemed.*

That thought pained like a wound. With a grunt he guided Vincenze up the black stone to the outcrop.

On the lee side the jumble of boulders formed an open ring, large enough, it appeared, to squeeze through. Sylvio unsheathed the short sword at his hip, hoping he had no need of it, and signalled to Vincenze to stay where he was. The first flakes of snow skirled round them.

Cautiously Sylvio stepped into the circle of rocks. It was clear. No ambush. He relaxed slightly, relieved there was nothing here to battle. The last of the day's light played oddly off the stone, ruddy like dried blood. Ashes drifted round his feet from the remnants of a fire from some alpine shepherd seeking shelter. Dried sheep dung cushioned the floor. Slowly, he paced the ring, studying the boulders. There was a small gap to the south that gave a relatively good view of the approach up the mountain, another, smaller niche that allowed only a narrow vantage of the north. There was only one escape. This was a prime place for ambush.

He heard Vincenze's muffled groan and that brought his attention around to the opening and his resolve to a decision. The need for rest overruled the need for a defensible position. Maybe they had not been followed into the mountains.

Sheathing his sword, he returned to Vincenze. "Come," he said. "We can rest in there awhile."

Vincenze nodded and accepted Sylvio's help into their hard shelter. For the first time since setting out on foot Sylvio risked a fire, such as it was, with lichen as tinder and dried sheep dung as fuel. There was a mountain spring nearby from which he refreshed their skins and scrubbed his face and hands as best he was able. The water was so cold his skin burned, but he bore it, soaked a rag to bring back for Vincenze who was sound asleep when he stepped into their rude shelter. With a shrug he let Vincenze rest, unpacked a bit of bread that was hard as biscuit now and carefully pared off a corner and dipped it into olive oil, chewing painfully and slowly. The cheese was beaded with oil and cracking, likely not fit for consumption, but he ate it nonetheless, along with a few slices of cured sausage packed in a crock of fat, and then chewed dried apple rounds. He needed the fat of that meal to help deal with the cold, he knew. What they really needed was something hot to drink, but without cooking utensils heating water for a thin broth would prove difficult. Still, the meagre meal took the edge off his hunger and discomfort and he watched the stinking flames of the fire as both the sun and temperature descended. Eventually exhaustion threatened to overcome him, and knowing he had to stay awake, at least until Vincenze recovered somewhat, he figured a careful reconnoitre wouldn't go amiss. He added another pile of sheep pellets to the fire, rose with the help of Aldo's staff and ducked out of the shelter.

There was a significant difference in temperature out here, the ever-present wind sharp. He hung against the rock for a few moments, allowing his eyes to adjust, letting his ears pick up the night sounds, which were few or inaudible over the moan of the wind. His torso throbbed. He flexed his shoulders, trying to ease his discomfort. Snow had fallen densely, blanketing the stone, but at least there was now this small respite.

There are people dying, Aldo's voice said. Sylvio flinched, glancing down at the staff. Unsettling to be carrying the thigh bone of his former prince, to have it there under his fingers gilt and garlanded with carving and gems. Even more unsettling to have Aldo speak to him through that bone.

Where, Sylvio thought? Where are they?

I don't know. I can only feel their presence near you, their inability to come to us.

How many?

Three. I am unsure. There is pain.

That could mean so many things. Shepherds who had fallen ill or suffered a slide, an ambush by beast or man. Anything was possible.

Sylvio gauged his surroundings, making out the scree ahead, the overhanging menace of the mountain walls against a densely black sky, the frigid shards of stars. Should he wake Vincenze? Should he investigate on his own? One could move quieter than two, and Vincenze was in no shape to move stealthily through the ragged road ahead. Truth to tell neither was he, but fine for him to risk himself. But then what if he should fall to some ambush and Vincenze have no warning?

With a curse he turned around and re-entered their shelter, bent and shook Vincenze awake. He passed the skin and some of their rations to Vincenze while he brought him up to date, all the while watching as Vincenze chewed, drank, nodded, watching as the man gathered his strength and resolve. A few moments later they were packed and wrapped into the heavy woollen cloaks they'd brought, the fire kicked out, and back into the wild wind.

There wasn't much hope of concealment out here. Even so they did their best to hug the walls, climbing higher up the pass. It was hard going, made worse by their condition and the snow that importuned them once more. By now they were well into the snow-line. They paused a moment to strap crampons to their boots, another precaution pressed upon them from that last farmstead. The going was easier after that. Panting from the altitude, pain and the tearing wind, their progress was slow but steady. They came upon a trail left by travellers, still evident despite the erosion of the wind. With signals they confirmed to each other what they read in the trail: shepherds, three, a small flock of sheep. They continued on. Then came upon evidence of a skirmish, many feet, two distinct types of footwear and the imprints of sheep hooves. Black stains splashed the snow. Blood, Sylvio thought. At some distance he could make out the bulk of animals, the very sheep he assumed, all slaughtered. Either the ambushers had no need of the meat and wool, or they were lying in wait somewhere alert to Vincenze and him. The carcasses were still warm.

Sylvio signalled to Vincenze, who acknowledged the scene and in return made a motion that he was going to climb further ahead, for Sylvio to draw his bow. Prudent move, given Vincenze was still in no condition to meet the demands of a bow, imprudent given the increased intensity of the snowfall. It took a moment for Sylvio to string the bow. In this cold it was stiff, so much so that Sylvio chaffed its surface to allow his warmth to transfer, then stepped into the space between stick and string, braced himself and reached to the side to pull the bow into an arc that would allow him to work the string to the horn nock at the end. A ginger flex or two of the string and he was satisfied all was well, rolled open the sheaf of arrows, knocked and crouched as he moved forward. Aldo's staff hung in the bow sock on his back, safe and out of the way. Even so, voices whispered there beneath his hearing, that of his father who lived in the bow; that of Aldo who spoke through the staff at his back.

Caution, they urged. Spirits hung in limbo here. Not dead. Not alive. Passing.

In that moment the clouds parted. Respite from the snow. There appeared to be a small copse ahead, haphazard and writhing in the wind, stunted shrubs. Vincenze cried out. Figures darted, alpine wolves, their eyes gleaming like green lamps.

No trees these. No shrubs. Sylvio loosed an arrow and brought down one of the wolves. That scattered the remainder of the pack.

"Nerezza aid them," Sylvio whispered.

This copse was one of men almost corpses, piked and left to die. A gruesome orchard standing amid the stones and the snow. They were dressed as soldiers or rangers might, plated leather jupons, and boiled leather helms. What folly this? Vincenze was bent toward one of the men, offering water from his skin. The wind was such Sylvio could hear nothing. The dead in the bones he carried cried out a warning.

Sylvio whirled, drawing another arrow. A man standing there, hands outstretched in a universal gesture of peace.

"Don't shoot!" the man yelled, his voice thin above the wind.

"For the love of the gods, don't shoot!"

Sylvio hesitated, trying to pick up details in the darkness. No armour there. Only the rough clothes of a mountain shepherd. "Identify yourself."

"Piero," the man called. "We've been searching for you. Friends sent us to guide you through the pass." He gestured to the dying. "We took out this band from Carmelo. Come. There's shelter and warmth not far from here."

Friends? Almost there? Almost free?

He lowered the bow and called to Vincenze who stumbled toward him and pulled him around, his face tight with exhaustion and pain. "That's not what I've heard," he hissed to Sylvio. "That one," he jerked a thumb over his shoulder, "says they were waylaid by an armed troop, all their sheep slaughtered."

"Shepherds?" Sylvio asked. But the dying were in armour.

Vincenze nodded.

Their visitor yelled, "Carmelo's scum!" and in a few swift strides was beside the man Vincenze had succoured and drove him brutally down the pike. A scream tore from him and lingered on the wind. Piero rose, shaking. "Will we never be free of his treachery?" He bent and scooped snow, rubbed his coat and face, spat and straightened. "Let's be out of this night. Nerezza has taken enough life this autumn."

Caught. Perhaps. But how to escape? Just he and Vincenze on this mountain, both of them stretched to the limits of their strength, and there beyond the blur of the snow he could see the shapes of other men, eight of them easily. Lives in the balance. Indeed, and more than those who suffered in that barbaric copse on which starving wolves fed.

Unsure, but seeing no other recourse, Sylvio followed the man who called himself Piero, knowing Vincenze would fall in with him. They walked on, leaning into the wind. The clouds lowered again and brought with them more snow. Periodically Piero called out encouragement, promising hot drink and savoury stew when they arrived at the outpost they'd taken over. Sylvio trudged on, hoping Vincenze would hold. Neither of them was in any fit state for this night's trek and treachery. And there were the cries of the recently departed, incoherent, lost. Not even Aldo could offer him any insight.

Finally Sylvio made out golden squares of light from windows, covered with oiled skins, could smell the fragrance of wood smoke which meant warmth and security. There, just ahead, the dim outline of a habitation carved from the face of the pass, not much more than a glorified cave that had a heavy cedar door banded and studded for strength and some measure of protection from the elements. Sylvio all but spilled into the space afforded behind that door, swimming in the wave of warmth that hit him. There were cheers and thumping hands on his back, people to help him from his cloak, pressing a mug of warmed sangria into his grip and leading him to a room beyond, deeper into the mountain that had a roaring fire in a natural chimney and where a copper cauldron hung and promised that stew Piero mentioned.

Perhaps friends after all? Some familiar faces from his previous life at court. If they wanted him dead would they not have dispatched him along with those others? He looked over to Vincenze who laughed with an old compatriot, nearly staggering with exhaustion and pain but laughing nonetheless. Likely from relief. Likely from want of relief.

But there was Aldo in Sylvio's head, the voices of the dead men in that gruesome copse. *Beware!* But what to do?

Stay alert. Find an opening. Use it. Somehow he had to find something to use.

Feigning an idiot grin he looked at Vincenze who sat across the board from him, the man all but asleep as he shovelled chunks of meat and carrots, parsnips and onions into his mouth. Vincenze wiped his chin with the back of his hand, lifted his mug to Sylvio who returned the gesture. Safe. They made it. Those thoughts were plain on Vincenze's face, drawn with pain and strain.

Which was Sylvio's last coherent thought for some time.

It was Calvino who first had word that matters had gone awry, informed as he was by the network he'd cultivated to protect his employer and the man Portelli sheltered. Sylvio and Vincenze had been taken captive to the Castello, and somehow disappeared during the peregrination from the Temple of Nerezza. Now there was word the flagship with Prima Violina from Almarè had sailed, and that the Breenai flagship held Dona Aletta hostage. At this very moment Il Principe raged, it was said, calling for blood and retribution.

"They'll come for us," Portelli said.

"To answer for all this," Calvino said. "It is most likely, Padrone."

"How many of our people went to the Festa?"

"None, Padrone. When the Maestro disappeared this afternoon they decided to observe the Festa within the compound."

Ah, the prudence and cleverness of them. "I think a hasty retreat should be made. Any chance of us getting through the gates?"

"Depends on how much people are willing to sacrifice in what is already a lean year. I think I can arrange for people to slip out several gates, with enough coin, and without the wagon train."

Portelli shook his head and stared out into the atrium where he'd positioned himself since everything had fallen apart. What he wanted to do right now was find the bottom of a jug of beer,

Danuto beer, sit in the cool evening of the village and watch as the candles were lit for Nerezza and set around the fountains and pools. Staff did that right now in the casa, lighting candles for their own dead. He watched the lights wink in the pool of the atrium.

How to proceed? How to tell the villagers who had placed so much hope on this trade caravan that now all their hope and more was likely lost? Would they resent him? Would they resent the fact they had harboured a man fallen from grace and sent into exile? Indigence and the prospect of worse could erode even the most steadfast of wills.

"I suppose you had best call a meeting, Calvino. We don't have much time, it would seem."

With a nod Calvino left the atrium. Portelli poured another mug of beer from the pitcher on the table beside him, swallowed a long draught. He promised himself he would get fully and completely drunk once all this was over. If he could afford the beer. The cost of this trade envoy severely depleted his reserves, and now if he were to sacrifice any hope of profit from his trade in cloth he would likely face bankruptcy. There were holdings he could sell off if need be, but loathe to do so because he always felt they really weren't his, that he held them in trust for the day Sylvio would once again be returned to his rightful place among them. There was his woollen mill and the farm where he raised sheep, all of it venerable family holdings.

And to whom would he sell those holdings anyway? All the rest of the traders were likely in similar predicaments now. Which left him to deal with foreign investors, and he'd be damned if he'd see one brick, one hectare pass to the Breenai.

He drained the mug, refreshed it, belched.

People arrived now in groups, knots of speculation and worry. Some of them set their candles in paper boats into the pool.

"What's this about, Sindaco," one of them asked.

He raised a hand and forced a smile. "Now let's not be hasty. As soon as the rest arrive you'll know everything." He scanned the atrium, watched the stragglers, saw their annoyance. It was a moment before they were settled, candles for their ancestors afloat in the pool.

"In a day filled with bad news I'm afraid I must give you more," he said without preamble. "And I will leave your response to this information to your own discretion." He swallowed another gulp of beer, and told them the news Calvino brought. Whispers rose among them. Again he raised a hand.

"To compound that there seems to be some sort of further political move afoot," he said, "Prima Violina has taken her flagship and set sail with the tide, before the market closes and completing what was thought to be strategic trade negotiations.

"Given all this it seems only logical that it's a matter of time before Il Principe sends his examiners to question us, linked as we are to the Maestro. And to prevent that, and any unpleasantness, I submit to you we leave in haste, in small groups and under cover of the Festa. If any of you wish to stay you have leave of the Casa Portelli. I do not foresee any hope in that decision. Myself, I will leave as soon as all of you who wish to depart have done so.

"As for your goods, the best I can offer is to secure them in the storehouses here." There was outrage now, despair.

"And what are we to live off this winter?" one of them asked.

"If Il Principe comes after us, all the wealth and goods of Simare will be of no avail. I do believe we are about to come to conflict, and in my opinion our best course of action is to fly for Danuto, secure the village and do everything to defy a head-of-state out of control." Their protests rose. He lifted a hand again to calm them. "I know, I know. It is treason of which I speak, but in the end, when you examine the facts, is it not Carmelo himself who has committed treason by selling us to Breena? You know what this latest tax means. You know the devastation it puts us under, and not just from an economic point of view. He has in essence made us all vassals of Breena."

There were grumblings of assent, anger, resentment.

"Calvino assures me," he said over them, "he can guarantee our passage through specific gates if we offer enough coin to cause blindness. And our retainers will be divided among us so we at least have some measure of protection on the road. Once out of Reena we can catch up with one another and gain strength in numbers."

"How do we know we can trust him?" one of them asked, gesturing to Calvino.

"Dona Aletta tried and passed him. I rely upon her ability as one of the stregare." He scanned the atrium, letting his gaze settle upon individuals. "We haven't much time. Those of you who wish to go should set to your business. Those of you who do not, I suggest you lend your backs and assistance." To add an imperative to his speech, he rose and gestured to Calvino, who accompanied him to his quarters. Behind him he heard the traders argue, disperse.

"There's much to do, Calvino," he said once they were in his antechamber. He looked around at the art and furnishings that had once been di Danuto's, out the windows where sunset flamed in the sky as though the world were on fire. "Let the staff know that once I have gone they are free to do as their conscience dictates. I release them of any obligation. They have leave to take whatever goods from the household they think will fetch them coin to aid them on their way. They are not, however, to break into the store-rooms, as the goods held there are in trust for those who flee this night.

"Send our most trusted retainers with grossi to those gate-keepers you think we can bribe, and assure our people passage. Have my own staff pack only what I'll need for a swift ride home, that is clothes for the road and weather, and coin to buy our way." He turned and looked at the small man, his bird-bright eyes, his face like a dried apple. "You are welcome to come with me, Calvino, to find a new life in Danuto such as it might be. I cannot think you will be safe here."

"There are places here I can hide," he said. "And information I can gather and have couriered to you. It would be better that way."

"Aren't you getting a little old for heroics?"

"But who would suspect such a man as me? The elderly are often overlooked."

Portelli gripped the man's shoulder, smiled. "In case we don't meet again, go with the blessing of the gods."

"And you, Padrone." He turned away. "I'll have strong coffee brought. You'll need it."

In the end all the traders but one chose to flee back to Danuto, and she offered her assistance to Calvino when she learned he would remain. "I can pass myself off as his niece," she said. "He will need someone to watch over him. And there are places a woman can go where a man cannot."

The only goods any of them smuggled were Danuto's famed horses, one and a spare for each of them. They left in small groups, what appeared to be family units, dressed poorly so as not to attract too much attention, and with the hope the fineness of their mounts would not leave them exposed. Given enough mud even the best of the horses were made to look worn, and with the cover of darkness the ruse might serve.

Portelli rode out with one retainer only, a man disguised as an indentured hand, weapons hidden under saddle cloths and cloaks. Just as he left the Piazza da Luna he heard the clatter and clash of an armed troupe, heard the jangling of the bell at the gate of Casa Portelli. There would be no answer, he knew. Calvino had barred the gate and said he would make for the back wall of the compound and scramble up and over into the alleys, his *niece* with him.

Portelli dared the main thoroughfares, trusting to his shabby presentation in order to reach the river gate quickly. Calvino assured him sufficient coin gilded the palms of the watchmen to guarantee his quick passage. In fact, when Portelli approached, the gates were wide open to the wharves, no lamps lit, and the guard house dark. His heart hammering he rode through. No challenge issued. In the distance he could hear a young voice chanting to Nerezza, clear and pure. Points of light glimmered out in the harbour, visible between the warehouses and forest of masts.

They were on the main road that ringed the outer walls of the city. It would be near to an hour before they picked up the road that veered off to the northeast and days later landed at Danuto. Instead, Portelli chose to follow a little used river road which would take him wide of the city and thereby avoid two of the gates and possible discovery. His plan, however, he soon realized was faulty. This was the Festa da Nerezza. There were candles in paper boats on the river, and those who followed their passage; he rode against the tide. At the next opportunity he took a road heading north and then east, and then north once more, always bearing north so he would eventually hook up with the other traders. Throughout the night he kept to this course, setting his mount to a brisk pace so as to put distance between himself and Reena.

He picked up the first group from Danuto an hour into his journey, and thereafter in small groups, growing in strength, riding at speed now they were away from Reena. They wouldn't be able to maintain such a pace for long, but while they could they asked all they could from their mounts and themselves. All through that night they hurtled up the road, through villages and hamlets, changing horses when needed. They still rode hard in the morning, made a brief stop at an inn where they bargained for fresh mounts which were easily had given the fine horses they offered in trade.

Coin passed palms as insurance against discovery should Il Principe's troops come calling.

Taking breakfast in the saddle, Portelli and the traders once again hurtled up the road to home. When finally they could go no more and needed to rest, they left the road for the cover of a woodlot, set picquets and hoped for the best.

An hour into their respite two of the retainers brought in a troupe of what appeared to be ordinary folk, bearing arms. When pressed, the confessed they'd heard rumour di Danuto had been taken captive and escaped, knew about the new tax, and wanted to join the people of Danuto when and if Il Principe came calling. They'd had enough, they said. What harvest they'd managed to hide was loaded and waiting to be brought to Danuto against what they suspected would be a long siege.

Portelli exploded into grins, clapping the newcomers by the shoulders and planting kisses on their cheeks. A little over a dozen in all, each mounted with a spare. Renewed by their faith, Portelli and his troupe set off again.

Over the course of the next days the weather changed from fair autumn to portend of winter. Mornings dawned to hard frost, rimming their blankets and sugaring grasses. The wind all but stripped the leaves from the trees so they stood umber and violet in the distance, the dark green of conifers emerging in clusters. Rain, driving and needle-sharp, chilled their flight and caused the steam to rise from their over-heated mounts. More and more rebels came to join the cause of Danuto, a supply train following along the back-country roads and byways where they stood better chance of avoiding notice by Crown officials. Traffic on the road increased noticeably. There were people on foot, wagons, small bands of armed troops both infantry and cavalry all with the look of ad hoc preparations. When questioned, they all had the same destination – Danuto.

Portelli found himself amazed and yet not. He knew why these people cast their lot with a man exiled and now missing. Sylvio's loss stood for all they lost themselves. And he realized, reluctantly, he'd be forced to find a plan of resistance, a way to give Sylvio a chance to emerge, wherever he was.

Their luck, however, did not hold. They were two days out from Danuto when Carmelo's troops caught up with them, rattling swords and shouting orders. When the dust settled it was all too apparent there were fewer troops of the Crown than there were traders and retainers. After the first shouted command to halt and put up their arms, the entourage from Danuto looked at one another, cheered and drew their own weapons as one, daring Carmelo's men to test themselves against formidable odds and this far from reinforcements. To everyone's surprise the captain of the troop ordered his men to stand down and fall in.

"If you'll have us," he said. "We've no more wish to spill countrymen's blood than you, and you could likely use some help this close to the Breenai border."

Portelli looked to the traders for consent. "There are enough of us to take them if they get out of line," one of the group shouted. Laughter erupted. Together they turned about and kneed their mounts into a gallop, once more toward Danuto.

Two days later in a drenching, frigid downpour they paused on the road within sight of home. Portelli chewed a collection of new profanities, all of them colourful and full of humour, because what they saw in the distance was indeed home, the village of Danuto, but undergoing reinforcement. A wooden palisade neared completion, ornamented with trebuchets, guard towers and main gate. A trench had been dug around the perimeter and the debris from that thrown up into an earthwork. Traffic passed into and out of the gate. The road had been churned into mud and workmen now laboured to pack it with cobbles and gravel, in fact paving the road. While all the rest of the country deteriorated under Carmelo's lack of care, here the people defied him and undertook improvements to infrastructure. With no funding, no support, they hauled and hacked and did what they must to fortify a village in defiance.

"By whose order is all this being done?" Portelli asked of one of the workmen, a man he didn't know and therefore plainly not from Danuto.

"And who are you that I should answer?"

"Sindacio Antonio Portell."

The man looked up from his work, the others within earshot pausing, grinning. "Pardon, Sindacio." Portelli dismissed the apology with a shrug. "Danuto's interim council," the man answered. "We all thought we'd give the Maestro whatever help we could, and reinforcing the village seemed a good place to start."

Portelli laughed then, despite being chilled to the marrow, saddle-sore and heart-sick. Here was a welcome! Here was defiance! "If only you could see this," he whispered to Sylvio who was not here to witness what people did as tribute to him. Wherever Sylvio was, Portelli could only hope he was safe and returning to them with all speed.

In fact Sylvio had the distinct feeling he wasn't safe at all. It occurred to him he slept, or thought he slept, and at that a very long time. Time was a river, then an ocean on which he rose and fell over languid swells; at other times tossed through storms that were agony. Rather, it wasn't the storms that were agony but his body. He hurt. No. Not hurt. He thought he might die. Definitely. Where his ribs had been bruised by Carmelo's men they now burned abominably, and that pain radiated to his shoulders, his arms, his legs. Sweet gods even his extremities felt as if they were on fire, as if someone pierced him with needles over and over again, which, he realized, was exactly what happened.

"He's coming round," someone said.

He forced open his eyes, although it almost proved more than he was capable, rolled his head to the side, felt the pitch and yaw of the vessel of his body. The pain of that submerged him again for a moment. Somewhere in the distance he heard, no, felt the tap, tap, tap of something sharp and stinging too near his groin. He flinched, tried to raise a hand against his tormentor, found himself incapable and bound.

The stinging stopped, someone saying in anger, "Where's that draught?"

"Coming, coming." Another voice in the distance, the sound of feet scraping on a gritty floor. He could feel the heat of flame near his face, again forced open his eyes. Not one flame, many, scores, lanterns burning throughout the room, incandescence like the sun. A face over him now, breath fetid, a hand pinching his nose. He gasped, choked on a bitter liquid. "Swallow, yes." More liquid. He swallowed, near drowned, coughing and retching. Still that bitter brew poured down his throat. He wanted to reach up and knock the cup from that hand, couldn't seem to make his limbs respond and in a few moments it didn't matter anymore. His vision greyed, narrowed, closed, a buzz in his head that spread like cool effervescence down his body. Tap, tap, tap on his body, in the distance. The ocean calmed for awhile.

He rose and descended through moments like this so that it became the standard by which he measured his life, as if this was all his life had ever been and ever would be. Pain. Consciousness. The bitter draught. Pain. Unconsciousness. Over and over. He thought at moments he spoke, but wasn't sure; was spoken to, but was unsure. Always that tapping. Always that pain as if his skin were flayed.

Time and its courses were foreign, and he lost himself on that ocean, incapable of either resistance or surrender. Sometimes he thought he was with Aletta and spoke to her but too often she dissolved into the light. Sometimes he thought he was on the road, fleeing for his very life, but then he knew he was sleeping because there was a hard surface under his cheek. And then when it was possible to string one impression to another and form a cohesive thought he supposed maybe he was ill for there was the smell of the sick room around him, of vomit and excrement, of blood.

Am I dying?

Or left for dead was his next thought, later, much later he realized when the ocean retreated and his world stilled. It occurred to him his eyes were open. He watched a beetle crawl by his face, emerald bright, a deadly jewel. Wasn't this what they called an assassin beetle? The kind that liked to feed from wounds? Beautiful, though. He could string together a garland of these and present it as jewellery for Aletta's throat.

Silly thought. You didn't fashion jewellery from insects. Although the Breenai did. Even so Aletta deserved better than chitin on her skin.

Aletta.

He stared at a shaft of sunlight that pooled on the stone of the floor beyond where he lay, bright white on black.

Aletta.

Singing in the harvest, kissing his mouth, whispers in the night of love, of fear.

He closed his eyes, felt the wetness of his cheek, the sting, the hard stone beneath his face.

When he opened his eyes again there was lamplight, a cloth running cool water over the fire of his skin, a hand, a man's hand brown from the sun and accustomed to hard work, an arm with a linen shirt rolled to the elbow, recently darned at the shoulder, there the face, a face he knew.

"Vincenze," he said, or tried to say, his voice failing. He tried to clutch the edge of the bed on which he lay, lean over, failed and vomited. Mercifully, he passed out again. At intervals he was aware of convulsions jerking his body, biting his tongue and the coppery taste of blood in his mouth. There were cool cloths on his painful skin, on his fevered brow, the smell of soap and disinfectant, of the harsh cold of winter wind when a door opened and closed, bright sunlight on the stone floor, golden lamp-glow from an oil lamp that burned at his bedside.

This time his rise to consciousness was steady and measured. He felt as weak as a newborn, as light as air. He lay on his side on a thin but clean linen sheet, under which was a mattress of sheepskins, another linen sheet over him and woollen skins piled atop that, a pillow of sheepskin beneath his head. It felt luxurious. A cocoon of softness against his tender skin. He touched the linen with his forefinger, paused, studying the chromium green vine that wound over and around his knuckles, up onto the back of his hand where it burst into beasts and flowers of cinnabar red and cadmium yellow, cobalt blue birds on his arm and manganese purple ropes, urns of brown ferric oxide and the pale bones in white lead carbonate, outlined and picked out as if in scrimshaw with carbon black. Stories and images crawled over his chest, and as he pushed away the blankets found their chapters unfolding across his belly, his thighs, his legs, even his toes.

He felt the surge of shock in his chest like a detonation of heat, tried to sit up and failed, his limbs boneless, his head spinning. "Please, the gods," he whispered and with a moan sank back, allowing those hands that had bathed him and nursed him to pull the covers back over his painted, painful body.

"I'll bring you some broth if you think you're able," Vincenze said, gripping Sylvio's hand.

"All of me?" Sylvio managed to whisper, his mind filled with the tattoos that shouted from his skin. He watched Vincenze's face, gaunt now, saw the darkness under his eyes, the twitch at the corner of his mouth that suggested strong emotion. Vincenze nodded an affirmation.

"I tried," he said. "I was weak. They had me bound."

The man had been exhausted and in poor health, worse off than he when they trusted to the deceit of men they thought shepherds. He felt Vincenze's hand leave his, closed his eyes to stop the room from spinning, sank back into the comfort of this bed likely Vincenze had arranged. When he heard something scrape across the stone he gathered his strength to open his eyes once more, found Vincenze settling himself on a stool, a bowl of brew steaming and savoury in one hand, in the other linen that he arranged beneath Sylvio's chin.

"Try a few sips," he said. "It's mutton but I've skimmed it so you should be able to keep it down."

Sylvio felt the spoon against his lips, the warm broth, sipped. It was delicious. He realized he was ravenous. "Slowly," Vincenze cautioned. Of course. He'd been ill, for how long he didn't know. He took another spoonful, glancing around what appeared to be empty space.

"They've gone," Vincenze said, interpreting Sylvio's interest. "I don't know why. As soon as they'd finished tattooing you they packed up, cut my bonds and made off, even left us provisions."

Courteous of them, Sylvio thought.

"I think they were Breenai. They spoke with heavy accents. And what they did to...." He looked away.

And what they did to him was very much something out of Breenai tradition: tattoo the accused as a mark of dishonour, brand him pariah for the rest of his days, without recourse to disguise or redemption. He smiled and then laughed, laughed at the genius of it, laughed with bitterness and tears and acknowledgement of just how twisted and clever and cunning was the boy he'd mentored all those years ago. Of course yes, mark him irredeemably with a perceived dishonour now that he'd dared to defy his Prince. Carmelo didn't want him dead, he realized. He wanted him very much alive so that when he chose he could reach out and pluck Sylvio back, play with him as a cat would torment a mouse. Strip him of home and title. Strip him of the means to support himself. Strip him of the appearance of honour and hope and all he held dear. But keep him alive. Always keep him alive because it was the only way Carmelo could assure himself Sylvio would never leave him.

Why had he not seen it before? The excessive grief and madness of the boy who lost his mother. The madness that drove him to execute his father and bring him back from the dead as assurance Aldo would not follow in Viviana's footsteps. And now Sylvio.

Why had he not seen this?

He waved away the broth, managed to say, "My staff?"

"They left it."

Surprise after surprise. He thought for sure they might have taken it for the gold and jewels that bound this bone of Aldo's. On the other hand this was also very much the style of Breenai troops. Leave no witnesses. Take no booty. Strike. Do damage. Get out. He'd seen it again and again throughout his years of banishment. It was what Vincenze reported only this past spring. Dead left with valuables and weapons. The tactics of terror. Dissolve a people from within.

What he needed now was information. He should ask for the staff. He should speak with the ghoul that was now Aldo, use that unsettling ability he had not asked for nor wished. But despite all his resolve his eyes were closing and Vincenze's voice growing distant.

The next time he woke he felt fresher, his skin not so tender. He couldn't bear to look at his body, to see the macabre work of art they'd made him, but did dare to run trembling hands over his limbs, as if to assure himself that he still was human. There were painful swellings scabbed by the feel of it. He could feel the lassitude of his muscles, the slack in his skin. There was an urgent need to use the privy and he opened his eyes onto daylight flooding the room from an overhead shaft. He followed that cone of light up into the darkness of the caverns above, saw the sharp glint of ice crystals floating there.

Winter, then. The first snows had come when he'd arrived at this place. How long had he been out of action?

He managed to ease his legs over the side of the cot that seemed to be carved from the wall of this shelter. There were sheepskin slippers of sorts beside the cot. He eased his feet into them, found his shirt cleaned and mended on the box at the side of his bed, slid that over his head and let it settle over his shoulders, his arms, without experiencing too much discomfort. That effort left him dizzy and holding his head in his hands, his arms braced on his knees.

When his head cleared he scanned his surroundings, taking his bearings. There the hearth in the natural chimney he remembered that first night he and Vincenze stumbled into here, a cooking crane there and spit. The long table. Benches, boxes, casks, a few pails. Treen on a shelf carved from the wall. Other sleeping shelves ran down the wall from his, one other place made up, likely Vincenze's.

His gaze returned to the box by his bed, the ornate staff there. Carefully he reached out to it, saw the green vines and colourful images on his hand and wrist, stopped for a moment in shame, grasped the staff with resolve and brought it to him. Immediately Aldo was there in his head. Sylvio just let himself open, too weak to do otherwise, submitting to this gift of his that was so unsettling and grown so expansive.

Ó Leannáin was still in the capitol, attempting to mitigate a growing disaster. They had word Aletta was safe, apparently through the most unlikely of sources, young Passerapina, the stray child Sylvio sent to the Casa Portelli.

Sylvio formed no reply, made no comment, just hung there in the flow until Aldo's voice ceased and remained in the background like a sigh of wind.

There were immediate needs, practical requirements, like finding a privy or at least somewhere to relieve his bladder. He levered himself up off the cot by using the staff, ignominious use for such a rare artefact, stood there a moment with the room spinning, felt his dizziness settle, stabilize, tried a step, then another.

By the time he reached the enormous wooden door he thought he would throw up, swallowed repeatedly and leaned against the cold stone of the wall. The door opened, letting in a blast of frigid air from which he was partially shielded by being beside the hinges. When Vincenze turned and closed the door, he jumped with fright, laughed briefly, and then scowled.

"And what do you think you're doing?"

"Inspecting the masonry." They laughed. "And hoping for a privy."

Vincenze measured Sylvio a moment, took a cloak from the wall and wrapped him in it, then helped him to another part of the cavern that served as latrine, an unsettling place to offer your bottom, hanging as it did over a chasm. Here the cold was so sharp Sylvio shivered violently by the time they made it back to the main chamber of the outpost.

Vincenze bundled him into a settle near the hearth, set a bowl of broth into his hands which he sipped in careful, slow measures while Vincenze apprised him of their stores and situation. The pass was closed for the season. There had been heavy snows, no evidence of anyone foolish enough to try their lives in the mountains this time of year. They were stuck in the outpost until a thaw.

Further back in the shelter was a pool and small stream which although cold continued to flow briskly. A good supply of turves and wood had been laid by, along with casks of salt pork and fish, a cold cellar of root vegetables, sacks of barley and corn meal, even a small store of flour, salt, dried beans, pinoli and best of all, apples. There were amphorae of wine and olive oil, even one of fish sauce. Flakes of good rope and twine, five bales of sturdy fustian and another three of coarse wool melton, thread, needles, hides. Tools were to be had, and a few arms. Altogether it would seem the men of the outpost lived comfortably in their winter isolation.

There was a second level apparently that led to the outside, stairs down the face of the compound. Vincenze was sure this was the only egress when the snows came so heavily that they buried the lower door.

"Any evidence of what happened to the men who ran this outpost?" Sylvio asked.

"None. But given what happened to the shepherds who were unfortunate enough to hazard upon our captors, I think it likely they're all dead."

"And these Breenai?"

"Either betrayed Ó Leannáin or were in the employ of Il Principe. On the other hand they may have simply been loyal Breenai, acting for their country."

"None of them a settling thought."

Vincenze nodded. "And after thaw?"

Sylvio shot him a glance, set his bowl aside on the table and leaned into the fire. After the thaw, indeed then what? Flee down the pass to Almarè, his tail tucked between his legs, forever an outcast, his country and Aletta lost and all hope abandoned.

"I don't know, Vincenze." And he carefully levered himself up and shuffled back to the comfort of linen sheets and sheepskins.

CHAPTER 3

Sylvio's recovery took too long for his liking. He knew he was a fractious patient, allowed his impatience to drown Vincenze and often without apology, resulting in a brisk measure of guilt on his part. Within days of his return to consciousness he stubbornly pulled on a fur coat that hung on one of the pegs near the lower doorway, pushed his feet into fur boots and hands into fur mittens. When confronted by Vincenze he growled that he wanted to locate the dead shepherds' bodies, to bring back their bones.

"All you had to do was ask," Vincenze said, buttoning himself into furs like Sylvio's.

Sylvio only glared at him, leaning on Aldo's staff.

He doesn't deserve that, Aldo said.

Shut-up, Sylvio answered. *Just let me think.*

That's the problem. You're not.

Well how can I with you in my head?

I didn't make you what you are.

Then who did?

No one. Anyone. Who knew? What made him a bone-speaker?

What gave him the ability to commune with the dead? He didn't know. Gods, he didn't know.

Ever since he could remember he had a simpatico with the dead, could feel their presence just under surface of his senses, but troubled by that awareness he'd learned to shut it out, to deny he could hear anything at all. When his mother died of fever, he could swear he heard her voice. Then later, before he met Aletta and had taken office in the capitol, his father slipped away, grieving for the woman who preceded him. Sylvio, as he had for his mother, carved an effigy of his father and added that to the family shrine. When he made his devotions he heard whispers, faint rustlings in the background. He never spoke of it. This was the territory of legend and hucksters who swallowed the smoke of opium and spouted hallucinations. What he heard was imagination, he was sure, part of his need to speak once more with family now gone.

The first person to suspect he was more than he appeared had been Aletta, from whom he could hide nothing. When finally she reasoned out what he was she brought him her knowledge with gentle words and worried brow, so unlike the aloof strega he knew. There had been no horror, no flinching. What she expressed was concern over his denial of his gift.

We cannot change what we are, she'd said. And he'd had no response to that other than, in the end, to agree and accept her subsequent proposal of marriage. He'd been too in awe of her, too humbled by her knowledge and grace. Because of her acceptance he, also, came to acknowledge what he was, unsettling as it was. That didn't mean he went out of his way to cultivate his talents. No, that came later. After Viviana died and he'd found Carmelo trying to saw a finger from his mother's hand. In the years that followed, more and more he found himself listening to those voices in the distance, hearing them like wind in leaves. And then, when finally Carmelo banished him for expressing his concerns and doubts about Carmelo's policies, and stripped him of everything he had, Sylvio examined, albeit with trepidation, the gift he had in order to craft the bows known as the arcossi.

"I could use your help," he ended up saying to Vincenze, part apology, part acknowledgement.

Vincenze glanced at him, twitched a smile and said, "We'll need the snowshoes," tucking two pair under his arm and hauled open the door. A blast of frigid air hit Sylvio in the face, sunlight as sharp as needles. His eyes watered. He blinked, stepped outside behind Vincenze, struggled with the toe straps on the snowshoes, gave up and let Vincenze secure them. Sylvio couldn't remember seeing so much snow. Plainly Vincenze had made brave effort in keeping an area cleared in the general vicinity of the main entry to the outpost, but by now the snow was piled near their own height, and the season yet early. There was worse to come, he knew, as winter deepened.

With care he mounted the slope of snow, reached the height and headed down the pass where he knew the dead shepherds found a bitter grave. It was a longer trek than he'd anticipated. Several times he paused, catching his breath, feeling the thinness of his reserves, the thinness of the air. Still, there was a grim beauty up here, utterly stark: white of snow, black of mountains, blue of sky. So different from Danuto and winters of snow like dustings of sugar, of stubble dull gold in the fields, of stone hedgerows overgrown with hazels and brambles where sometimes he and Aletta would wander and talk about everything and nothing.

Now even that life of exile was denied him, pariah that he was. He pulled himself straighter, head lowered so Vincenze might be spared the garish artwork of his face. Exactly what he looked like he had no idea. He'd not seen himself in a mirror, hadn't been completely hit with what he'd been made, but what he could see by examination didn't leave him much hope. Breenai punishment this tattooing might be, but the world knew of it, spoke of it in whispers and fascinated dread.

Without a word he started off again, controlling his breathing in this spare, sharp air.

He knew they were upon the killing ground before Vincenze called out sight of the first bones. Sylvio heard the dead, heard Aldo's warning. He looked up and out to where wolves had unearthed the corpses and carrion birds had dispatched the bodies with indifferent efficiency. Bones lay scattered, partially buried by snow or scoured by the incessant wind. Sylvio found them all unerringly, guided by sibilant whispers that had once been the voices of the living men. A family here: brothers, sons, cousins. Six in all, three that had been piked, three that had been concealed behind an outcrop. He filled the sacks with every bone he could salvage, mandibles, femurs, it didn't matter. He thought he should weep for the tragedy of it, but found himself numb, only able to listen to their disembodied voices calling to him, giving him their last living moments, pleas there, promises. He felt hollow, a living conduit for the ancestors of this land he called home and made his heart.

Several times he paused in his gathering, leaning on Aldo's staff. Vincenze worked for him then, taking instruction as Sylvio called out a little to the left, a little deeper, guiding Vincenze as he was guided, balancing the conversations of the shepherds, of Aldo, of his father and ancestors, of the living man with him. He felt his strength flagging, knew he'd overextended himself, but stubbornly refused to give in.

When they made their way back to the outpost Vincenze shouldered the sacks, which left Sylvio to shuffle his way along in the cumbersome snowshoes, stretching his strength. The day had grown to late afternoon by the time they made it back inside, Vincenze's first care for Sylvio, getting him bundled onto the settle, making up the fire. Annoyed with himself, but knowing he had little choice but to accept Vincenze's unquestioning care, Sylvio submitted, giving half an ear to the man's chatter. All the while Aldo and the shepherds were in conversation. And beneath all that his own thoughts ran on and on like an engine unable to stop. He sipped the bitter tea – he'd forgotten to stir in honey – and drifted, drifted, and eventually slept with the dead.

The days and weeks that followed took on a rhythm of their own, slow, methodical, gone down deep to a place Sylvio had never been. He was too numb to feel fear. The only emotion he periodically experienced was one of disgust, disgust of himself, of his body, of the freak he had been made. As quickly as it surfaced he buried the emotion, sometimes turning aside from the work he had started with bone, sinew and glue, alternatively to cut and stitch himself new garments that covered everything but his face and his hands. This latter was quiet work he could do by the hearth, requiring nothing of him but the steadiness of his hands and eyesight. Often he fell asleep with his sewing in his lap.

As his work progressed, he appropriated one vessel for use as a glue pot from their small store of cooking utensils, melting together an olfactory assault on the senses that would serve as glue for the laminations he would undertake. Part of his time he spent sorting through the cords of wood stacked neatly in an area to the back of the outpost where currents of air circulated and kept the wood dry. At first he wasn't hopeful about what he'd find, but to his grudging pleasure there were staves of ash and yew, prime wood for bows, and of lengths long enough that with careful splicing he'd be able to craft weapons of considerable strength and power.

There were other bucked logs, red oak, beech, spruce, that would serve for a bowyer's bench. Certainly there were tools enough that he could manage well: axes and adzes, in-shaves, draw-knives. A broken bit of glass would serve very well for a scraper.

So it was, sometimes with Vincenze's assistance, he put together the rudiments of a bowyer's shop beneath the shaft of light that came from that opening far above. It provided even, cool light, perfect for the task he undertook. The work was meaningful, requiring nothing of him but his concentration and propensity to detail, but in that concentration he discovered new depths to this thing that he was, this bone-speaker, in fact, this cucullatus.

Fret-saw in hand, he gently sliced away slivers of bone for these rarest of bows he undertook; here Marcello who had been a father and brother, his livelihood the herding of mountain goats, his passion this land they called Simare.

You are our hope, Marcello would say.

Why me?

Because of what you are.

And Sylvio would lay aside these pale vestiges of what once had been a walking, talking, breathing man whose only voice now was the whisper in Sylvio's head.

There was Raul, the brother. *Use me well and I will honour this land.* Gugliehno, the son: *I wanted to live! Give my life meaning!* And with them the cousins and companions: Nuncio, Tancredo and Fedele.

Sylvio walked the paths of their lives, knew their hopes and their fears, and through them stretched beyond into the world of their ancestors. There were times he felt he walked two realities, the one beneath his hands in the making of these arcossi, the other within where a landscape utterly vast expanded. He thought he might drown, but didn't. Thought he might lose himself and his sanity, but instead found strength, and in time he learned to gently, but firmly, close the door on this legion, this cacophony that never slept. And in honour of these fallen he carved effigies, adding them to the pouch he carried at his hip with the hope that one day he might find what was left of their families and give them this one, small gift for their shrines.

Days passed one into the other. He couldn't say he was content, but the work gave him purpose and allowed him to explore the voices of the dead who lived with him; most of all this work kept at bay his longing for his wife and friend, apparently safe in Almarè according to Aldo.

His strength returned little by little, helped along by the meals Vincenze brought him else he would have forgotten to eat. There was no need to hurry. There was every reason to heal, which physically he did. While he'd gone to spare muscle and sinew, the hair over his entire body disappeared, destroyed by the onslaught of the tattoo they'd made him. The scabs and swellings sloughed away. And while he appeared strong, he felt a physical weakness he couldn't quite pinpoint, a general malaise he put down to his own disgust. And that malady of the spirit was something to which he resigned himself, knowing that should he ever manage to devise a successful plan to release his country of oppression and domination, for him there would be no return to a life of fulfillment. Not without Aletta. And there was no question he would be unable to reunite with her. In the eyes of the world he wore his dishonour and his shame for the rest of his days. The traditions of the Breenai were too legendary, too known. Wherever he went that knowledge would prejudice opinion. It didn't matter that he knew he was blameless. It didn't matter that he had the good opinion of those close to him. No, in the eyes of the populace, in the eyes of strangers, he would be a freak, a traitor, tried and condemned by virtue of his skin before he even had opportunity to speak any defence or allow his actions to bear witness. For Sylvio his exile was utter and complete, and only this one task remained, to give Aletta the gift of a free Simare.

As the weeks passed the snow mounted. They found the upper

egress of sensible design, the internal setup of the outpost even ingenious. Most days Sylvio fashioned bows, splicing and shaving staves, laminating thin slivers of bone to the heartwood, over that sinew and more wood, tillering, always testing. Vincenze helped where he could, stirring the malodorous pot of glue, carving horn tips, carefully ravelling linen cloth for the fine, spun threads that he gathered into bundles and plied, a twist counter to a twist, rubbed liberally with beeswax he found among the kit to clean weapons.

They worked, they ate, they slept and did it over again, marking off the days, measuring the snow as it mounted and the temperature descended, some days simply staring into the fire in a lassitude of numbing cold.

Through it all Sylvio held an inner council with the dead, expanding his senses, expanding his ability, so that through the conduit of Aldo's staff he found himself able to communicate with little Passerapina who wore the brooches made from her dead grandmother's legs, with Ó Leannáin who wore a an intricately carved torque fashioned from the a finger of a man he didn't know but used as a conduit. And through these they listened to the ancestors, to their council, to their guidance, devising plans and discarding them, developing others and considering them.

Eventually the temperature rose. Snow retreated, little by little. The lower doorway again was usable. Their stores held well, being provisions for a troupe of six not two. There were a dozen arcossi in all Sylvio manufactured, all in varying stages. When the pass opened the bows would provide them cover, a disguise as traders come over the mountains to Almarè. By now Sylvio knew he couldn't just go walking into Almarè and announce himself. Carmelo's spies were everywhere, watching for Sylvio who now was all too easy to identify. He would find it difficult to secure any assistance no matter where he went, branded as he was.

This particular afternoon Sylvio stood outside, boots on his feet, cloak over his shoulders, hood drawn. He'd walked down the pass a little way toward Almarè, taking with him his own bow the Breenai had left him, sub-vocalizing a conversation with his father who spoke through the bone. Aldo was part of that discussion, speaking through the staff Sylvio was now never without. He assured them both he wasn't going far, just far enough to see how the snow had retreated, whether they might at long last put into action the plan they'd devised all winter long.

From where he stood he had a clear vantage of the pass down the mountain for some distance, winding as it did around boulders and scree, eventually breaking free onto ochre alpine meadow where drifts remained like frozen waves. Beyond that clouds enclosed the mountains, a rolling vista of white and grey, above that the sharp, clear sky. An eagle soared there, black against blue.

He brought his attention back to the pass. No snow impeded the trail. He and Vincenze could leave as long as the weather remained fair, enough time for them to put behind the influence of the mountains. The descent to Almarè would be on the side of prevailing winds and therefore wetter than the lee. What they didn't need was to be caught in the caprice of spring storms.

For no reason other than he wanted to open his back and stretch, he stepped into the bow, pulled the string into place, nocked an arrow, sighted and let fly, watching as the arrow sped in a high arc out and down the slope, landing easily four hundred yards beyond, buried in the snow. He closed his shoulders, lowered the bow, watching the place the arrow had landed. With the same measured movement he unstrung the bow, slung it over his shoulder, turned his back and walked back up the way he came.

Vincenze turned from where he was at the hearth when Sylvio returned to the outpost, slumping into the settle.

"We'll start packing tomorrow," Sylvio said in answer to the question on Vincenze's face.

Vincenze nodded and pulled out the pot on the crane, ladling out chowder he'd put together from salted stockfish, lentils and root vegetables. He handed a bowl and spoon to Sylvio, took one for himself and eased onto the bench by the table.

"I'll build a sledge of sorts, then," he said.

Sylvio grunted an assent, knowing they'd have need of some method of transporting the goods he'd made all winter. A sledge dragged behind a man would be the easiest solution. And there would be no point arguing with Vincenze about who would pull the sledge. Vincenze as much as mothered him these days, and despite Sylvio's early protests, Vincenze continued to serve him, wary of Sylvio's new distance, and, Sylvio was sure, wary of his bizarre appearance.

It took no more than three days for them to put together provisions for the road, a few luxuries like a cooking pot and spoons, pack trade goods in waxed bags, sweep the outpost clean and turn their backs on a winter that forever changed their lives.

On that fateful night of the Festa de Nerezza, Aletta crawled into the bunk of the cabin she'd been provided aboard Almarè's flagship, Passerapina tucked onto a palette at her feet. Aletta laid there, blanket to her chin and watched the retreating lights of the harbour until they disappeared from view. All she could see was the phosphorescence of their wake. She wept, quietly and bitterly, as she'd not wept since she was a girl her first night in the school of the stregare. She'd been sixteen.

That was the night she'd been sterilized, clinically and carefully, part of her early instruction. She never knew who it was. There had only been a voice in the darkness of her anaesthesia.

Remember what is between your legs can be a weapon used for and against you.

Afterward she laid desolate, shattered, spilling silent tears where she curled like an infant on the invaded bed. For days she walked through the cloisters of the Accademia della Stregare unable to meet the gaze of her instructors, her sisters, sure she wore the dark stain of her hurt. Shortly after that, when the terror of the experience subsided into numbness and the lessons began to take hold, she realized at some point all of the novices carried with them the same desolation. It was a profound knowledge she remembered thereafter. It was the last time anyone placed her in a position of compromise.

So she was barren. It was what happened to all the stregare, she later learned. It was what focused all their heightened ability into an illuminating lens. A breath, a twitch, a rise or fall in body temperature were all clues the stregare learned to read, the inflection and timbre of voice sounds that resonated with revelation.

She learned all her mentors had to teach and more. She went out into the world on loan from the Accademia della Stregare, gained a reputation as an impartial, unerring truthsayer, and when invited to attend as handmaid upon La Principessa Viviana, accepted that invitation over all others because Viviana wanted her not for her ability, but trustworthiness as a companion.

It was a subtle but marked difference that set Aletta apart from many of the other stregare who found employment as arbiters, magistrates, consuls.

But tonight that impartiality, that cool reason could not win over the tide of despair that swept her out of the harbour and into exile. She could be widowed for all she knew. No. Not widowed. She knew as certainly as she breathed that Sylvio still lived, and that knowledge was not a result of long training. It was simply the blind faith of love.

Innamorato!

Oh, gods, yes, he was very much her life. He was breath and sustenance to her. The orbit of her choosing. It was with him, and only with him, that she refrained from her gifts unless invited, that she stood vulnerable and willing to accept all he had to share.

Sylvio di Danuto. The man to whom she wed herself and understood as she understood no other.

Finally, lulled by the sway of the ship, she slept.

When Passerapina woke her with coffee and biscotti she pulled herself together, submerged despair, need and desolation. She would be of no use to anyone, little say herself, if she were to allow herself the indulgence of self-pity.

And there was the immediate question of this little bird known as Passerapina. Aletta patted the mattress of her cot, an invitation for the girl to join her, watched as Passerapina scrambled up beside her, legs tucked carefully under the folds of her linen shift. Better clothes would have to be acquired, warm garments for winter as a start, and a better diet that would bring the bloom back to those sallow cheeks and sparkle to the harshness of those bird-bright eyes.

"You've bathed and combed your hair," Aletta said as opening.

Passerapina nodded.

"How did you come by the means?"

"I asked one of the people who serve the Prima."

Clever girl. "And have you eaten?"

The girl nodded.

"Where are your family? I will have to make arrangements to return you to them."

"I have no family."

Said with evenness, although there was defiance and despair there, Aletta could hear. It was a familiar thing to the child, she knew. "You've been alone for some time."

Passerapina nodded.

"You've always lived in Reena?"

Passerapina indicated no.

Reticent child. Cautious child. Indeed she would have to be to have survived alone on the streets of Reena. Answer the questions. Offer nothing extra. It would take work and time to gain this child's trust. "In order for me to decide what I should do with you I'm going to need a little more information. You have my word that while you're in my care, if I can prevent you any harm I will. You're, of course, not going to believe that. You've probably heard that before. But you trusted me enough to come with me as my handmaid. I'm asking you to trust me a little further."

Passerapina nodded her head in agreement, reached out tentatively and touched Aletta's cheek, snatched back her hand, fingers lingering on the bone brooches at her shoulders. Aletta felt the alertness of the girl, sensed a conversation she couldn't hear.

"From where did your family come?"

"We had a farm." The girl's fingers pressed against the brooch. "Outside Reena," she said. "We raised..." she cocked her head to the side as though listening, "poultry?"

"Birds?"

Passerapina nodded. "Yes. Lots of them. Ducks and geese, chickens and ... I don't know how to say that!" She flung her hand away from the brooch, her face twisted with frustration.

That confirmed for Aletta the girl spoke with her ancestors, that the brooches were conduits made from the bone of some relative. So young to be burdened with such a gift. "Mama and Papa, Nonna and Nonno, Zio and Zia – they were all killed by soldiers. Nonna made me hide in the bath house. The soldiers took everything.

"After they left, Nonna made me take her brooches. I didn't want to. But she wouldn't stop."

"Your nonna was dead?"

Passerapina nodded yes.

"And you can hear her now, when you touch your brooches?"

The girl shot her a look filled with fear.

"Peace, child," Aletta said, wiping the girl's tears with a corner of the sheet. "You don't need to be afraid. You're not the only person who can speak with your ancestors. There are others like you." The girl inhaled sharply. "And it's a gift about which we must help you learn."

Aletta indulged another suspicion. "Do you believe me?"

Passerapina nodded, her eyes brilliant with concentration.

"Do you understand why you believe me?"

"You're telling the truth."

"But how do you know?"

She shrugged, a frown flitting across her brow. "I just know."

"I don't think you do."

"You're lying," the girl said. "You know something about why I can tell if you're telling the truth, about why I can speak with Mama and Nonna and the others."

Sylvio, what did you send me? "You are, of course, correct. I was testing you."

"I know. But why?"

"I had to be sure."

Passerapina's eyes narrowed. "That man, the one I met in the street and sent me to you – he's your husband."

Aletta nodded.

"And you're worried about him."

Amazing child! Now Aletta was the one being interrogated. "I am." No point being devious with this remarkable thing.

"He's the one everyone's been talking about. The *exiled?* man?" She shook her head. "What does exiled mean?"

"Banished, sent away so that you can never come back."

"Why would someone be exiled?" She said that last word as

though tasting it, rolling it about in her mouth.

"They might be considered dangerous. Or they might have done something to displease the person with the power to exile them."

"Why are you worried about your husband?"

"I'm not sure you'll understand, my little bird, but my husband, Sylvio di Danuto, is very much loved by Nostro Principe."

"Then why did he send him away?"

"Because he's also afraid of my husband."

"That's stupid."

"It is, isn't it?" She watched a smile flit across Passerapina's face, like a touch of sunshine there and gone. "But you mustn't mistake Il Principe for stupid. He's in fact very, very clever. He just has a hard time letting people know how he feels." And has a hard time letting them go. He fears abandonment. Indeed yes she should have seen this before. The attempt to take his mother's finger. The abomination he performed upon his own father, she was sure but had no proof. Keep the ones you love around you forever, bound for all eternity.

She drew a long breath, let it go and with it matters she could not immediately solve. There was, however, this girl, this strange wee spirit Sylvio sent her.

"What would you like to happen to you now?" she asked, watching the girl's face for signs, signals.

Passerapina showed no surprise, her dark eyes like hard coal. "I would like to learn to be like you, to be able to tell if people are telling the truth."

"You can already do that."

"I would like to learn more. And I want to learn how to make these dead people shut-up." Her face betrayed her exasperation.

"They just keep on talking and talking and sometimes I just tell them stuff it, and they do, but then they always start up again and sometimes I can't sleep. And I want to learn how to be your handmaid. I'm not sure what that is, but I think I would like it. I can tell from the way you talk about it. I want to be like you. And I want to be like him, like Maestro di Danuto. He just tells all those dead people to stow it. I could tell when I met him. There were such a lot of them talking to him and he didn't even pay any attention." She flushed then, looked down to her lap. "I shouldn't have said all that. Pardon, Madonna."

Aletta took Passerapina's chin under her fingertips, lifted the girl's face so they could look at each other. "I'm glad you did say all that, Passerapina. And it's perfectly fine to hunger for knowledge and the ability to control your gifts." She dropped her hand. "So, let us begin. I expect you to tell me when you don't understand something I say or tell you to do. I expect you to listen with your gifts so you'll be able to tell when I'm saying something other than the words I speak. Do you understand?"

Passerapina nodded. "Like right now you want to bathe and dress and start gathering information so you'll know what to do about the Maestro."

Aletta smiled. Oh yes, clever child. "Exactly so. Do you think you can fetch me what I need to do the first part of that?"

"Yes, Madonna." She slid off the bunk and marched from the cabin. In a moment Aletta could hear that clear, piping voice making imperious inquiries on behalf of her lady.

Later, refreshed and better able to meet the demands of this her first day of exile, Aletta took the air above deck, informed through Passerapina that they were free of any pursuit and well out to sea. Violina joined her presently, leaning heavily on a cane, her face lined with pain.

"Does it vex you?" Aletta asked. "The arthritis?"

Violina gave a half-hearted smile. "There was a time I would have skipped across this deck and been happy to do so. Now the sea is nothing but a cruel lover. The dampness you see."

"I do." Aletta said. "We can sit if you'd prefer."

Violina barked a laugh. "Give in? Don't be foolish." And so they strolled, slowly and carefully, leaving the personal behind for the pressing problems of state and diplomacy and trade. It was agreed Aletta would take an advisory position in Violina's court, without requirement of her use of gifts. It was a prudent move that placed Aletta under state protection. It gave her access to high-level meetings and reports. It gave her opportunity to track the whereabouts of her all too important husband.

Arrangements were made for a monthly income, housing. It was agreed Aletta should screen her own personal staff, given she likely could perform a better check than any security.

When they were near to the close of their arrangements, Aletta was aware of Passerapina halting, staring out into the distance of the sea. She was utterly rigid, all her attention focused inward just as her gaze was stretched out to the limits of the horizon.

Violina shot Aletta a sharp glance. She could feel the Prima's question, admired the prudence of the woman who held her tongue and waited for explanation.

"Don't lose yourself," Aletta whispered to Passerapina. "Attach yourself to me while you're listening."

The girl flung out her hand. Aletta caught up her fingers in her own, felt their cold, amazed at how small was her hand. It was easy to forget she was so tiny, so young, with that force and intelligence so large in her. The girl let out a whoop. Tears tumbled down her face. A grin flashed across her mouth.

"He's alive! The Maestro! He's hurt, and galloping in a coach to the mountains of ice, but he's alive!"

Aletta's grip tightened. "How do you know?"

"A man. He's not dead, but he is. Aldo. His name is Aldo. He's sort of a door. He stands between the ancestors and us. He's with the Maestro."

"How can this be?" Violina whispered. "Aldo is in Reena with Il Principe."

Passerapina whirled to her. "No! Yes! He's in both places."

"How can this –"

"Aspetta." Aletta turned back to Passerapina. "Ask him where is his staff, the bone staff he carries."

"It's with the Maestro."

And so. Yes. And so. What she suspected all those years ago was true. Carmelo had found the ancient rite, had been successful, and condemned his father to half-life all so Aldo would never leave him again. Oh, Carmelo, my Prince, what have you done?

"Aletta?" Violina said, a sharp breath.

"The child speaks the truth. Aldo is both with Sylvio and his son. He is the living dead. His son has made him thus."

"Gods."

Indeed yes. She was sure they laughed if they listened at all to what mortals contrived. She pulled at Passerapina's hand slightly. "Don't go too deep, child. You'll lose yourself."

"They're all yammering!"

"Then shut them out. Take your hand from the brooch."

Passerapina tore her hand away from the brooch. "They're still talking!"

"Tell them they're hurting you. They'll stop."

Passerapina's eyes screwed shut, her lips compressing into a thin slash. A smile broke across her face. "They listened! They stopped!" She turned to Aletta. "They stopped!"

Aletta glanced around the deck, at the sailors who threw them glances, paused in their endless tasks. This wouldn't do. Not at all. There was uncertainty, the superstition of those who rode the caprice of the sea.

"We should retire, Prima," she said. "I'm afraid I have taxed you."

And so with care they turned to Violina's cabin and settled her with a brazier and hot drink.

As the days passed Aletta put on the mantle of her role as lady in waiting and advisor to Prima Violina, just as Passerapina wore her new role. The days were full. She exhausted herself in tutorial of the girl, in deep discussion with Prima Violina. Even the captain of the ship came to her upon one occasion to hear a dispute from below decks and determine who was culprit and who was injured.

It was the nights Aletta found difficult, hours that were a solitude of her own thoughts and her own fears. More often than not she took to her cabin window or the pitch and roll of the decks, watching the stars wheel and the waves swell, always searching the horizon for some sign of pursuit either friend or foe.

Four days out from Reena they rounded the cape and turned north once more, now toward Almarè and the broad harbour and delta of Marè itself. Dolphins dove at their bow in these rich waters, in the distance the black and white of orca who fed not only from these lovely creatures, but the sea lions who lolled on rocky outcrops. Above the whine in the rigging the sky was a cry of birds – cormorants, gulls, boobies, terns, all diving and swooping and shrieking. In the distance she could see the white-stained cliffs of the cape, ribbons of flight as flocks wheeled and turned in the metal-bright sky. A command barked out across the deck, carried from captain to first mate, first mate to master of the watch. Hands set to ropes, heaved, trimming sails as the helmsman adjusted course, easing the wheel around to a new heading.

Ever there was that ache where Sylvio's presence should have been, He was alive, damn them all. Alive and trying to find his way to Almarè. Day after day she thought this, even as she helped Passerapina pack their few belongings in a coffer the carpenter fashioned for her.

And then the days swept away with the sea and they sailed into Marè. Passerapina's eyes were like bright buttons as she took in the marble and gilt beauty that was this legendary city on the water. Flags and banners streamed out as they sailed into the roads. A boat left the wharf, moving with speed to where they anchored. That would be one of the Prima's staff, she suspected. She noted this for the child who was under her care and tutelage, pointed out the Marè Palace, the round dome of the Senate, the Coliseum Maggiore, the amphitheatre where plays and concerts were held. The girl remained quiet, taking in all Aletta had to tell her, her fingers pressed to one of the brooches.

The next hours passed in a blur: passage to the mainland, litters to the palace, staff taking charge, setting up quarters for Aletta and Passerapina, hurried toilette and refreshment, hurried meetings and discussions. That day slid into the next, and the next. Meetings about the state of affairs in Simare, of the instability of her government and Prince, of reports or lack of as to Sylvio's whereabouts. Plans and debates, discussions and arguments, all while putting together her own staff, introducing herself to the head of the Accademia della Stregare in Almarè, setting up lessons for the girl, attending her new duties as handmaid to Prima Violina.

At night she collapsed into bed in a miasma of exhaustion. Industry was the only way to counter her fear that Sylvio wasn't safe, that something had gone awry, that the reports Passerapina gave her through the network of the dead were false or misleading or misunderstood.

Over the weeks the debates about Sylvio and Simare were divided and often descended to argument. It was agreed Breena poised itself for invasion, but there was disagreement just how that invasion would take place. Some felt it would be an outright occupation with troops and an overthrow of Carmelo. Others felt Breena would keep him as a puppet in a country they owned in a very real, economic sense.

And then there was the problem of what to do with refugees. There were not many, as yet, but officials worried there would be a flood. A lot they knew about the spirit of the Simari. But Aletta offered no opinion. She observed. She listened. And she waited. It was what a strega did; all but the latter.

As to the latter she had all of the former to stop her from screaming her frustration, her despair that perhaps the news Passerapina fed her was misunderstood. The girl was so young to be burdened with such gifts, and because of that Aletta told no one of what she'd discovered in Passerapina, shrugged off the tutors and the lessons as simply insurance the child would receive the best care Aletta could offer. She kept the girl shielded from court interest, cleared the child's care-givers herself under the invasion and demand of her ability as a strega. Both she and Passerapina went everywhere with an armed escort. And there were the invisible ones, the ones who tasted food, who checked linens, who scrutinized every facet of their lives. Every one of them cleared by Aletta herself, and bound to her in a way that no other could bind them. It was an invasive procedure, a violation of their innermost selves, this power of the stregare. A touching of minds, dominance established in the knowledge the strega knew the truth of everything you said, everything you did.

In the end Almarè's inner politicos decided to cast their security net wide, and most of all to watch for any sign that Sylvio di Danuto, her lost and vaunted husband, had found refuge across the mountains. Generally it was agreed he would mount an armed coup. It seemed the logical thing to do. Depose the despot. Return the balance of trade.

Fully five weeks after they arrived the remaining Almarè trade ships returned, and with them Julio, the Prima's trusted steward. He brought disquieting news of riots and revolt, of people streaming out of the capitol. The police, the standing army such as it had been, all were in a state of complete collapse. There was looting and hunger. Breena had offered to send troops to keep the peace, which Carmelo accepted and kept in the capitol. There was a Breenai fleet in harbour that sent regular patrols along the coast, interrogating fisherman and raiding villages. It had been put about that Sylvio di Danuto was an outlaw running from his Prince's justice. Anyone known to harbour him would be taken under arrest for interrogation. There was, interestingly, no reward posted for his capture.

All through that winter they watched, they waited, they debated. She was plied with questions which she deftly avoided. At one point Prima Violina remarked, while Aletta oversaw her agenda for the day, "You're remaining extraordinarily detached from all this."

Aletta looked up from the agenda in which she was making notes – a scheduled tour of upgrades to the public bath houses. "Am I?'

"Don't be coy."

Aletta returned her attention to the agenda. "I assure you I'm anything but coy."

"You've offered not a word of advice throughout all these discussions."

"I am your handmaid, Prima. It would be a gross lack of decorum to offer comment."

"You *are* being coy."

"This tour is going to take the entire day next week, Prima. I suggest you have me defer any other meetings. I've arranged for a litter and several rests throughout, even one immersion into a hot pool. I know how you don't wish the people to see you labouring with your affliction."

"My affliction?" Violina let out a cluck of exasperation. "I've managed quite well all these years with the demands of this damnable arthritis without you running interference for me."

"Of course, Prima. Shall I cancel the hot pool?"

"No! My dear Dona Aletta di Danuto, you are as bad as Julio."

"Then I should think she is doing very well indeed," he said, entering as he always did like a breath of sharp, clear air. "Your tea, Prima."

"Oh damn the tea, Julio! I'll be in my study."

"Of course, Prima. Just as soon as you drink the tea."

She glared at him, waved at one of the ever-present staff to take the tray to her study and made her way, stiff and plainly in pain, out of the room.

"You shouldn't provoke her," Julio said when they were alone.

Aletta drew a slow breath, smoothing the silk over her knees, aware of how much she'd changed over the weeks. Gone were the worn linens and fustians she'd worn labouring in the fields of Danuto, gone the wooden shoes. She'd been pinched and pampered, oiled and waxed, primped and painted into the iconic strega, gold dust on her eyelids, kohl around her lashes, jewellery in her hair and silk on her body.

She looked up at Julio, a flat stare she knew could be disquieting, very much the inscrutable face of the truthsayer she was. "It isn't my intention to provoke the Prima."

"She has been more than gracious."

Aletta thought of a retort, instead set her pen aside, leaned back in the chair and studied Julio's aquiline features, the steady gaze, the smooth dome of his head. She could hear his concern, both for his mistress and for her. "Of course she has been gracious. And I am grateful. But my thoughts and my heart are my own council."

For a moment he watched her, then inclined his head and left the room.

She picked up the pen and continued to make notes.

So the days went. Autumn became winter, and winter here was more a misery of rain than of cold, a sheeting grey downpour that drummed through the day and into your dreams. Everything felt damp, the sheets, her clothes. Braziers and fireplaces blazed throughout the palace, the hypocausts running at maximum to keep the chill from the woman who ruled over this world of marble and art.

And then one day the sun broke through the clouds, pale but insistent, a promise, a hope. Passerapina told her Sylvio had been making bows, bows from ancestors. Aletta turned her face up to the light and warmth, and closed her eyes.

The rain stopped a few days later. The sun transformed from weak to brazen, a heat upon the skin that went to the bone. The linens dried. The pavements dried. Steam rose from the harbour where ships rocked on the tide, warping in, warping out. A pelican perched upon her balcony the afternoon Passerapina came careening to her side, her eyes sparkling, teeth flashing, all but vibrating with excitement.

"I passed my first exams!"

Aletta drew the girl to her, feeling her small frame grown strong and firm.

"And Nonna says that Aldo says that the Maestro is coming down the mountain!"

Sylvio!

Aletta bent and pulled the girl into her arms, weeping.

So it was on that same night when candles for the dead winked on the harbour, and the acolytes of Nerezza chanted from the towers, Maponos Ó Leannáin made his way through the halls of the Castello, summoned by the prince to whom he was ambassador.

Not for the first time he was aware of the wickedly sharp edge he walked. Any mistake, any miscalculation and his life was forfeit. Be calm. Stay composed. Wear that non-committal face. These were the weapons he used in his treasonous, traitorous bid to keep his beloved country from invading Simare and leaving misery and enslavement as their legacy.

There had to be a better way.

Yes, his people were crowded into impossible villages and towns that scrabbled up the sides of mountains as relentless as death, their only wealth that which they took from the rock – gold and silver, iron and nickel, gemstones of a quality that brought them great profit and little comfort. The commodities Breena lacked were food and water. Dairy they had, afforded by the goats and sheep that clung to the mountains and alpine meadows. Fish they had because of the rich waters off the coast. But grain, produce, the lush orchards and farmsteads of Simare and Almarè they lacked. The lakes and streams of fresh, potable water were rare to Breena. Linen, cotton, silk were textiles of great worth in his country; their wool was abundant and yet worthless as compared to the cloth of their neighbours.

And while Breena could afford to purchase all she needed, this present administration resented their lack. Why should Breena not have these commodities for her own? Why should Breena not expand her borders and allow her knowledge, her skill, to possess and improve what they claimed? Make the world Breena.

And Simare was so ripe for the picking, so ready for plunder and possession.

Except that Ó Leannáin had a fundamental disagreement with that position. As did others of his countrymen. But unlike those who spoke out against Breena's imperialistic policy, Ó Leannáin chose to work from within, using his influence to gain power and station. So it was he found himself ambassador, treading this perilous path, and now on his way to meet with Il Principe, the royal counsellor and father, Aldo, who was the living-dead and an ally, and a senate who were either pawns to or protestors of this crowned head.

And while all these people he attended upon should have been involved in this most sacred of festivals, they were instead gathered here at the behest of Carmelo who, it was said, was incoherent with rage.

Ó Leannáin could hear that rage now as he approached the Sala de Pubblico. "I'm expected," he said to the guards who cast nervous glances at him and over-shoulder. They swung the bronze doors open, bronze from his own country it should be noted, but fashioned by these remarkable craftsmen, and he stepped into a scene of chaos.

Like an explosion Aldo's thoughts thumped through him, warnings, cautions. Carmelo, still in the ceremonial robe of heavy silk, wheeled toward him, pearls and gold plaques flying out from the bone crown as he turned. The heavy kohl around his eyes had smudged.

"Where have you been? I summoned you hours ago."

Ó Leannáin bowed deeply. "My apologies, Principe. I had to oversee trade transactions aboard my flagship and only recently received your summons." He unfolded from his obeisance. "How may I serve you?"

"He's gone, damn you! You were supposed to help me find and keep him here!"

"Who has gone, Principe?"

"Di Danuto! Who else?"

He looked around the room at the senators, at Aldo, back to Carmelo. "Did he not return with the procession?"

"No!"

"Do you have scouts out looking for him?"

"Of course!" Carmelo flung himself onto the throne, one muscular calf exposed. "I've even sent word to all the gates."

"Then wherever he is I am sure your men will return him safely to your presence."

"My men? My men! More like yours." He buried his face in his hands. "Oh gods, what have I done?" And he wept deep, wracking sobs.

Ó Leannáin looked at the senators, caught in clumps of confusion. They'd been rendered virtually powerless by Carmelo's strategies, here as a token to good governance. Their murmurs rose and fell, hushed beneath bent heads and furtive glances. Outside the windows he caught glimpses of lights in the harbour, and there, off to the west a glow too bright to account for festival rituals.

He touched the torque at his throat, heard: *The cucullati are busy this night.*

A messenger burst into the room, looked at the Prince who wept on the throne, over to Aldo who stood like a silent spectre, hooded and cloaked like one of those cucullati but that his robes were not red. It was plain the messenger tried to compose his revulsion of the former prince when he crossed the floor to Aldo and delivered his news in whispers. Ó Leannáin heard immediately. *The west quarter is burning.*

The merchants' quarter, the compounds of all the traders of Simare who kept offices and lodgings in the capitol of Reena – on fire.

Aldo motioned the messenger to depart, bent and touched his son's shoulder. Carmelo twitched away, flung up an arm to ward off his father. His loathing was as clear as a scream when he said, "Don't touch me!" Aldo gripped Carmelo's shoulder tightly, the fingers like pale claws. "What do you mean there's a fire? Where?" Carmelo looked over his shoulder, out to the west where there was now a definite brilliance. Dogs barked, shouts and screams rose up to the windows. You could smell the fire now, oily and noxious. Bells rang out, stuttering and imperious, a doleful cry to the citizenry.

One of the senators dared to say, "We need to contain it, Principe."

Carmelo turned back, stared at the senator. "What do I care?"

"It is upon the backs of our merchants the Grossi Bribe is paid, Principe. Without them…." He shrugged, glanced at Ó Leannáin.

Ó Leannáin said, "Without them the Crown will have to open the treasury. My ship will be sailing within the fortnight to return with Breena's payment for providing Simare with protection."

"You blood-sucking scum."

Ó Leannáin smiled, reinforcing this subterfuge. "You invited us, Principe. We merely provide you with a service you are unable to provide for yourself."

"The fire, Principe," one of the senators said.

"Yes, yes! I know the bloody fire! Send out someone to deal with it. See to it."

Aldo straightened from his son, turned to the senator. Only shadows of his face, pale and eerie, were visible inside that deep hood. He gestured the senator to the door. The man all but fled the room, two others in his wake.

Carmelo turned his attention back to Ó Leannáin, dragged his sleeve across his face, leaving streaks of khol across his cheeks. "I want you to use some of that expensive service to find di Danuto." He smiled then, an icon of innocence and beauty. "I know I can trust you to do that."

"As you wish, Principe." Ó Leannáin bowed deeply, backing from the room, straightened when he reached the doors, turned and left.

When he reached his chambers he dispatched messages to key people in the security forces Breena had stationed in the city, one to assist with the fire in the merchants' quarter, one to take several small parties and question gatekeepers as to Sylvio's whereabouts. He knew there would be no news, but went through all the necessary forms to satisfy his commission.

Throughout the following hours he ran reports from his desk to Carmelo. The messages that ran between Aldo and he were of another kind entirely. The fire had leapt the merchants' quarter and now engulfed the Via di Dios and major temples. There was concern the fire-wall might not hold if the wind shifted and would rage through the poorer districts where wooden buildings stacked one upon the other like kindling. Carmelo's response was to demand what was being done about finding di Danuto. And there was, of course, the matter that none of this was within Ó Leannáin's jurisdiction. He was am ambassador. Nothing more. Still, he set up his quarters as a communications station so that those senators and officials who laboured to save the city their Prince ignored would have a place to work. The government buildings were now engulfed in the fire. Books from the famed library were being ferried to the harbour where boats had been commandeered to transport them further up the coast to Imalfia.

Then the wind shifted. The firewall failed. Fire leapt through the slums of Reena like a greedy, roaring beast. And then a disturbance broke out near the harbour, festival-goers likely drunk on new wine and frustration, goaded by the fire that escaped containment. Like the fire their heat spread, combusting through the streets into a conflagration of another sort. Ó Leannáin sank to a window sill and looked out over a city that had once been the awe of the known world.

The moon hung huge and bloody and smeared with roiling black clouds. Little could be heard above the roar of that fire, although periodically an explosion burst through the air, and screams hung like sirens in the confusion that was this night.

By morning warehouses along the wharves were engulfed. Ships stood out in the harbour. Many upped anchors and made for the open sea, their business unfinished, the season ruined. Throughout the next four days Reena's officials battled to keep things under control. Ó Leannáin slept in snatches, putting himself at the service of the senators who struggled to mobilize an infrastructure stretched beyond use. Somehow, though, these remarkable people, these Simari, halted the fire's progress. Citizens and police, firefighters and mercenaries, all had pulled together in the end to save this their jewel. The fire wasn't out. But it was contained and under control.

On the fifth day that news was relayed to Carmelo. There was no response. Senators and ministry heads did what they could, but it was now a case of implementing emergency services for overburdened hospitals and care workers, those attempting to find shelter and food for the thousands who were now homeless. And that required funds. Which were non-existent in the public treasury. And that meant convincing Carmelo to open the royal reserves and dispense largess. Which wasn't happening.

In the end the senators came to him, pleading that he seemed to have the ear of the crown, that he could use his influence and persuade the prince where they had failed.

Exhausted, angry, and trying to hold onto the threads of his subterfuge, he capitulated and demanded an audience with the prince, and when he was denied cracked off a message to Aldo to find out where was this beautiful boy. In his chambers. Ó Leannáin went there in a towering rage, cold, concealed. Attendants attempted to prevent his entry. Ó Leannáin merely glanced at them. They withered, opened the doors onto the royal chambers. The heavy curtains of Carmelo's private rooms were closed despite the early afternoon, a brazier lit and burning heady incense and weed that would have dropped a strong man into a stupor in minutes.

Carmelo lay upon his back, skin golden in the light, a contrast to the crimson silk on the bed. At the moment his face was buried between the thighs of a girl who was likewise engaged with him.

"I thought you'd want to know the fire is contained, Principe," Ó Leannáin said.

Carmelo let out a grunt and thrust his pelvis up at the girl who noisily attempted to complete her job. The prince stilled and then shoved the girl from him, dragged a hand over his face and rolled onto his side. He grinned. "She's primed. Want some?"

"Thank you, no."

Carmelo slid off the bed, eschewing any attempt to conceal that sculpted, oiled, perfect body. He crossed the floor to Ó Leannáin, kissed him on both cheeks. The honey-sweet-sour musk of the girl swept over him. "And di Danuto?" Carmelo asked, pulling back.

It took all his control to remain composed, to keep his face unreadable. The boy trailed his fingers down Ó Leannáin's cheek. Ó Leannáin took it in his own, turned the palm to his mouth and pressed a kiss there, folding the prince's fingers closed when he was done. What he didn't want was for the boy to touch his torque of bone. "There is no word, Principe."

Carmelo shrugged and turned away. "Don't come into my presence until you've found him." He climbed back onto the bed and shoved the girl onto her belly.

Ó Leannáin bowed and turned his back on the wet sounds behind him. When he reported to the senators he wanted so much to offer then the Grossi Bribe, but knew he couldn't, and instead planted the thought that perhaps they might find some legal way to seize the royal treasury. Surely there had to be some provision should a head of state be found insane or incompetent. In the end that was exactly what they did, which served both of Ó Leannáin's purposes. And just as insurance he had a unit of soldiers dispatched to overtake the traders from Danuto, a risk he realized, but sent nonetheless with the hope these last vestiges of Simare's own force would throw their lot in with the traders.

The days and weeks that followed were the most trying of his career. There was concern typhoid and cholera would break out. Carmelo screamed and threatened, albeit ineffectually now that mercenaries and public servants were being paid by the senate. Ó Leannáin listened with a benevolent, nodding face, withholding comment, biding time. There were those senators who now openly spoke against their crowned head. Carmelo's tantrums magnified.

Ó Leannáin took to touring the disaster relief efforts, escorted by his own people. He was vilified among the citizenry, the enemy, the root of their misery. But he bore it. As he must if he were to bring about the change he hoped. It wasn't uncommon to hear people speaking of the hope of di Danuto's return, of fleeing to the village of Danuto to find refuge.

Shortly after that it was brought to Ó Leannáin's attention that a crack team of Breenai were missing. When he made inquiries with the prince Carmelo told him to mind his own business; what should Ó Leannáin care what he did with hired mercenaries? That had been followed by a silent warning from Aldo, a warning he met with despair and relayed to Sylvio who was by now likely close to the Almarè pass.

The royal treasury only went so far. The funds ceased flowing. The relief efforts halted. New building and reconstruction remained plans on the senate floor.

Ó Leannáin dispatched messages back to his government. He also made alternate plans of his own, waiting for the right moment to implement. And so the winter waxed. People starved in the streets. Dogs fought over carcasses left to rot because there were no funds to pay the bureaucrats and staff who oversaw public welfare. Ó Leannáin found himself subsisting off lentils and rice, which was better fare than had many. Nerezza's cucullati, who were rare enough, roamed ceaselessly, so that the colour red, and more importantly the colour red in a cloak, came to be feared.

The winter waned. Fishing boats and small barques should have appeared in the harbour where only his own flagship swung to anchor, standing well out for fear of contagion. Carmelo spent the winter in a drugged and drunken euphoria. His questions about di Danuto had ceased after those Breenai mercenaries went missing.

And then, when the first flush of green came to those few growing things left in the city, Ó Leannáin received one of the messages for which he'd been waiting – a courier from Breena. He'd been recalled. That could only mean Breena was poised for annexation.

That night, without farewell to the prince he'd come to engage, Ó Leannáin slipped out of the city, took a lighter out to his ship and made sail not to the north, but south around the cape and then north once more to Almarè. The Grossi Bribe went with him.

***

Sylvio found the noise of the village market an assault, the sound and stink of humanity foreign. There were stalls with early greens – lettuces, spinach, kale that over-wintered and a tray of delicate wild strawberries – a butcher with crates of various fowl, a tethered lamb and goat, and a pig recently slaughtered and flayed. Yard goods hung from awnings like gaudy banners, merchants barking the quality of their wares. Baskets and cheese-makers, a potter with his winter's production, a confectioner with marzipans and sugared almonds and candied fruits.

Sylvio paused by the tray of strawberries, remembering mascarpone and strawberries drizzled with honey. He remembered sharing the bowl with Aletta. He fumbled at his purse, remembered it was empty and backed away. Instinctively he looked up at the merchant, embarrassed to be caught wanting, only to be met by a look of shock, and it was then he confronted for the first time what the rest of his life would be like, the revulsion with which he'd be met.

He raised his gloved hands and pulled the hood further over his face, filtering this fine spring day, bent his head and turned away. With a gruff comment to Vincenze he made his way to the outskirts of the village, which wasn't hard to navigate, there being only the main thoroughfare that led eventually to the capitol of Marè.

Some distance out there ran a dry-set wall of stone bordering a field of spring wheat; to the left the road fell away to a bank carpeted in spring violets and bordered by tall cypress. Doves mourned in the gentle light. Somewhere a cuckoo called. Sylvio pulled himself up onto the wall and watched the bounce and froth of the stream in spate, letting the warmth of the day penetrate his cloak and his body. He felt weary, stretched thin, wondered if he'd ever feel well again and if that sense of being unwell were more a malaise of the mind than of the body.

A grey cat leapt to the wall, startling him out of thought. It blurted a greeting, eyes liquid amber, bunted its head against his arm and when he wouldn't relent and dispense caresses, it pawed at him with claws sheathed. Despite himself he smiled.

"Finding affection where you can, eh?" The cat purred when he put his hand to its head, rubbing its ears. "Lost or on the prowl?" The cat quacked a response. "On the prowl, I'll wager." It leapt away, down into the field of wheat and bolted for cover.

Sylvio felt more than heard what caused the cat's escape: the rumble and thump of a wagon pulled by beasts. He glanced back along the road, gripping Aldo's staff. Sure enough a wagon lumbered toward him, pulled by plodding oxen. Two men sat the driver's board, one flourishing a whip over the heads of the oxen.

There were eight other people mounted and keeping pace, the ones in the fore clearly armed and armoured. The crack and crackle of the whip sent the doves clattering from the stream bank. Sylvio kept his place on the wall. He could feel a note of simpatico shiver from the staff under his fingers, vibrate through his back from his bow. Vincenze. Yes, there atop the wagon. Hitching a ride?

"That your friend?" the man with the whip shouted, a round, ringing voice that would do well in the market or a crashing good song in a tavern. Sylvio watched Vincenze bend toward the driver, clearly saying something. Sylvio was too distant to overhear, or even catch the subtleties of facial expressions. Still, this didn't sit comfortably with him. "Then hop aboard, man," the driver yelled, waving to Sylvio. "And be quick about it! Can't stop these beasts, or I'll be all day getting them going again! I want this road behind me by nightfall."

Sylvio slid from the wall and walked toward them, keeping his head down and his wits sharp, aware he was inspected. Despite his attempt to conceal his painted body, he realized he didn't make for an innocuous figure. Damn, but there was nothing he could do about that now. It was either the garish freak or the silent one mimicking a harbinger of death. Better the latter, he thought, even though his cloak was grey rather than red.

He made for the rear of the wagon, and managed to launch himself onto the platform amid bales and crates and barrels. There were two women tethered to the rings of the wagon walls, a man who looked as though with one effort he could rip wall, rings and all clear from the seats. Slaves? Or indentured labour. Which would make the driver, allowing these goods were all his, a trader.

Sylvio made no attempt at introductions and instead settled down on the back of the wagon, bracing himself against the side-wall and a bale of something that had the sharp fragrance of pepper.

So then a trader in the exotic. Which could mean many things.

He overheard Vincenze offer gratitude, heard the name Massimo – the trader's name, then – and nodded to his companion when Vincenze settled himself adjacent.

"Bound for Marè," Vincenze said, his voice low. "I've offered him our swords on the road in return for passage."

Sylvio nodded, his voice a murmur so that Vincenze had to lean close to hear. "And we are?"

Vincenze shot him a sharp glance, picking up Sylvio's caution. "Who we are. I told him I can cook."

Which he could. Sylvio gave him that. He nodded to the women who huddled together, folded one upon the other.

"Working girls."

They didn't look much like women who plied their favours for coin. They looked more like plain country women who had been taken from their homes, and certainly not from these parts with their fair hair and blues eyes. Northern Breenai then.

"A trader in the rare and hard to find," Vincenze said. "Apparently of some repute."

Sylvio smiled to himself, thought, of course. He indicated the chained hulk of a man who was also fair, blue-eyed.

"Prize fighter, I've been told."

Of course one always kept a pet fighter chained. "Well at least we're not walking," he said.

Vincenze grunted a laugh, and settled back. "We keep watch at night, with one of Massimo's men."

Ah. So this was how it was to be. Following Vincenze's lead he leaned back, sliding into half-sleep while Aldo and the others whispered through his mind. Mostly he rejected what they said, considering other plans, other possibilities.

Their journey that day wasn't exactly what could have been termed comfortable, but then he remembered the racketing, jouncing ride he'd had fleeing to the mountains the previous autumn, what now seemed an age past. He'd been Sylvio di Danuto then, beloved and berated of his liege lord, flying for his life and some hope of recovery for his country.

Hope? What hope now? Others he was sure would council a coup d'état. Invasion most likely. And then what? A puppet government? Loss of everything that was fundamental to a country of artisans? The dead gave their own council, but that path was one that was fraught with more changes than he thought any citizen of Simare would countenance. And, were a man honest with himself, that path the dead counselled was yet still a monstrous thought to Sylvio. While the people of Simare had a reverence for their ancestors, he was not sure just how far they, or he, would be willing to take that. There had to be another way, but on his life he could not think of one.

Carmelo why? Why do this?

He did manage some sleep, fractured as it was. By nightfall they'd made it into a town of decent size. Sylvio and Vincenze unhitched the beasts and saw them stabled, watered and fed, allowing a good currying for the horses, and took their own supper, a simple bowl of risotto and onions, aboard the wagon. The women and fighter were fed as well, unchained and allowed to make use of the privy and to wash. They, like the beasts, were bedded down in the stables, secured against escape. It was Vincenze who undertook their care, shying as they did from Sylvio, whose reaction was to turn away and draw his cloak about himself, climb up the wagon and sit there hunkered against the coming darkness. He didn't bother to string his bow. The possibility of trouble this night seemed unlikely, Marè being what she was – well-governed, peaceable – and there were the gates of the inn's compound to breach.

Vincenze returned after some time, stood watching Sylvio for long moments. Sylvio knew the man measured his mood, no longer knew how to approach him, how to lighten this darkness that would settle upon him since his disfigurement. Sylvio, for his part, hadn't a clue how to put this life-long friend at ease, give him some word, some gesture that would set things right. Too much had happened. Too much had changed. As it was he left Vincenze to make up his own mind and for himself remained adrift in debate with the voices inside.

It was Massimo who came out to them some hours later to keep watch, something that didn't surprise Sylvio in the least. He knew it was to be a night of interrogation, subtle or no made little difference.

With a groan Massimo thumped down to the bales, the punch-work lantern throwing wild shadows. By now the moon hung above the rooftops, full and cold, the light it cast blue and pale. It lit Massimo's clean-shaven face. Sylvio placed him at around thirty, that lean sort of good looks that beguiled women and won friends. Massimo flashed them a smile.

"So what brings two travellers like you on the road to Marè?" he asked passing a jug of beer and mugs to them.

When Sylvio didn't answer, or accept the beer, Vincenze took the lead. "Bringing our bows to market."

"You're bowyers then?"

Vincenze nodded.

Massimo shrugged when neither of them accepted his hospitality, poured for himself. "From Simare?"

Fair enough observation, Sylvio thought, given their accents. Again Vincenze nodded.

"Things aren't good there I've heard."

"What have you heard?"

Massimo wiped his mouth with the back of his hand, smiled. "The usual gossip that flies before trouble. The capitol's burned.

People are fleeing. Sounds like a shit-storm to me."

"Pretty much."

"And your friend there?"

Vincenze shot Sylvio a glance, who remained silent, keeping his hood well over his eyes and avoiding the light of the lantern. "The Maestro? He's mute."

"Is he?" Massimo turned his attention fully to Sylvio. "From birth, or is this a recent affliction?"

"How long do you figure it will take to get to Marè?" Vincenze asked.

At that Massimo laughed and drained his mug of beer. "Four days if I've a mind. And I think I've a mind." He heaved himself up. "Right, you two have the watch to yourselves. Thieve from me and I'll hunt you down." He smiled again. "Just business, you realize."

"Of course," Vincenze said, returning the smile that was all tooth.

The remainder of the night was without event.

Over the course of the next four days Sylvio and Vincenze slept by day as best they were able, kept watch by night, and gauged the mood of the countryside. Unlike the villages and towns of home, all seemed peace and normal activity here, the roads well maintained and policed against brigands. Fields were ploughed and seeded, livestock pastured. Business, commerce and manufacture flowed in the normal course of things. There were public bath houses and medical facilities, courts and markets, theatres and arenas. Soccer and bocce were played in streets and on greens, voices raised in the usual banter of people content and at play.

Sylvio remembered a time this was the norm for his own people, when industry was rewarded instead of taxed and stolen by an administration who betrayed every sacred trust and office.

As Massimo wanted, they entered the outskirts of Marè four

days later, a sprawl of humanity that spoke clearly of affluence. It was around noon by Sylvio's reckoning, given the height of the sun and the activity of the people who seemed to be closing shop for lunch and the afternoon break. A brief pause was made at the gate where their business was stated and paperwork checked. Sylvio watched closely as Massimo and the head porter spoke. There were gestures, glances his way, all suggesting he was a topic of discussion, whether because of his physical state, or for some other reason he was unsure. Whatever the reason he nudged Vincenze who said in response, "I know. I've been watching. I don't like it."

Sylvio grunted a response.

"Time to take our wares and our leave?"

Sylvio nodded, and together the two of them hauled the sledge down from the wagon. The belt with his quiver was buckled on his waist, bow and pack slung over-shoulder, the staff in his left hand, sword on the same hip. Vincenze likewise prepared, and together the two of them walked away from the wagon, nodding thanks to Massimo, who grinned widely as they passed, pocketing a purse that hung heavily. Not twenty paces out an armed guard surrounded them. Sylvio turned back to Massimo, who shrugged.

"Don't be offended. It's just business, you understand." He patted the purse that now hung from his belt.

A reward then. Someone was looking for them. Who?

Without thought Sylvio ripped his sword from the scabbard. "We don't want trouble."

"Come with us and there won't be any," one of the guards answered, motioning the others to close in. Sylvio heard Vincenze swear, draw his own sword.

"Who pays you?" Sylvio asked.

"The Prima."

She put a bounty on his head? Were they that desperate to find him. And did he want to be found? Was he prepared for what would happen if taken to Marè Palace, faced the well-meaning, high-ranking officials who would have had all winter to debate and consider their options. His options. What they would ask of him.

And if a man were honest, we would admit he was not ready. Not yet, gods forgive him, not yet. He knew what they would ask of him, and he had no alternatives to offer to a plan of armed conflict, of civil war, of deposing Carmelo and replacing his misrule with ….

What? That was the nut of the problem. With what or whom should they replace the legal crowned head of Simare?

He looked at the guards, how they hemmed in Vincenze. Of course. There was the fact of his own tattoos, of these men likely mistaking him for a Breenai traitor in the company of Vincenze. Mistaken identity. A chance. Forgive me!

"I'm not at liberty to follow," he said. He bowed, barrelled into the guard beside him. That threw the man off-balance, enough that Sylvio was through the gap and pounding away, his hood sliding back and exposing his face. A woman screamed. Dogs barked.

He whirled around as he ran, checking for Vincenze, yelling, "Drop the damned bows, man!" Saw him seized, the despair in his face, Vincenze who had always stood by him and suffered for his loyalty. Sylvio roared then, an explosive cry of anguish and frustration, spun back around and dodged his way through the crowd as he sheathed the sword and yanked the hood over the grotesque painting that was his face. He could hear pursuit behind him, men yelling at pedestrians. He veered off onto a side-street, leapt the running board of a carriage to hide from pursuit. A woman's face was at the window, her look of horror. He vaulted back to the street, taking another road, then an alley, and another that wound like a goat-track down to a small piazza, and there struck up another lane that took him east and then south, although after a few more twists and turns he lost all sense of direction.

There were now no sounds of pursuit, and being winded he slowed to a jog and then a walk, gulping air, taking the mood and milieu of the area. He was in trouble, he knew, without coin to buy food and lodging or the ability to find his way to Marè Palace, wandered through what appeared to be a residential area, stone walls and wooden doors heavily hung with iron that periodically opened onto courtyards that were modest.

He'd been irrational, he knew, haunted by the past years and more recent months of deception and subterfuge. There could have been many reasons for the guard to answer as he did, some of which may have had to do with Sylvio's own safety. The purse at Massimo's hip could have been a simple reward for Sylvio's delivery to the Almarè authorities. He knew from communication with Aldo throughout the winter that Aletta now resided in the Marè Palace, safe and awaiting him, as were many others committed to restoring Simare to a just rule.

And were a man honest with himself, he would admit that perhaps it was his own shame and indecision that caused him to bolt. He had no tools at his disposal to help him deal with his disfigurement and the constant horror with which he'd be met for the rest of his life. And how was he to meet Aletta again knowing that now he could only ever be a freak to her? How, on a larger scale, was he to command any respect or authority for the betterment of his country?

There were no answers for him, not even from the dead who now spoke like the thud of blood in his heart.

Why Sylvio ran Vincenze could not understand, and when he leapt to retrieve his friend he felt himself pulled back, held by strong arms and words of caution. In despair he cried, "Let me go after him!"

"We're to bring you to the palace," one of the guards said, the man who had spoken to Sylvio. "And I've already said more than ordered."

Vincenze looked over at him, judged from his bearing and the way the others regarded him he was the captain of this crew. He also judged a mistaken identity. "I'm not who you think," he said.

"Sylvio di Danuto?"

"No. His friend. Vincenze."

The captain swore, gestured to two of the others who ran off after Sylvio. "My apologies. We'll find him. Don't worry. In the meantime, if you're able, will you come with us peaceably to Marè Palace?"

What else could he do but acquiesce? The captain barked another order, and two others turned back to the gate where horses were stabled. He should have noticed that, had been too concerned about Massimo's potential treachery, about trying to protect the man he'd served in one form or another all his life. There had just been too many betrayals, too many sacred trusts shattered.

"Can you ride?" the captain asked, offering him the reins of a mare.

Vincenze nodded and rose into the saddle. The horse shifted weight but responded well to knees and a soothing hand. "You will find him?" Vincenze asked, turning his mount's head where the captain indicated.

"We've cast a broad net."

"So have our enemies."

"Don't worry. We've been watching for you for months."

"And lost him when you had him." The captain looked at him sharply, but Vincenze let the accusation hang between them. The man nodded, accepting Vincenze's disapproval. "And you should know if he doesn't want to be found, he won't." That was perhaps braggadocio, but he also knew Sylvio, and given he wasn't fighting a battered body and a race that deprived him of sleep and reason, he was pretty certain the Maestro would find a way to blend into the shadows. But that assessment was of a man he'd known, not the man with whom he'd come down from those mountains of ice. That winter and those mountains changed Sylvio, more than the tattooing, more than the recovery from his severe beating. Vincenze had been sure Sylvio would die. His recovery had been so slow. And after, when he was again whole, Vincenze watched his friend retreat behind that canvas of colour and form that was now his body, listening, he was sure, to the voices only a bone-speaker could hear. There were times he'd catch Sylvio gripping the staff, his eyes wide and unfocused, seeing into an inner world Vincenze feared. It was as if Sylvio stood on the margin between life and death, an unwilling but very adept conduit.

A cucullatus. Indeed. It was almost as if that was what Sylvio had become, one of the red-hooded few that guided the living to death.

It took every restraint he knew not to just cut this horse from the tight ring in which he rode, make his own escape and find Sylvio, reason with him and guide him to safety. There would be no sense in that. Better, despite his loyalties, to go to the Prima and bring every reason and argument to bear, mobilize a larger net, draw Sylvio to safety so they could all start planning a rescue for a nation held hostage.

Within the hour they rode through the gates of the Marè Palace, a frisson of marble and gilding, like a confection jutting out into the huge lagoon that lay like liquid turquoise. They dismounted. He was led through to the captain's superior, where a report was rapped out, and from there handed off to a steward with an armed escort who took him through to the palace proper, passing through mirrored halls, corridors hung with portraits cracked with age, floors awash with mosaics and painted tiles. Light flooded the passages, running as they did along the outer perimeters of the palace, almost like enclosed loggias.

There were fruit trees in bloom in the gardens and courtyards beyond, petals raining like pale pink snow onto the gold of daffodils and tissue-white narcissi. He could hear birdsong, someone strumming a lute as they passed, laughter, discourse, the buzz of a community at work and play.

They turned down another corridor, interminable in length, trotted up a flight of stairs and after a few more turns and twists and what seemed hours they halted before a set of doors where a person sat behind a desk. One of the escort made a comment to the official there, who told them to wait a moment, rose and slipped into the room beyond the door. When the official returned she gestured to Vincenze to follow. The escort were shed. He stepped into the room. The official said, "Vincenze Mambelli, Signor Febbo," bowed and retreated. The door closed with a decisive thud.

The man addressed as Signor Febbo was none other than the Prima's own steward, Julio, whom Vincenze remembered from his days working with Sylvio in the Castello. Julio's brow wrinkled although he smiled, gesturing to Vincenze to take a seat.

"I must apologize for the confusion and subterfuge," he began. "Wine?" Vincenze shook his head. "Water then? No? Ah, of course, Please excuse our ineptitude trying to bring you and the Maestro safely here. The best of intentions sometimes are not enough. You'll wish to refresh yourself, naturally, but first the Prima wishes to speak with you, and I am then to show you to quarters where I hope you will be comfortable."

"Prima Violina?"

Julio nodded. "If you'll wait here a moment I'll have her informed you're here." He turned away from the room, leaving Vincenze to pace out his frustration and impatience on the rug of the foyer. When Julio returned he led Vincenze through several rooms to a private office where Prima Violina sat behind a desk of black lacquer, sparsely but elegantly gilded. An ancient oil lamp of thin alabaster sat on her desk, its turning so thin you could see the black and madder scene in its bowl. She had a sheaf of papers in her hand, apparently reading, her hair bound into a headdress of voile and silver thread. Over her shoulder another woman bent and read with her, pearls and red enamel beads cascading in ribbons over the curve of the woman's cheek. She straightened, staring at him with a face that might have been carved from ivory, wide mouth and eyes like flint that were outlined with kohl. It took a moment for him to recognize her. She was thinner than when last they spoke, half a year ago in the atrium of Casa Portelli, all softness gone, completely unapproachable and very much the strega.

He inhaled sharply, stilling his apprehension, turned back to the woman he'd been brought to see, made a gesture of obeisance when Julio announced him.

"I understand we've failed you for the moment, Signor," Violina said.

"I am assured your people are combing the city now."

"So I am to understand." She gestured to a chair. "Come. There is much to discuss."

And so with a sigh he sank into the cushions that were now too soft, and with well-watered wine to hand he recounted all that had happened since that night in Reena when a festival for the dead marked a passage of considerable magnitude. The telling was long, broken by the attendance of Ó Leannáin and a few of the senators, by questions and digressions, food brought, and then lamps lit as the telling gave way to other information. Throughout it all Vincenze watched Aletta who remained standing, striking because of her detachment and self-possession. She made no comment. She observed in that intense, unnerving way the stregare had. And late into the evening when discussion had devolved into debate, he realized just as Sylvio had travelled an inner road that took him beyond approach or understanding, so had the woman Sylvio loved as no one else.

It was Ó Leannáin in the end who said, "All our debate boots nothing without the man on whom all our hopes lie." That brought Vincenze's attention back to the room and the discussion at hand. "With the Prima's permission, I suggest we retire for the night and hope our people bring di Danuto in quickly."

Nods and murmurs of assent went round the room, and in knots senators and officials left. Vincenze lingered at a gesture from the Prima, as did Ó Leannáin and Aletta. Julio, as always, hovered nearby, ever the indispensible, perfect servant.

"I'm afraid there's more," Ó Leannáin said when they were alone. "It would seem di Danuto hasn't told you all he knows."

Vincenze raised a brow at that, looked over at Aletta, who nodded, once, almost imperceptibly.

"He is capable now of shutting out all communication we've been feeding him through the network of the dead. He can eavesdrop, but he has learned something none of the rest of us can, to keep his own thoughts shielded, even his whereabouts."

"It is as you fear," Aletta said, speaking for the first time. "You warned the captain who brought you here that if Sylvio didn't want to be found he wouldn't." So she heard, despite his best effort to conceal that not only from what he said, but how he spoke. "And I very much fear he will not want to be found, not yet."

"What's your reasoning?" he asked after a moment, studying her, wondering if that mask of a face concealed the warm, engaging woman he remembered in the village.

"What is happening to our country is more than political," she said.

"Gods, what are we facing?"

"I wish I knew."

But Vincenze very much had the feeling Aletta had a keen insight into what they faced, but because of either her training or her love of country and the man to whom she was wed she kept her own counsel.

Giving Almarè's police the slip was one thing. Remaining hidden was quite another when you were a glaring, visible figure out of nightmares. Were Sylvio to shed the cloak and hood, he'd have them running for amulets of protection against the painted freak he'd become.

A solution presented itself in a line of laundry strung between balconies. He shifted the angle of the bow-sock slung over his shoulder, letting it ride high for a moment. As he hoped, it caught on the white linen sheet he targeted, dragging it from the line and in the process brought the rest of the laundry tumbling down to the street amid cries of surprise and anger. In the ensuing confusion he bundled the sheet under his cloak, lowered the height of the bow and continued on up the winding road. The houses here were modest, mostly poor labourers living in narrow spaces that rose three and four honey-stone stories, kitchens above, bedrooms beneath and common room on the ground floor. Balconies of white-washed wood jutted out into the street, many already hung with early flowers that would cascade into waterfalls of colour by the time the season turned to autumn.

By nightfall he'd wandered into an area of artisans' shops, and as it happened came across what he took for a bow-yard, given the iconic sign that hung over the compound's gate. There was a light in the porter's window, a dog in the yard judging the incessant barking beyond the stone wall. He marked the street, wandered a bit further until he came to one of the city's many bridges. It was cool, dank and stank of rot beneath the arched span, but as he suspected there was a niche in the pylon into which he inserted himself for the night.

With his knife and a bit of twine he fashioned for himself a mask of linen that would serve to enforce the ruse he planned to adopt in the morning, leaving only holes for his eyes, his nostrils and his mouth. Without a mirror he could only hope he covered all the artwork of his face and neck. Better this, however, than the hood and cloak he wore. While the mask would draw attention, he hoped his new disguise would prevent people from thinking he was a harbinger of death, or worse a pariah marked with his shame and loss of honour.

Disguise done, he removed the mask and chewed on a dried strip of meat from the leather pouch in his satchel, drank deeply from the skin of water he'd kept, again tied the mask into place and braced himself against the stone for whatever rest he might find. And while the dead whispered in his sleep, Aletta's face washed like balm through his dreams; in the end the linen on his face was damp not only from the night but the tears he shed silently and alone.

By morning he pulled himself together, stiff with resolve and resignation, and made his way back to the porter's door at the bow-yard. He asked for the Maestro of the shop when challenged by the spotty-faced boy who lounged carelessly against the doorframe of the office, leaned into the impudent face when the boy smirked and looked off in another direction, and said in a low growl, "You'll tell the Maestro he's needed at the gate if you've a mind for your hide."

Brash and without any intention of following through on his threat, Sylvio watched the boy gulp, nod abruptly and slide through the industry of the main yard, trot up a short flight of stairs to a door where he knocked and disappeared. Within a few moments he returned ahead of a fellow with a face like a dried apple and who walked with a limp. Sylvio felt the scrutiny, watched speculation spark on that face and disappear, accepted the hand that was thrust at him in salute and welcome.

"Beppe. And you would be?"

Who would he be? Certainly he didn't wish to reveal himself, not yet, not with the Palace looking for him and he with no plan formulated for himself or what he would do about his country. "Fabrizio," he answered. "Thought you could use a hand in the bow-yard."

"Did you?" Beppe glanced at the bow-sock over Sylvio's shoulder, jerked his head in that direction. "Your hand?"

Sylvio nodded, un-shouldered the bow and handed it to the fellow who undid the strings, drawing out the long, graceful arc of wood, bone and sinew. Beppe turned it over in his hands, weighed it, ran gnarled, scarred fingers over its length, fingering the bone wear-plate, the horn tips that were carved into likenesses of Nerezza, pursed his lips and looked up at Sylvio. His eyes were like glittering buttons. "May I?" Again Sylvio nodded, following at the fellow's gesture into the main compound. Beppe coughed an order for a butt, to clear the area, stepped into the bow as people scrambled and with difficulty teased the angeli string into place. He cast an apprising glance at Sylvio.

"Ninety pound?"

"One hundred and ten."

He raised a brow, nodded, turned his attention back to the bow. Sylvio could hear his father stirring, protesting, answered with a thought to be at peace, watching Beppe as the impact of what he held hit him. Beppe's lips parted, his eyes widening slightly. He cast another glance back at Sylvio who said nothing, hiding as he did behind the linen mask.

"Arcosso," Beppe said.

Sylvio nodded, handed him an arrow that was a bit of frippery, footed and splined with walnut and a shaft of balanced ash. Beppe received it not without notice, nocked the arrow, drew a test, and then to Sylvio's surprise this bird of a man took his stance, opened his shoulders and drew fully and let fly. The speed with which the arrow streaked was invisible. Only the resounding thunk of it hitting the butt gave truth to its flight. The silence of the yard was profound. The arrow had gone cleanly through the butt and embedded deeply into the wood of the door behind.

Beppe's lips pursed again as he stepped into the bow, took the tension off the string and let the loop slide down from the tip. He handed the bow back to Sylvio. One of the workers trotted across the yard, wrestled the arrow free and trotted back to hand Sylvio the arrow. With a gesture Sylvio turned it to Beppe.

"A gift?"

"Call it a bribe," Sylvio said.

"And you wish me to employ you?"

He nodded.

Beppe barked a laugh. "What brings you to Marè?"

"What makes you think I'm not from Marè?"

"Your accent."

Fair enough. Careful man. "I'm on a journey," he said, which was truth enough, "and I need time to consider, and gainful employment until then."

"You in trouble?"

Was he in trouble? Dear gods, yes, so much trouble he was about to lose his ass if he weren't careful. "No."

Beppe gestured to the mask. Sylvio said, "Burns, a disfigurement."

"Five denarii a week, half a denarii docked for food and lodging. We dispense new hose and doublets spring and fall if you're here that long. No intoxication during working hours which are dawn to dusk. We serve a midday meal in the compound for the workers. After hours you can find oblivion for all I care, just be sure to be sharp for work in the morning. We work eight days on, three off. Don't bring your whores back here." He gestured to one of the bowyers. "He'll show you to quarters. You can start by sweeping and fetching materials for the journeymen."

And so Sylvio began yet another life, that of Fabrizio. He let the routine of the days encompass him, rising with the others at dawn, taking bread and strong coffee into the yard where he swept, fetched wood, tools, horn and sinew, minded the glue pots, stickered raw staves when they shipped into the yard. Lunches he took on his own, and the others seemed not to mind, in fact appeared more relieved than anything to have his strange appearance removed for a short while.

In fact he gulped his lunches on the way to the bath house which was deserted this time of day, scrubbing in the chill water with haste and secrecy for fear of being found. He was never late returning.

In the evenings he offered to take a watch at the gatehouse, relieved to avoid the questions and curiosity of his coworkers, and when the porter returned Sylvio walked through the darkened compound into the bunk house he shared with ten others, slipping onto his cot fully clothed.

During off days he spent time at a small shrine to Nerezza he'd found, setting out the icons of his family, his father and mother who were long gone, and those others he'd collected over the winter, his thoughts on Aletta who might as well have been dead for the distance there would be between them when finally he met her again. If he met her again. At such times his mother's voice surfaced in the community that now resided in his head, her voice a gentle admonishment, and the sadness that engulfed him often was more than he could bear.

By the end of the first month working for Beppe he'd saved enough coin to buy himself a used set of clothes: breeches and serviceable doublet, hose. He still had the sheet he'd pilfered and sewed for himself two new masks. He'd have to think about gloves soon, as the leather of the ones he wore were showing signs of wear. He'd also have to think about fitting them closely to prevent blistering, as he'd discovered in those first days of the bow-yard.

Spring slid toward summer and Sylvio found himself tinkering with staves while others weren't looking, irritated with a minor flaw here, a lamination there, and then found himself offering a brief word on occasion when he could see a bowyer going astray. One bowyer talked to another it would seem, and by the time the summer heat and humidity descended on the delta of Marè he was being sought for advice. Finally Beppe approached him one morning when bread and coffee were spread for the workers and said, "You might as well earn your keep and start in on bows. It would seem you know your way around."

Sylvio nodded and set to selecting wood for his bench, using the axe he'd brought with him, and hastily crafted wedges to split and rough out the shapes he needed. The other tools he required were loaned by the other bowyers, just appearing in his work place without comment, a silent affirmation and acceptance. He returned them at the end of each day, sharpened and oiled.

By the close of his work week he was selecting staves and using a borrowed drawknife to remove excess wood. He'd have to see a smithy soon to make the blade for his own.

If you're here that long, Aldo said, a reminder that there was work of quite another magnitude waiting for him. Sylvio glanced at the staff that was always at his side, either in his hand when he sat idle or walked, or resting nearby when he worked.

He'd found since coming down from the mountains his hip had

given out, likely something fractured or worn from the hardship of the winter and the multiple beatings he's suffered, and Aldo's staff had become more to him than a conduit, now a necessary accessory to his mobility. He glanced over at the thing, still beautiful and with a power and sinister aspect only he understood.

I will not take an army into Simare, he thought. *Leave off!*

Then what?

Gods, he didn't know! But he would not bring bloodshed upon his people.

They're amassing here in your name. They're calling to you as a saviour.

I'm no saviour!

It's not a matter of choice.

No, it never had been. He turned back to the bow and fitted horn to the yew core, daubing the foul-smelling hide glue to the dark heartwood. Within he shut out the babble that had arisen, letting out a grunt of frustration that turned heads. He bowed his own, recognizing his growing dependence on the mask that hid the horror of his face and the emotion that increasingly tore him apart.

But there was the grace of the bow-yard, of these artisans who worked wood into tools that could mean survival on so many levels.

It was during one of his off days, when the heat and humidity were a palpable pressure on the skin, that Sylvio bought himself a loaf of bread from the baker he'd come to frequent, and a hunk of the hard, tangy cheese the dairyman carried who kept a stall in the local market. He decided to splurge and purchased a half-bottle of wine, likely rot-gut, but would be welcome for the day he had planned for himself.

Despite the heat he was still masked, covered from head to foot in cloth and leather. Sweat ran down his spine, plastered the linen mask to his face and his neck. He felt as though he'd suffocate, and for that reason chose a route that would take him out of the city for a little while, somewhere where he might find solitude and an opportunity to lay upon the bank of a backwater of the estuary. A place to strip and bathe, to lie in the shade and carve some shape into the confusion of his thoughts.

It was a relief to be out of the city, away from stares and jostling bodies, to hear birdsong without the rattle and bang of carts and wagons, horses and the constant cacophony of voices, living and dead. He'd hitched a ride on an outbound wagon, jumped off at a cross-roads and cut across orchards and grain fields, pasturing ewes and lambs, cattle, until he came upon a small stream that likely sheltered some excellent fish. There were willow growing here, providing a cool curtain where finches warbled and flitted, catching flies. The stream was brisk, with a sandy bottom scattered with limestone boulders that hunched against the flow and sent ribbons of froth downstream.

The area was deliciously isolated. He stripped and took his clothes into the water, scrubbed them and himself and for a little while just sat there in the shade and the water to his waist, letting the current tug. Such a simple pleasure. Such a simple thing, a bath, alone, in this grotto of green and dappled light.

He remained there until his fingers wrinkled, distorting the pattern of vines that were now part of his body. If a man were to be honest, he'd have to admit the artist who branded him was brilliant. All of Sylvio's life revealed itself in these patterns. He'd seen the arcane symbols on his face that spoke of the ritual of life and death, clearly given to the artist by someone who had studied in Nerezza's temple, someone like the Prince himself. These gave way to personal images of import to Carmelo and Sylvio, indicators of their own relationship: books and scrolls, horses and hawks, the chamber of the Senate and the domes of the ossuaries. There were bucolic vignettes, exercise grounds, and the archery field; games of bocce and wrestling and the rough and tumble of soccer.

It was all there, a perverted tribute from the boy he'd mentored, a boy who loved so deeply that he couldn't bear abandonment, and breached all boundaries, committed every taboo to assure he would never be abandoned again.

It was with a heavy heart Sylvio pulled himself out of the stream, draped his clothes over mounds of mint that grew wild along the bank. With a few of the sprigs he rubbed himself down, protection against stinging insects, tied on a breechclout and lay himself upon the ground, letting lassitude take him.

He knew in his heart he should make his way to the palace, listen to what the living had to say, instead of just the dead. He should formulate a plan, find a way to bring Carmelo not only to justice, but to reason. And were a man to be honest with himself, he wanted to see Aletta, even if from a distance. You didn't love someone that long, that deeply, without feeling as though a part of you were missing.

But she was gone. Carmelo effectively divorced them when he had Sylvio tattooed.

Even so.

At some point he dozed. He woke with a start, shivering with cold, cursed himself for a fool and dressed with haste. By the time he'd crossed the fields, the orchards, and gained the main road dusk was falling but he managed once more to hitch a ride, this time with an inbound wagon hauling untreated hides. Gods, but it stank, and negated the tranquility he'd enjoyed earlier, but at least got him through the gates before nightfall.

He realized by then he'd formulated a plan. The magnitude of it threatened to overwhelm him.

A light burned in the porter's window when at length he made his way back to Beppe's shop. He called a word of greeting, only to be met by a message that the master of the shop wished to see him.

Without stopping to drop his belongings, he went directly to Beppe's office, knocked, was called in. It was a modest room furnished with economy, a table that served as a place for Beppe to tally his accounts, ledgers stacked neatly, a lamp of good quality, heavily banded coffers that were locked, a chair with a back for Beppe, two stools for guests, a window that opened onto the yard.

One of the stools was occupied by a man in Marè's official livery. Beppe gestured to Sylvio to take the other stool.

For a long moment Beppe looked at Sylvio, then shook his head and sighed. "I'm sorry, Maestro. It would appear the ruse is up."

Ah. That explained the man in official livery. Discovered. Time gone.

"It was not my intent to deceive you," Sylvio said.

"Despite evidence to the contrary, I believe you."

"When did you suspect?"

"That first day, but I didn't think Sylvio di Danuto would humble himself to work in my shop." Beppe gestured to the mask. "Was that a ruse as well?"

Sylvio swallowed. "No."

"I won't ask."

"Thank you."

Sylvio turned to the other man. "I gather you're to escort me?"

The man nodded. "I've men stationed nearby if Maestro Beppe here would be good enough to send a runner? There are a great many people depending on your safe arrival at the palace."

Beppe barked for a servant, sent the maid scurrying.

Sylvio rose. "It has been an honour, Maestro."

Beppe shook Sylvio's gloved hand. "It has been mine. I'll have a servant bring the rest of your things."

"Not necessary. Divide what's left among the apprentices." He indicated the bow and staff he carried. "I have all I require." Turned and left the room, his escort with him.

It was unfair of him, he knew, to ignore their concern, the words of welcome and relief that greeted him when he was announced into the Prima's cabinet. Their voices trailed away into silence. He stood there a moment, watching, observing, listening to another swell of voices inside his head, silenced them also. With some last vestiges of grace he bowed, remained standing there in the glow of the lamps that flickered in a fragrant breeze. The doors to the balcony were open. It was now so still in the room he could hear the lap of waves in the lagoon. Somewhere in the night a nightingale sang a cascade of song.

The Prima's steward, Julio, indicated a bench, which Sylvio declined with a gesture, offered wine, which he also declined. Julio retreated to his place beside the door. Sylvio let the moment of uncertainty stretch, taking in every face, every movement, watching their concern, weighing their responses; a raised brow from the Prima where she sat in a large, carved chair softened with pillows; a steady observation from Ó Leannáin who stood by the open doors, his saffron shirt billowing over fustian trews that were hanging loosely without the traditional wrappings from ankle to calf. Vincenze had been the first to grin and step forward in greeting, frozen in place by Sylvio's cool response. There was dismay on that familiar face.

And there, like an icon and unapproachable, Aletta, her eyes heavily kohled, her face framed with moonstones and gold that hung without a tremor. Her dark gaze was on him, but of emotion there was nothing, a betrayal to him of her deep immersion into the disciplines of the strega. He watched her for a long moment, wanting to take her by the shoulders, kiss her, whisper his need of her, his love for her, but instead turned his attention back to the woman who governed here and had risked a great deal in this political game.

He knew he should say something, assure them he was well, that he was capable of making the necessary decisions to rescue his country from the perilous path on which Carmelo set them. He should throw back his hood, and reveal to them the extent of what had been done to discredit him. He should tell them about Aldo. He should tell them what the dead whispered over these past months.

But instead he stood there, hiding within the safety of his cloak and his hood, bow on his back, staff in his hand, waiting to see how they would proceed, and how that, in turn, would determine his own actions.

"We are relieved to have you with us at last," Violina said at length. So it was to be casual diplomacy, a lead line to determine the waters they navigated. The silence stretched out. "We should have made it clear to our security forces that you might misinterpret their mission."

"There was no misinterpretation," he said, keeping his voice level and low. That raised question on her face, a quick glance to Ó Leannáin, back to Sylvio. He relented and offered, "I needed time to think."

Time to think? He could see the question on her face, incredulity there, even astonishment. There had been an entire winter to think. But in truth he'd spent that winter adjusting to his new situation, to the fact he was branded for all time, that he walked each and every day with a host of others who were silent to the rest of the world. And it was only recently the magnitude of the task before him carried weight.

"I believe you have news you wish to impart," he said. "But let me assure you there is nothing you know that I don't already."

That apparently stunned them further, even the cool and assured Ó Leannáin whom he now knew to be a bone-speaker of no small consequence. The only one in the room who seemed completely unaffected by his statements and his composure was Aletta, who watched him unflinchingly.

"Then you know about the burning of Reena?" Violina asked.

He nodded.

"And the riots across the country?"

Again he nodded.

"And of people fleeing into exile or to Danuto to join the resistance force gathering there?"

"He knows all this," Aletta said. "We can tell him nothing. He knows Breena has sent security forces into Simare, that our country is all but annexed and under occupation. He knows you will council an invasion by a liberation force, the deposing of Il Principe." Her gaze never left him. He merely nodded once in response.

"Then what do you propose?" Violina asked. "I haven't risked my country and these people for nothing."

"I propose I take a bath, change into fresh clothes if you will accommodate that." He raised a gloved hand to fend off her objections and questions. "It is late. We're all in need of a moment to reflect."

Violina shot Aletta a glance, clearly seeking verification of Sylvio's veracity let alone his sanity. Aletta answered, "I have never used my gifts on my husband, and don't intend to start now."

Ah, my Aletta, he thought. Pain ran through his chest. He closed his eyes momentarily against it.

A shrill voice broke the tension of the moment, beyond the door at his back. Violina gestured angrily and Sylvio heard the door open, turned to see what commotion came to them. A girl, a bird of a creature, burst by Julio and scuttled to Sylvio, clutching his cloak.

"Nonna said you were here! Please help me shut them up! She's all I have against them!"

The moment the girl made contact with him he knew who this was, had felt the shadow of her during those long communications of the winter, a small and unwilling conduit completely unprepared for the magnitude of her gift. He bent down to her, touched his gloved hand to her pale cheek, looked at her dark eyes.

"Passerapina," he said, no more than a whisper. "Basta, Passerapina. Ascolta me."

She stilled then, listening as she was told, her dark eyes bright and intent on him. He touched one of the brooches at her shoulders, felt the voices of the dead slam into him. She cried out, but he smiled for her, hoping she could see that within the depths of his hood; in moments her tiny form relaxed and tears slipped down her face. Such a small child to bear such a gift. He thumbed away her tears and smiled.

"I told them they were hurting you, to speak to me instead. Do you understand?" She nodded. "We will spend some time together tomorrow, and I'll teach you."

She inhaled raggedly, her eyes wide. "Do you promise?"

"I give you my word."

"Dona Aletta tried, but it wasn't enough."

"I'm sure. She's a very good strega, but what we are is different."

She pushed back the hood of his cloak and he allowed it, letting her see the horror of his painted face, the scenes and traceries there for all to read. He heard gasps in the room. But Passerapina smiled, bright as sunlight on water and raised her fingers to his temples, his eyelids, his nose and cheeks. Her touch was warm, full of wonder and he found that difficult to bear. "You're pretty," she whispered and hugged him.

He rose with her in his arms, swallowing emotion and shame, turned back toward the room and all those staring faces, only to find Aletta at his side, her eyes liquid with unshed tears. There was so much he wanted to say to her but not here, not now. Instead: "She found you," he said.

Aletta nodded, her gaze steady upon his.

"And you brought her with you."

Again Aletta nodded, the jewels tinkling around her face. He kissed Passerapina's brow and passed the girl to his wife's ready embrace. "We *will* have our moment," he said. "Just not at this moment."

"I know, Innamorato," she said. "I'll have a physician sent to your quarters." Ah, so she had heard that. She smiled. "Some things don't require my gifts," she said.

He pulled the hood back over his head, turned and left with Julio. The room was full of outrage, he knew, most particularly from Prima Violina, but this was not his concern. Not now. Indeed no, not now. The place to which he'd journeyed might as well be among the stars for all the familiarity any of them would have, Ó Leannáin among them. Bone speaker the Breenai ambassador might be, but what Ó Leannáin heard was but a faint whisper compared to the legion that walked with Sylvio even into his dreams.

The room to which he was shown proved an adjacent suite to Aletta's, discreetly indicated by the efficient and urbane Julio. There was a servant to wait upon him, and after Julio bowed himself out the young man appointed to him inquired if he wished to bathe, perhaps take a massage and a light supper. Sylvio grunted an affirmative and allowed himself to be led to the private bath, undressed and scraped with oils and scrubbed with salts and then, after the luxury of the hot plunge pool, submitted to the kneading and gentle pummelling of a masseuse who worked with oils to relax and calm the cords and knots from his limbs. There was a warmed linen robe for him, sheepskin slippers for his tingling feet, and there in his room a tray of goat's cheese and fruit, prosciutto and olives, crusty bread and spicy green oil. A gorgeous hand-painted jug proved to contain fruited wine which he drank with relish.

Just as he was sinking into a delicious lassitude his servant admitted a physician who checked his greeting momentarily when he saw Sylvio. It was a reaction to which he knew he must become accustomed, and in an attempt to make them both feel at ease he gestured for the man to come forward.

Sylvio's servant said, "Dottore Vittorio Leonelli, Maestro."

"It would appear my wife thinks I need a physician," Sylvio said.

"Where would we be without our wives?" the physician replied, sinking into the chair Sylvio indicated. He set a satchel beside his feet, folding his hands over the black linen of the robe over his knees. "And why does your wife think you need to see me?"

"She likely suspects I haven't been sleeping particularly well."

The physician smiled at that, taking a slender tube from the satchel, and sought leave to listen to Sylvio's heart. "Big breath," he said, and Sylvio complied, "and let it go," which he did. The tube moved. "Another. Let it go." The physician rose, gently loosening off the back of Sylvio's robe, repeated the process on his back. Out came a notepad and pencil of graphite. Sylvio listened to the scratching of the physician's thoughts, answered, "Not particularly well, no," when queried further about the quality of his rest. "But given the circumstances…."

"Understandable," the physician finished, scratching further. "Appetite?"

"Also not wonderful."

"And also understandable – "

" – given the circumstances." Sylvio offered a smile he didn't feel.

"Weight loss?"

Sylvio looked down at his body, semi-reclined as he was in the chair. "I suppose a bit. But, again, understandable."

The physician set aside his notes and pencil, leaned forward over his knees toward Sylvio. "Now tell me about your artwork."

Sylvio felt the shock of that, straightened in the chair. "What about it?"

"Were you awake the whole time this was done to you?"

"No."

"You were drugged?"

"Yes."

"Do you know what they gave you?"

"Some form of poppy. Vincenze helped me recover."

"And Vincenze is?"

"A friend."

"A good one apparently."

A good friend indeed. Faithful, resourceful, loyal Vincenze who followed him unquestioningly, sacrificing his own life and hope of domestic bliss in order to protect the man he not only called friend, but Sylvio now knew whom he revered. Not a position with which Sylvio was comfortable. It was a long fall from such a height.

Sylvio nodded to the doctor, an affirmation.

"How long did you endure this?"

"I don't know. Vincenze's uncertain. Perhaps two weeks."

"And your health before?"

"I'd been beaten several times, recovering from the first lot when I was set upon again. And then, this." He gestured to his body.

"Are you experiencing shortness of breath?"

Sylvio nodded.

"Palpitations?"

"Sometimes."

"Were there swellings?"

Sylvio indicated there were. "But there had been a lot of bruises from the beating, and then all these...."

"Tattoos."

"Yes."

"Tell me, the location where you were held, were there any beetles?"

Bright as emeralds. In his delirium he thought he'd string a necklace for Aletta. "Assassin beetles, yes."

The physician pursed his lips, looked down a moment and then sat back, pencil in hand again and scratching across that book of notes. Without looking up he said, "I'm going to draw a small quantity of blood which I want to examine."

"This isn't a normal examination of a man put through extraordinary circumstances."

The physician glanced up briefly. "No."

"Care to tell me?"

"Not yet. I need to take a look at what's going on in the stream of your blood." He reached for the satchel. Sylvio watched as the physician set about taking a sample with professional detachment, placed a square of linen at the puncture, folded Sylvio's arm up and told him to keep it there a moment. The phial was placed in a small wooden box, the remainder of the equipment packed away. His arm was inspected again, swabbed with something that was cool to the skin and smelled astringent, bandaged.

"I'll be back tomorrow after I have my results and we can talk. I suggest you take your ease, despite the pressures and demands upon you." He rose and left.

When alone again Sylvio dismissed his servant, who tidied briefly and bowed his way out, letting Sylvio know if he was required he'd be sleeping outside the door. He took a small pouch from his effects which had, miraculously, stayed with him through all those misadventures and terrors. From it he withdrew the figures of his long deceased father and mother, set them upon the small altar which stood on a side table of fruitwood, and lit a few grains of incense in the small brazier. There was no need to intone any prayers. His family were with him in that community carried inside his head. He simply wished the comfort of their icons, of ritual that was familiar and ancient.

He blew out the lamps and slid between the linen sheets on his bed, watching the night air stir the drapes, the moonlight illuminate the spirals of smoke rising from the brazier at the altar. At last, when he thought all rest had deserted him, he slept.

He woke to the smell of fresh bread and coffee, felt the warmth of a breeze off the lagoon touch his skin. The servant – Marco apparently – stood ready with a banyan in his hands, and Sylvio rose and slid his arms into the voluminous linen, sat in the chair indicated for him and allowed himself to be served. There was even sweet butter, which he slathered on the still warm bread, feeling it smear across his chin as it melted and dripped. It was with a ridiculous sense of abandon that he wiped it away with the serviette he was provided, and found himself grinning like a boy. The coffee was rich, strong and hot, the bath and massage he took afterward going a great measure toward restoring his physical sense of well-being.

Marco provided him with a selection of clothes from the storehouses, and despite what was required of decorum, he chose a short-sleeved robe of grey that had a subtle smattering of embroidery at the hem, held at the waist with a belt studded with silver plaques, brown fustian trews and plain leather sandals for his feet.

He spent the rest of the morning tutoring the child, Passerapina, teaching her the things he had learned without any guidance of his own. While the extent of her ability as a bone-speaker was impressive, even daunting for a child so young, there was nothing there that Sylvio hadn't faced himself, and didn't feel she would be able to control given enough time and tutelage.

Toward the end of their session she kept reaching for his hands, running her fingers over the hard knobs of his knuckles where vines twined and birds flew.

She looked up at him, her face intent. "If I'm good, can I be painted too?"

Sylvio closed his eyes, swallowing the lump, unsure how to take her innocence and tarnish it with the truth of what had been done. "It's not because I'm good that I've been painted," he answered at length.

She frowned. "But you must have been. It took a lot of work to do this, I think. And there are stories all over you."

"Quite so, my little bird. A lot of work. And a great many stories. Not all of them happy. Don't wish for this, Passerapina. It isn't beauty at which you look."

Her fingers strayed to the bone brooches at her shoulder, her eyes widening. He knew to what she listened. He knew what her ancestors told her, and he watched dismay take the sunlight from her face.

He nodded to the question there in her eyes. "It's a mark of shame, yes."

"You've been bad?"

Despite himself he smiled. "Yes. I've been bad."

She leaned toward him conspiratorially, her eyes wide. "What did you do?"

"I didn't love someone enough." She frowned again, confusion there. "You'll understand one day, Passerapina. I promise you, despite all we'll do to protect you, you will understand." Gods, how to look at the disappointment there, how to bring back that quicksilver smile? "But enough. You've spent enough time with this wicked old man. Go now. There are things to explore today, and if you don't show up at the academy my wife will be very upset with me." She hugged him then, a warm, living body of muscle and bone, of question and horizons yet undiscovered. Gently he set her back. He smiled and watched her face light up. "I promise we'll spend more time together yet." She clapped her hands then and left, the nurse who accompanied her taking the girl's hand and leading her out of the door.

"They're waiting on you, Maestro," Marco said. "I'm afraid several messages have been sent."

And so he went to listen to the arguments that would be put forward in this council. There would be representatives there from Almarè's Senate, the Prima herself, Ó Leannáin, Vincenze, Aletta. He decided, albeit with a great deal of discomfort, to eschew a robe and hood that would hide his disfigurement. It was a tool, he realized, one to be used as any other.

Although he'd visited Almarè in his capacity as Ministro, he'd never been inside the enormous chamber where law was debated and legislated. It was built in the round, of marble and gilt, frescoes of the founding of the capital, gods and legends that ringed the enormous enclosed amphitheatre. Pillars supported the dome where light fell and dust motes sparkled like snow in the mountains. A senator had the floor at the moment, attempting to shout over the calls and jeers that echoed through the chamber.

All came to a standstill when he entered. A herald might as well have brought them all to silence. This was becoming predictable, and he felt annoyance flash hot and urgent through his thoughts. He paused there in the entrance, took in their faces, replayed the phrases he'd caught when he entered, sifted through what the dead said within, and bowed deeply toward the raised box where Prima Violina sat resplendent in robes of red. Aletta sat to her right, Ó Leannáin to her left, Vincenze behind.

He felt Aldo stir, fingered the staff. He straightened from his obeisance and crossed the floor to where his escort led him, and seated himself beside Aletta. Prima Violina made a formal introduction and belatedly applause rose round the room in welcome. At a gesture the senator continued with his argument that Almarè should indeed raise a liberation force to aid those in Simare who stood for freedom and the overthrow of a monarch who no longer upheld the good governance of his people. And what was the rest of the world to do while this threat ruled? Were they to stand by and watch trade and commerce suffer because of the ineptitude of one man?

Round of applause to that. Stir of resentment from the community Sylvio carried in his head.

Another senator gained the floor, arguing that Breena had all but occupied Simare, that if he were to understand the situation in Simare a peace-keeping force had been sent from Breena and now controlled the capitol, the passes and shipping lanes. Even now fishing boats and small traders were slipping away under cover of night and sailing round the peninsula to seek refuge in Almarè. Some form of policy and provision would have to be made for these people. Either Almarè was to commit to involvement in Simare's affairs, or remain neutral, and given Simare was a major trading partner, to remain neutral was out of the question. And who knew where this would end? First Simare. Then Breena might look to Almarè.

From elsewhere the question arose as to the resistance movement in Simare. How accurate were the reports that while many Simari fled, others had travelled overland to Danuto where a veritable fortress had been established in defiance of the crowned head and the occupation force. That even now Carmelo sent foreign troops to besiege Danuto.

This submission was countered by another: what if Carmelo

were deposed? What then? Did Almarè or any other country have the right to dictate to Simare who would or would not lead the country? And who would that person be? Would a police state ensue to ensure legal election? Or would the liberation forces appoint a leader?

Almost as if orchestrated the attention of the Senate came to bear upon Sylvio, who was embroiled in a very real inner argument. He knew the people in this room all looked to him for an answer. Indeed, the community within suggested an answer, one he refused over and over again.

He retreated behind the mask of his face, little by little learning how to use what had been intended as a way to render him powerless. Moments stretched out into uncomfortable minutes. He felt Aletta stir beside him, settle. Heard Ó Leannáin speak a sharp word to the small portion of that inner community. Aldo rebutting.

He turned his attention to the Prima, not at all surprised to find himself looking into her direct gaze, saw the frown, the question there, the frustration that he didn't acknowledge openly. He refused to offer some support, even a token hope. Unfair of him he knew. He owed her much. But this was necessary. For a long moment he held her gaze, unflinching, without remorse or quarter until at length she looked away, back out to the floor of the Senate.

Silence hung around them, shifting with the shafts of sunlight that pierced confusion and frustration. But he would not speak. He would give them nothing, because what he had to give was abomination of the worst kind, a plan so monstrous in its scope they would surely reject it out of hand, shut him away as mad.

Indeed what he had resolved to do was mad. Utterly. Unless you knew Carmelo. Unless you'd watched the boy grow and develop. Watched how he'd suffered for want of the love and attention of a father wedded to his country. Watched how he'd shattered and reformed into a twisted parody of devotion when his mother died. Carmelo had to be shown another path, but because of the enormity of his need this path was one of darkness and eternal servitude. There could be no other way. And in the end he knew the people of Simare would accept this decision, immersed as they were in their relationship with the dead.

Sylvio knew this now. Just as he also knew he must bring Carmelo to this understanding on his own. Where he would go, no other could follow.

And so committed to an exile greater than he'd ever imagined, he waited in silence until the debate of the Senate resumed. They meant well. Whether they debated in an attempt to find a solution to Simare and her ruler out of self-preservation or a higher ideal mattered little. It was part of a play that must be allowed to unfold.

Finally someone asked the question he'd been waiting for: "Will the esteemed representative from Simare say nothing in response to this debate?"

Again he watched all attention shift to him, heard the Speaker recognize the honourable Maestro Sylvio di Danuto. He could feel the tension of the moment. Reluctantly he rose to his feet, felt the staff in his hand vibrate to Aldo's presence. He wondered how he looked to these men and women, whether they saw the grotesque creature he'd become, or whether they saw through the mask to the man beneath. In the stillness that enveloped them he heard someone cough, heard the rustle of cloth as someone shifted on the cool stone benches that rose ring upon ring.

He could have chosen a preamble, some diplomatically phrased explanation, some platitude to ease the way. Instead he chose to be direct.

"I will not lead an invasion army into Simare. Not now. Not ever."

For a moment they sat stunned. He watched their faces, watched as disbelief gave way to outrage and then erupted into a chorus of question. He raised a hand to bring them to silence. It took some time, but they settled.

"I am not required to give you an explanation. But I will." He felt Violina bristle beside him, was aware she likely asked herself where was his gratitude, his recognition of the extent to which she'd sacrificed and risked in bringing him here to refuge.

"If I were to lead an invasion army of willing liberators," he said, "what concessions is that going to require?" He raised a hand to the burst of outrage in the chamber. "Let's be honest, shall we? Although we are comfortable neighbours, Almarè will want some guarantee this situation won't happen again, that her own borders are protected. That will lead to benevolent offers of military support, perhaps even bases both land and sea. Between you, you'll decide upon a leader and an interim government. Good intentions all, but intentions that will not solve the problem that has occurred, and undermine the very foundation of what it means to be part of the land we know as Simare. And how, exactly, will these actions be that much different from what Simare's neighbour to the north has done already?"

There were derisive comments now. But again he raised a hand to bring them to silence, scanned the room slowly, allowing his attention to linger here, there, marking those who protested, those who remained silent.

"You're all asking yourselves," he said, "what is so special about being Simari? And I will answer you, it has to do with our reverence of our ancestors, a reverence that is quite profound, in fact so profound we are the only people of the world who commune with our dead." He turned his attention to Ó Leannáin, saw the question there. "Yes, we commune with our dead. It is something unique to us. It is something we carry in our bones." He saw understanding colour Ó Leannáin's face, watched him turn his attention inward and trace the path of his own lineage.

Sylvio looked back out to the senators, felt the tension, the eruption that was about to occur. "Doubt me? Then go and retrieve the arcossi I brought with me when Vincenze and I descended from the mountains. Your men confiscated the goods when you attempted to seize us. See if you are able to use the bows. Or if the bows are unruly."

It was Ó Leannáin who had given him that clue, half a year ago when they stood in the warehouse of Casa Portelli during the fall market. It was Beppe who confirmed it that day in the bow-yard when he'd tested Sylvio's bow and had only been able to handle it because Sylvio settled the spirit of his father who spoke through the bones laminated in that bow.

"No," he said. "There can be no invasion force. This is a matter regarding Simare's ancestors, and will be settled by Simare's ancestors. I will not lead an invasion."

He looked down at Aletta, saw her trying to contain the woman and wife, loved her for her strength and her unflagging belief, and left the chamber amid voices flung in frustration.

If he thought to find a moment's respite, a pause in which to think and plan his next steps, he was mistaken. When he finally settled himself on the balcony of his suite, a breeze from the lagoon a caress on his face, the physician was announced and spent some short but devastating moments with him. A parasite in his body, it seemed. Quite advanced. The prognosis was not good.

Sylvio looked back out to the turquoise lagoon. There were trading ships rocking to anchor, masts like spears against a cloudless sky. Fishing boats tacked toward home, sluggish and laden. Birdsong peppered the air, rising from the garden below his balcony and with it came the scents of flowers and herbs, brine and spice. There was such beauty to be seen if a man chose to see it, if a man were honest with himself. There was beauty enough to last a lifetime if he had the courage to set aside his fears and let beauty grace his days. All his days. However many there might be.

"There is, of course, a treatment I can prescribe," the physician said. "But it will take many weeks, perhaps months or longer."

"Which I don't have," Sylvio said, turning back to the man. "What I have to do doesn't encompass time for treatment."

"Is this worth your life?"

Sylvio watched a bird stuffing grubs down the throats of chicks in the tree that grew beside the balcony. Summer. All things growing, burgeoning, coming to the fullness of their days.

"I have no choice," he answered.

The sun westered when he realized the physician had gone. Watered wine had been set on the table beside him, a lunch untouched, a plan formulated and a message sent to Aletta asking – in his heart begging – her to join him for dinner. He allowed his servant to bathe and dress him, once again choosing simple garments that hung loosely in relief from the humidity and the sensitivity of his skin.

When Aletta entered she was dressed as the woman, not the strega, the heavy khol and jewellery set aside for her own natural beauty and a gown of linen fitted under the bust and cascading in soft folds, her arms bare but for one plain bracelet. Her hair was pulled up from her neck against the heat and spilled in unruly curls. She filled the room with her presence. He remembered how she could do that, how she could command attention whether she took on the role of strega, woman, wife or field-worker. Gods how he had missed her.

He rose and closed the distance between them, drew her into his arms, drowned in the scent of her, the feel of her, tasted those lips that were so familiar and whispered her name into the evening as though by saying it he would keep her here forever. He was aware that he trembled, aware that she did also, felt her tears on his neck, heard her whisper his name like a prayer. For a moment he forgot the grotesque creature he'd been made, both outward and within. But then reality asserted itself and he set her back from him, looked into her face for some sign that she found him unbearable, hideous, could find nothing but her concern and worry.

"Passerapina's right," she said. "You are pretty."

He snorted a laugh and led her to a chair where a light supper had been laid on the table for the two of them. When he's settled across from her, dismissed his servant and poured her wine, he looked at her steadily, aware that he broke her heart over and over again, and that this time would be no exception.

"This isn't a reunion, Aletta," he said, wanting to give her more, tell her more, drag her with him through all the dangers and tensions he had yet to face. She pushed food around her plate, looked out to the balcony. Evening sun gilded her face, for a moment rendering her an image that might be found in a temple. How she managed to do that he had no idea. "I'm sorry." And that sounded so inadequate. I'm sorry. For what? For losing his position at court? For banishment? For exile? And now this? This journey he was about to take that might very well mark the end of all things bright and good between them, she who had been the very foundation of all the joys of his life?

She kept her gaze out upon some point beyond the balcony, out upon the sinking sun and the lagoon. "I know you are, Innamorato. And between us there is never need for apology. You know this. Just as I know you go to a place I cannot follow, though I would, though I would use all my knowledge and power as one of the stregare and wrest this information from you." She turned her face back to him. He saw her eyes glitter with unshed tears."But I have faith in you, and so I refrain from using my craft on the one man I swore I would never."

And so he let it rest at that. They ate. They caught up on small details, skirted larger issues, and when at last he found himself beside her in the warm night air, listening to the warble and whistles of a nightingale lost in a rapture of song, he discussed with her the larger issues at hand, what he was to do, where he was to go, and the care of the curiosity they knew as Passerapina.

She left at dawn, with a promise she would rendezvous with him in Reena at the Festa da Nerezza. By then it would all be resolved, one way or another.

CHAPTER 4

He came down from the mountains with ice in his heart and stone where there had been hope, all possibility of a life replete with wife and hearth and home flayed like flesh from bone. There was only purpose. There were only the miles to cross and the embrace of what he had become. A man could wish otherwise, were he honest. A man could deny what he was, hide from the gods, forsake all that he held dear and true and good and sweet and run from responsibility toward oblivion and promise of peace.

But, no; such were the fabrications of idle dreams.

He stood for a moment below the summit of the pass, looking back up toward Almarè and the decision that had brought him here, turned and looked toward Simare and his home where his heart yearned to be, and aware of false promise of rest.

The air was thin here. He remembered that giddy sensation, the feeling of drinking air in an attempt to fill his lungs, drowning in the sky. He heard the cry of an eagle, looked up into a hard, bright sky and watched the bird glide along a thermal, effortless, the embodiment of freedom. His cloak snapped around him, fretted by a ceaseless wind. Behind him he'd passed the door to the outpost. Nothing stirred there. Utterly abandoned. Only the voices of the dead who, at night, now appeared like tendrils of smoke from an old fire. They were sweeping toward him, more and more as he journeyed, and he knew it would continue as he came nearer and nearer to Carmelo.

This was not a place to pause, he decided. Too cold. Too windy. And he very much felt the malaise that was upon him, the sickness that ran not only through his soul but his body. With Aldo's staff in his hand, his bow and pack on his back, he continued his descent, hoping to reach the shelter he remembered from his last journey.

You should not travel alone, he heard Aldo say.

And who would molest him, he thought. He was a painted horror, a hooded cucullatus, a harbinger of death. What thief, murderer, assassin would dare to touch him now? Risk the notice of the gods? Interfere with the order of the spirit world?

No, he was safe. He could go where he would, ask what he wished, gain entrance to whatever he desired. But always, always he would be alone.

By careful husbanding of his strength he indeed did make that shelter of rock in which he and Vincenze had once taken refuge. But unlike the last time he'd taken comfort, there was no stack of deadfall or sheep dung with which to make a fire, evidence of the absence of shepherds on the mountain and therefore even modest prosperity among the hill people.

He ate dried rations and drank from the wineskin, this only as part of a grim understanding that he had to take care of himself if he were to physically undertake this journey. When he did sleep, fitful as it was, he dreamed of Aletta and a life that had been, woke in a panic when he realized this was a life no longer his.

Throughout the next days he travelled slowly but progressively, descending the mountains through cloud cover, down into foothills and cover of green, through stands of fir and pine, hemlock and yew that dripped with moisture, further down still into sunlit meadows where the nimble mountain herds grazed and birdsong replaced buffeting winds. He tried not to think, pushing the voices that were always with him to the background.

Once more he found the shepherds' trail, rested at way stations he and Vincenze had visited, replenished his pack from the dried stores he found there, sometimes lighting a fire and taking comfort from polenta or risotto. Sometimes he even lingered awhile when there were bathing opportunities and a bunk. On such occasions he took time to probe the depths of the community with him, to sort through the families and names until he could find the thread that would lead him to Passerapina and touch her gently with his thoughts.

Aspetta, pupetta, he'd say. *It's the Maestro.* And he'd hear her quicksilver joy, laughter like sunshine. *You're learning well. I'm pleased. Tell Dona Aletta I'm fine.*

And he'd break the communication, fearing to tax the child. Always he'd leave an exhortation for Passerapina's grandmother, to guard the girl and protect her from the mob that waited beyond. He listened to Aldo. He listened to his father. And he'd sink into the rhythm of his journey.

When again he came upon that farmstead he'd visited last fall, there were still signs of habitation. He took cover within a copse and watched throughout the day. It appeared the farmer and his wife were still there, the children as well. There were hands in the fields, bringing in the barley and oats. Women bent in the market garden, plucking the red plums of tomatoes or swinging bushels up onto a cart near the dry-set wall that neatly divided one section of the farm from another. He was pleased to see them prosper still, cautiously moved through late afternoon shadow and circled around, gaining another vantage. Here he found a hamlet of canvas, whether migrant workers or refugees, he didn't know. A dozen tents. There were carts in the drive-shed, more than he remembered, and certainly more than one farmer required.

There was no easy way around the farmstead, not in daylight. Resigned to wait, he settled himself into the shadows and dozed intermittently, unafraid of being found, not with the host he carried with him. Laughter roused him; the dead cautioned him. In the guttering light of torches he saw a trestle had been erected, around it the workers, farmer and family taking their evening meal together. The caution came from within the house, a soul preparing to pass. He needed to collect her, this grandmother, this woman who with thousands of others would act as judge and jury.

In what was to become a familiar ritual with him, he approached the house, shrouded in hood and cloak, the staff in his hand, the bow at his back, a figure of darkness out of the darkness. He made no attempt at secrecy. Still, he went undetected until he stood by the old woman's bed. A young girl sat on a stool by the bed. She let out a shriek. Sylvio raised a hand in a gesture of peace, lamplight flowing weirdly over the patterns on his fingers. He said nothing, only turned to the bed where the old woman watched him with dark, knowing eyes and lifted withered, bent fingers to the hand he offered her.

"You've come for me," she wheezed.

He nodded, took her cold hand into his own and with thoughts as gentle as an evening breeze guided her out and away. The lamp guttered, evanescent. There was a thump, a door crashing back on hinges, a voice raised in question. The girl, wide-eyed in the torchlight from the window, stammered out a few broken phrases, fear, anguish and then the farmer he remembered stood in the room. His headlong rush checked when he saw Sylvio, who wondered just how strange this would all look.

"Gods!' the man stammered, grabbed the girl and wrapped her

protectively.

Sylvio said nothing, wishing he could, wishing he had some word of comfort or gratitude to give to this man and finally said, "She went without alarm or pain. She bids me tell you of her love and pride. Your family is safe." He strode for the door, paused. "Mark the Festa de Nerezza this year." And let himself out into the night.

Word of that occurrence seemed to travel ahead of him so that even though he took to travelling by night, the farmsteads, hamlets and villages he passed left offerings for the cucullatus who passed through. Often he caught the pale oval of a face in a window, watching for signs of the spectral man followed by a host of the dead. And indeed the host that came with him had grown to an army as the days and weeks slid by, a shimmering, shifting stream of gossamer and dreams. There was always an evening meal waiting safely in the area's ossuary, surrounded by lamps or tapers lit in homage to the dead. He was never molested, never questioned by porters or gatekeepers. Even brigands on the road gave him a wide berth, their fingers twitching through warding signs, their gazes averted especially should he encounter them at night when his host was most visible.

That long summer girded him in warmth, allowing him to lie in shadow free of the cloak and garments that swathed his painted body. He bathed in sun-spattered streams. When it rained he took shelter in the houses of the dead, feeling dead himself.

It became evident to him that villages either had been abandoned or now burgeoned as people sought the safety of numbers. Whole settlements he passed were little more than echoing memories of what had once been a vibrant community, curtains and trestles, linen presses and crockery still intact behind doors unlocked and unbarred against theft or invasion. Yet others had thrown up hastily constructed walls, often three and four families to a home where before there had been one. There were rude wooden structures leaning haphazardly against stone buildings. And here the vermin that came with overcrowding and no provision for planning and sanitation swarmed, so that that the ossuaries no longer were the quiet, still haunts of the dead. Cholera and typhoid ran rampant, plague and dysentery. The dead that followed him out of these villages and towns were legion, their voices ones of rage and retribution.

As that long, golden summer turned to autumn the host at his back now trailed behind him for miles, the shimmering tail of a dark, slow-moving comet. The evenings turned cool. He slept through days of rain, chilled and cheerless in the shelter of a barn or temple, ossuary or simple copse. He felt the thin rattle of his breath, wanted nothing more than to sleep day through night through day again. It became more and more difficult to tread the ocean of voices in which he now swam, more and more difficult to find the anchor of his father, or Aldo, to trace the path to little Passerapina and her quicksilver laughter and thereby to the harbour of Aletta.

They'd be sailing soon. A rendezvous to come. But first he had to close that distance and confront the boy he'd failed.

Then it happened in one town an assembly of people came to him one night, bringing their dying, seeking the blessing and advice of the cucullatus who roamed the land. There was fear, yes, he could see this plainly by the torches they held. But he gave them gentle words, for what else could he do? And touched their dying to take them into the host he would bring to Carmelo.

Finally, he broke his silence and told them who he was and why he travelled. To his surprise they accepted him. They accepted the plan he proposed. And it was then one of the elders brought to him the red hooded cloak of Simare's revered, the mark of those who stood at the doorway between life and death.

He held the fine red wool in his hands, fingered the felled

seams, the crests of Danuto and Simare that had been blazoned at the hem. "You do understand what I go to do will create a new regime of cucullati?"

They understood, they assured him. What he proposed was the natural embodiment of what it meant to be Simari. And their acceptance, their understanding, struck deep to his heart and he could have wept for his love of them.

It was then he left behind the cloak of disguise and put upon his shoulders the cloak of what he was. Thereafter his passage through the towns and villages became moots, and from them couriers rode to other centres, spreading news of what was to happen in Reena. This he followed through his association with the ancestors, and at last made connection with the other few bone-speakers of the land, preparing his plan, laying the groundwork for not only Carmelo's reparation, but the good governance of this land unique among nations.

And then he was there. Miraculously there, looking up at the gates of burnished bronze, standing silently before the mercenary sentry in the toll-booth who gaped and waved him through. Behind him Sylvio heard the door of the toll-booth slam shut, heard the bar bang down and the bolts thud home. Cucullati were one thing. He was quite another.

It was a deserted city through which he walked, the moon riding high and cold overhead. The cobbles underfoot were blue in the moonlight, shadows dark and stark. Dogs quarrelled over carcasses of what he didn't know. He passed by the burned out hulks of buildings, picked his way over the calamity of carts and stalls fallen into ruination. Three people, scuttling in rags and in harness, hurried out of his way with a wagon pulled hastily behind them, plainly pilfering from the detritus of a civilization fallen to decay. He could have wept but that he had forgotten how by now. After awhile a man could become numb to such misery. After awhile a man could lose himself.

The moon had set by the time he found the Via di Dios. The temple of Nerezza was as he remembered, well-tended despite the extremity of the city. He took the steps slowly, weary beyond exhaustion. Inside, the braziers still burned, endlessly, fragrantly, lit for the goddess who took them all to death. She was still as overwhelming and inscrutable as the first time he'd seen her. He fell to his knees before her likeness, bowed his head to the red terra cotta floor and then prostrated himself.

I've done all you asked, he thought. *Let me rest just a little while.*

And he slept the sleep of the dead, although the dead slept no longer.

The news that came with the refugees that summer was cause for gossip and a morbid sort of fascination. Whole towns lay abandoned beyond the mountains. Others bulged against walls and capacity, and drafted every able-bodied person to take sentry duty both day and night, four and five families to a household – can you imagine! – people recruited to forage, to reinforce walls, to carry the dead to the temples and assist the priests in their sacred and terrible duty to the goddess Nerezza. What was happening in Simare?

It was said the village of Danuto had become a city, that an army of resistance gathered there in defiance of Il Principe and several legions of Breenai mercenaries that had arrived by ship early in the spring. No good would come of this.

And had they heard about the cucullatus who now roamed abroad? Sure sign Nerezza sent one of her servants to harvest. And what of the host who walked in the wake of the cucullatus? What of them? Why did Nerezza not take them to rest? Or was there no rest to be had while her representative, while Il Principe himself, all but ignored his sacred duty to Her and the country that had always revered its ancestors. Yes, perhaps it was that, because had you heard he'd broken trust with Her, that the Prince had murdered his father and then snatched him back from the Goddess' embrace? Apparently it wasn't a stroke that afflicted Aldo. No. Aldo was the living dead. Had you heard?

No. What madness, this? What cause to so betray the trust of country, of duty, but most of all to betray the love of family?

And now, now! Had you heard? This cucullatus was none other than their own Sylvio. Di Danuto! And he would bring that boy of a prince to justice, yes he would, Sylvio and the ancestors who walked in his wake.

What then? Why, then there was to be a new regime, a new form of government and by all the gods, by Nerezza herself, between mortal and ancestors, never again would Simare suffer as she had.

And so it went wherever Aletta travelled, whether overhearing comments in the markets, in refugee camps she visited, or the instruction she gave at the Academy. Even at court and the Senate, when she attended Prima Violina, people spoke of little else. In fact, the senators wanted to know exactly what this cucullatus meant and she found herself in the uncomfortable position of having to explain some of her country's most sacred offices and myths. Only now she knew they were no myths. The cucullatus with an army of the dead was none other than her own husband. Ó Leannáin suspected it and Passerapina confirmed it. Sylvio was making for Reena, and with him he brought the gods knew what.

Throughout the summer she found herself living two lives, one of the strega who remained impassive, the arbiter of justice; the other the woman and wife who kept to the solitude of her own company, given relief only through the child Passerapina who she thought of more and more as her daughter.

She had finished an evening meal with the girl after having attended a performance Ó Leannáin had given in the opera house, the proceeds of which went to the Simari refugee camps. It had been a remarkable experience, to finally hear that cultivated, round voice soar a capella, to hear the emotion, the control, the unabashed skill. The experience had left the girl quite animated, one of the reasons Aletta now cuddled with her in the comfort of an overstuffed chair. Passerapina smelled of lavender, scrubbed and pink from the bath, a camica of linen draping round her knees. Aletta had allowed Passerapina to remove her cosmetics, a task in which the girl delighted and which seemed to settle the hectic flush of the child's cheeks.

"I like you better without all that stuff," Passerapina said after awhile.

Aletta looked down at her. "Oh you do, do you?"

"You don't look so mean."

Gods! "Do I look mean?"

"Yeah. Like no one should ask you anything cause you know the truth of everything."

Aletta laughed. "Keeps people honest, Passerapina. They don't lie to the stregare."

Passerapina thought about that a moment, and then: "Why are people so afraid of saying what they mean?"

"Maybe because they're afraid of getting hurt."

"Is that why Nonna and the others tell the truth?"

"I expect so."

"You can't get hurt if you're dead."

"Not that we should look to death as a way to escape getting hurt."

"I think it would be boring to be dead like Nonna."

Aletta laughed. "And why is that?"

"Because it seems all Nonna does is either yabber on and on, or sleep. Or at least I think she's sleeping." She looked up at Aletta. "Do they sleep?"

"I don't think so. I think they're just, well, weary of talking."

"I liked hearing the Ambassador sing."

Aletta smiled, keeping pace with Passerapina's quick shift of conversation. "Why is that?"

"Because he tells the truth when he sings. He's not saying one thing and meaning another."

"It's hard when you're a diplomat," Aletta said.

"Why does it have to be?"

"Because sometimes people get upset at what you might say, so you have to find a way to say things so they won't get angry."

"Like asking someone instead of telling someone?"

Oh yes, this clever girl! "You're learning fast, my little bird."

"He's not very good, you know."

There was no need to ask who. She knew. Passerapina often dropped information about Sylvio like this, just matter-of-factly, as though she'd just received a letter from him. How did they do this? How did these two living people find each other through that overwhelming population?

She swallowed her apprehension, asked, "What makes you say he's not very well?"

Passerapina shrugged. "I don't know. He just sounds, you know, tired."

"He's walked a long way."

The girl nodded. "He's walking at night now. He says children are afraid of him, that mothers warn them he'll come for them if they aren't good."

She could hear Sylvio saying such a thing.

"He says he loves you and that I should go to bed."

Her heart stuttered. She swallowed, watched the girl scramble out of the chair and go to the care of her governess, turned her face toward the open terrace where night stole definition from the day and her thoughts darkened with the loss of light.

He travelled now by night, alone in the company of Simare's ancestors, not well, she knew. Not well at all. She knew he hadn't told her everything the physician said, and the physician was keeping his own counsel, and all of that could only mean there was something very gravely wrong, something Sylvio would go to such lengths to hide from her, to keep her from worry and despair while he went on this impossible pilgrimage. Alone. Utterly alone. She wanted to weep for the desperation of it, for the raw fear that threatened to undo all her carefully schooled rehearsals as the strega and the unquestioning companion upon whom she knew he relied. But she wanted to know. *Gods, Sylvio, what ails you? What have they done to you?*

She caught her breath when her servant announced that the Breenai ambassador wished a word. She paused, considering sending him away. To receive him she should dress again, put on the mask of the strega. When she hesitated further, her servant said, "He is quite insistent, Madonna. I told him you were not receiving guests."

She slumped back into the chair and cradled a cup of wine in her hands. Fine, then. Let him come. Let him see her at her worst. *What care I?*

She gestured her acceptance, took a long drink from the heavy wine, felt sweat bead at her temples. Ó Leannáin bowed when he entered, all feline grace and secrets. It would appear he made no effort about his appearance; he was dressed in a calf-length leine, sandals on his feet, apparently incapable of dealing with the heat and humidity of Almarè's summers, coming as he did from a more northern clime.

"Wine?" she asked.

He nodded, took the chair across from her.

"You gave a spectacular performance this afternoon."

He smiled, a brief lift of the mouth, and by that she measured his agitation. "I needed to see you."

"And I'm being seen." She gestured irritably at the servant to leave off lighting lamps.

"I've just learned we're to sail in two weeks."

She let the wine touch her lips, watched him over the rim up her cup. "The Prima just received word," he said, "from the captain of her flagship." Which would explain why she hadn't learned of this earlier in the day during her regular run of duty. "I thought you'd want to know immediately."

"Thank you," she said, which didn't even begin to encompass how she felt. To sail! To travel home again, to perhaps find the possibility of a life of quietude with her husband and the addition of this child she had taken as her special charge. It was tempting to slip into that life of anonymity, to fill her days with simple tasks, her greatest burden to act as an arbiter of justice for the village assizes. Sylvio could return to the bow-shop. They could raise Passerapina between them.

Such delusions, she thought. As if any of that were now possible. Carmelo still had to be brought to justice, the country healed, the government reassembled and economy kicked and cajoled back into operation.

And what of Sylvio? What was it he concealed from her? What further games did the gods play with a man so deserving of his retirement and rest?

"I gather Violina will be sailing on her flagship," she said.

"She has a vested interest, yes."

"Of course." And so she would have to oversee those preparations as well as her own, remain the strega a little longer.

"Has Passerapina been in touch with the Maestro?" he asked when she offered no further comment.

"Why?'

"I don't seem to be able to find him."

She shrugged, alert to the question inside his question. "He's alive."

"I've always been able to trace him through Aldo."

"And you're saying?"

"That I can no longer find Aldo."

Ah, so we come to the crux of his tension. "Passerapina was in touch just this evening." She studied him in the dim light, reading the way he sat, the way his hands fell in a studied illusion of relaxation; he was anything but, she knew. His tension was palpable to her. To read what he wasn't saying took a few moments, and then she realized this usually guarded man had let down his defences. "I think you better ask me what you really came here to say."

He looked up at her sharply, tossed off his wine – so he *was* distracted – rose and crossed to the open doors of the balcony where he leaned against the frame. She watched him carefully, alert now to his tension, alert now to the reason he sang so well this afternoon. It had been a lens, a focus for everything he now felt.

"I've been thinking since that day in the Senate," he said, "about what Sylvio said regarding a bone-speaker's ability arising from a tie to Simare. It hadn't occurred to me before."

"And why should it now?"

It was some moments before he answered, "Because I have some decisions to make."

"About?"

Again a long pause, his back to her. It occurred to her she had come to think of him as a friend. Over the months they'd been thrown together in many political and social situations, and she'd come to have a grudging respect for his intelligence, his candour, the risks he took in the name of what he felt was just and good. Did she know him? Not really. They'd never discussed matters personal.

"About what I am, and what I'm to do about that."

"You're worried about being perceived as a traitor?"

A pause there, then, "Not really. I can bear that. It's more trying to reconcile why it is I have abilities it seems apparent no Breenai possesses."

Ah, Sylvio's observation. She'd wondered about that at the time, wondered why that comment had been directed to Ó Leannáin.

"May I ask a personal question?" he said.

"Of course. But I may choose not to answer."

He lifted his shoulders in a shrug, still watching the growing darkness. "Do you observe the traditions of Simare?"

"What do you mean exactly?"

"Do you have a shrine with you? Do you have icons of your ancestors, carved from bone, to which you address your thoughts and reverences?"

"Of course."

"Can you hear them?"

"No."

"And that doesn't bother you?"

"No."

"Then how do you know they're listening?"

"How do we know anyone really listens? We choose carefully what to say and to whom we say it, if we've learned anything in life. Why this interest in things Simari?"

"It hadn't seemed of import that my mother never told me who was my father," he said, "that we lived in Breena alone, that as I grew and discovered I had this ability that there were no others who could tell me about what I could hear.

"And then when I started to put the puzzle together, I tried following the paths of the dead to find my own ancestors, and found I couldn't, so assumed I was an aberration. It wasn't until Aldo made his presence known, when I was appointed ambassador, that my suspicions once again came to the fore."

"And you suspect what, exactly?"

"That my father was Simari."

"And the significance of that, beyond the obvious?"

He turned back to her, his face shadowed. "I suppose nothing, really. I've already committed treason." He laughed then, bitterly. "And why should I trifle over treason when I have committed so many other crimes in the name of justice?"

"It's just that you felt being a bone-speaker somehow set you apart, gave you righteous cause."

He dipped his head in acknowledgement.

"And now that you can no longer hear Aldo, you question even that."

Again that gesture of his head. "I almost envy Sylvio."

Her heart tripped through a tattoo again. She found herself on her feet, anger driving her toward him. She hit him hard across the face, a backhanded act of fear and outrage. Envy Sylvio? Envy the fact he'd lost everything? Envy the fact that he laboured to bring to justice a boy-prince whom he loved as his own son, laboured beyond all sensibility and caution for his own health, even his own existence? She would have hit Ó Leannáin again, but that he caught her by the wrist, staring at her, his eyes wide with shock. "How dare you!" she hissed. His eyes narrowed, his face closer, those eyes like lakes. He pulled her toward him, his other arm sliding round her back. She turned her face away, wrenched her wrist from his grasp. "No!" She backed away from him. "No!" In a rush of realization she asserted her training, cleared away her own emotions that had muddied this entire encounter and saw now the extremity of the man, his sense of loss, his loss of control. "You're confused, Maponos. Think. Think!"

He slumped against the door-frame, running his hand over his face, gathered a long, shuddering breath. "Gods, Aletta, forgive me." He looked up at her. "I am not myself."

"You've never had to face this sort of crisis before," she said, trying to retrieve some grace from this moment. "Living a life of absolute certainty has its perils."

"It does."

"You need to think about what you will do when this is all over." And it would be over. One way or another. Sylvio journeyed toward that end.

"New territory for me. I have a niece I need to think about, find a way to protect her from her uncle's infamy. I have a life to rebuild, an identity to find." He looked out to the night. "I suddenly realize I've spent my life weaving webs and left myself marooned, that I'd come to rely upon my gifts and talents to the exclusion of all else."

"A danger we all face. Hasn't it occurred to you the dead with whom you've become comfortable are also distracted? That they, too, bend all their thoughts toward one event only?"

He looked back at her. She could see him smile, that dazzling gesture that could so easily disarm, only now he used it without guile. "I hadn't thought of that, no. What a fool I've been." He shrugged. "It would seem I must beg your forgiveness for many things, Aletta. I have been selfish and more than a little inconsiderate this evening. Who but you would understand the full gravity of what we're all facing? And who but you would bear it all with such grace and silence?"

He crossed the room, touched her cheek. "Sylvio, although he goes to an uncertainty, is a man with many gifts, not the least of which is you." He bowed. "Pardon me for disturbing the peace of your evening." He turned and walked away.

"Maponos," she said. He halted, looked over his shoulder. "I am glad to be counted as a confidant. I fully expect you to be aboard ship with me when we sail for Reena and the Festa de Nerezza." He smiled and left.

Three weeks before the Festa de Nerezza the elders of Danuto met with their Sindaco, Antonio Portelli. They met because their besiegers upped stakes in the night and left, tents, baggage train, foot and horse alike. All that was left were the arcossi with which many of them had been armed, smouldering cook-fires and the question of what had chased them away. No one was sure, exactly. Some of the sentries said they'd seen a strange low-lying cloud surround the mercenary camp, heard cries and sharp orders, and then the army had set off down the road, the cloud following in ragged ribbons.

Hadn't drinking on duty been restricted? What did that matter when the army was gone? But what should they do now?

"I think we should send out a scout," said Portelli. "And while the scout is gone, I think we should prepare an envoy to ride to Reena."

Was he insane – they wanted to know. An envoy? To Reena? What with all these reports of cucullati abroad, of the riots and ruin in Reena. There would be no market this year, that was for damned sure. So why go? Why risk?

"Because we need our own intelligence from the capitol. Because we're not much of a resistance holed up here, and eventually all these people who have come to join us are going to get restless without a besieging army holding them. In fact, I think we should go en masse to Reena. Take our grievances to the Prince, in a show of force."

Madness, plain and simple, but mad enough that they agreed, caught up in their defiance, in their sense of righteous cause, sentiments Portelli did everything to encourage in the days that followed as he ordered, cudgelled and cajoled together a rough lot of artisans and farmers, labourers and professionals, even a number of security types who knew their way around swords and armour. While preparing for this massive march, Portelli received a courier from the next town. There was to be a rendezvous in the capitol. Sylvio himself had ordered it, with him the authority of the ancestors. Directly after that Portelli took news from their scouts: the mercenary army had scattered, some making for the hills to the north, apparently abandoning their units and defecting back to Breena. Others had died in a skirmish that appeared to have had no bloodshed, only dead bodies along the road, faces twisted in horror; it was as if they died of fear. A very reduced number were trickling back to the capitol.

Mayhem, Portelli thought. Utter mayhem and madness had besieged his country. But madness enough that it somehow made sense, if you were Simari, if you knew the bond there was between the living and the dead, and so Portelli took it upon himself to shoulder the mantle of responsibility and do what Sylvio had asked of the entire country.

Go to Reena. With overwhelming numbers. And hold Carmelo accountable.

Grand plans, he thought. He wasn't quite sure how he would manage to undertake all that, but something would occur to him along the way, he hoped. Gods, he hoped.

And so, as he had every year for eleven years, he headed a caravan – this time a motley army – down the broken road to Reena, with hope in his heart, and growing uncertainty in his thoughts. It was a jostling, dusty, noisy travelling village he led, growing as the days passed, stretching for miles along the road and over the verges. This time there were no carts and wagons of merchandise, no herds of horses. Their armed escort had become an entire countryside of insurgents, and they travelled with the swelling hope of justice, bolstered by rumours that ran rampant among them of cucullati abroad, heading toward retribution in Reena.

Rain pelted them and still they marched. Drenching sunlight dried them and they kept to their purpose. They shared provisions. They shared songs. They shared the burdens they had shouldered these long years and found cause and solidarity. Whole refugee camps emptied and gathered in their wake, villages, cities and towns, farmsteads and businesses.

It was a slow, rambling, shambling journey, songs and stories erupting along the length of the populace, the cries of children, squawk and squeal of livestock. And despite himself Portelli found himself buoyed by their conviction, day upon night, night upon day, until finally the red tiled roofs of Reena showed in the distance, the towers and domes of temples and public buildings.

For a moment the clouds of the afternoon parted. Light played over the darkened hulks of buildings that had burned in the riots of last autumn, accusing fingers of stone where there had been homes and studios, the fabric of a city known for its beauty and ancient traditions. From this vantage he could see the enormous obelisk of the Gigantico, its eternal light diminished in the shafts of sunlight. Beyond it, out in the empty harbour, clouds brooded on the horizon. And then as they came closer still, it was apparent the open gates, those works of burnished bronze, hung broken on their hinges. A city in ruin, at its heart the decay that rotted all else.

As a measure of precaution, he sent scouts ahead, to reconnoitre the city. The remainder of his ragged crew he'd encamp outside Reena's walls. Better out here where they had room to manoeuvre, and better a night to finalize their plan of action for tomorrow, for tomorrow was the Festa de Nerezza, and surely the goddess would aid them in bringing her errant son to justice.

In the half-light world Aldo walked he hadn't expected this weariness that forbidden sleep could not abate, or oppression that relief from the community of the dead could have afforded. Dead was dead. Or so he'd thought when blood coursed and breath fed the stuff of thought and life and awareness.

He looked out across the harbour where the Gigantico stood sentry. By now the sun hung low on the horizon. He remembered red and gold, purple and indigo, and failed to find any relation to this grey world. It was getting harder to remember these things: the feel of wind on his face, the sharp smell of the sea, the taste of salt on his tongue. And with that failing sensory world he found he wandered in a dream of the past. Such seduction there. To sink into the easy comfort of what had been and there to find immolation.

But, no. He called up anger. Anger to keep him sane. Anger to keep him here in the now. Anger to drive him to attend this immediate task and those yet to come, those endless tasks yet to come.

Yet how to sit in judgement on his own son? Carmelo who had murdered him and forced him back to half-life, back to this world of grey and memory, to a bleak existence of purpose and infinite days.

He broke trust, the ancestors hissed.
He created abomination.
He defied the gods.

For love of family, Aldo thought. For love of us. Twisted and insane though that love might be, it was for love of his mother and him that Carmelo did what no other had attempted. Brilliant boy.

Pathetic creature. *Gods, what have I made?*

He turned away from the view of the harbour and made his way slowly, with deliberate care, toward the Sala de Pubblico where his son had him summoned. It was difficult to walk, to coordinate a body he no longer felt he commanded. So much of his existence now occupied a place of time and distance instead of here and now. The immediacy of living no longer concerned him, yet he remained engaged. In life he had been a man of duty, and in this half-life it was all that gave him any definition. His duty. To serve his people and his country. And in this, he knew, he was absolved of the horror of abomination. In him he would make this half-life have meaning and honour. It was Sylvio who showed him that. Sylvio who even now gave everything he had in the name of honour and justice.

He heard Carmelo's anger long before he ever arrived at the chamber, felt Carmelo's rising hysteria reverberate through his head. By the time Aldo shuffled into the room his son was in full flight.

"What do you mean they're gone?" Carmelo screamed, his voice echoing in the cavernous space. "They can't be gone!"

Courtiers and officials ranged around the room, affecting studied attitudes of indifference, but their very silence spoke too clearly of their awareness of an unpredictable situation.

Wake up, Sylvio, he thought. *We are soon out of time.*

The mercenary officer stood before the throne of bone, hands on hips, fingering his empty scabbard. "Gone, Principe. My troops are gone. And those accursed Simare bows left to rot. We were brought here to maintain security, not to fight ghosts."

Aldo watched understanding stiffen his son's face.

I warned you, Aldo said. *But you never listen.*

Carmelo let out a growl of frustration. "Then why didn't you maintain the siege with the force you had remaining?"

"With a few score? I'm not about to put my troops at risk."

Carmelo leaned forward on the throne. "But that's what we pay you for!"

"Not anymore. In fact not for some time."

"Get out!" He thrust himself up from the throne, flew down from the dais. "I don't need you! Get out!"

The officer bowed and backed away, a smirk on his face.

Carmelo whirled to the courtiers, to the ministers and servants of high office. "Who's in charge of security these days?"

One of the senators stepped forward from the crowd, bowed. "You appointed yourself, Principe."

Carmelo checked his anger, his mouth working, then, "Can no one give me word as to the situation in Danuto?"

"There is an encampment outside the city's gates," the senator answered, now quite isolated from the other courtiers who had given themselves some distance.

"What? And they're what? Just camped? Preparing to enter for the market? For the Festa?"

"We don't know, Principe."

"Then send someone to find out."

Aldo now crossed the floor and stood beside his son. *There is no market this year.*

Carmelo spun toward him, his face blotched with anger. "What do you mean there's no market this year?"

You've stripped them of everything. There's no market. They come to petition you, and to bring you to justice.

"Justice? Me?" He laughed loudly, turning to the court. "They come to judge me. I, the Prince of Nerezza. I who am their lawful ruler."

You who have betrayed every sacred trust.

Carmelo turned back to Aldo. For a moment Aldo thought his son would strike him, would finally release him from this endless misery. He wished it. Gods, how he wished it. "We'll let Nerezza decide if I have failed the gods, shall we?" With that he turned and stalked through the door behind the throne that led to private chambers.

Aldo watched him go, knew he should give the boy time to cool. But there was no time for Carmelo. As it was he'd delayed too long, allowed the country to teeter on the brink of disaster. With a gesture he dismissed the court, listening to the grumbles of senators who accused him of doing nothing, heard their frustration, their fear. Most of all he heard their fear.

He heard Sylvio then, clear and harsh: *Bring them all to Nerezza tomorrow.*

Fog trailed through camp when Portelli received the steward he'd left behind a year ago. Calvino walked with a more pronounced stoop now, shockingly thin, this year of hardship and privation showing clearly on his face. He smiled now, bowing to his former employer.

"I cannot stay long, Padrone. I've been sent by Aldo."

Portelli gestured him toward the fire, poured coffee for the man. "What news?"

Calvino slurped, hugging the mug under his chin. "A ship from Almarè's in the roads, flying the flag of the Prima. Aldo says Dona Aletta and Ambassador Ó Leannáin are aboard. The Maestro is already at the temple. We are to be there for the Festa. It is what the Maestro has instructed."

"The Maestro? You've seen him?"

"No, Padrone. He sent word to Aldo."

"Has he said why we're to be at the temple?"

"No, Padrone."

No. But certainly there was to be some manner of accounting this evening. The arcossi they'd brought with them, scavenged from that eerie exodus of besiegers, had been untouchable since they made camp outside Reena's walls. Ancestral icons people carried with them seemed to shout with long-forgotten voices. And now Sylvio back from the dead as it were and gathering everyone for the Festa. It was as if the world were preparing for a night of madness.

He and Calvino exchanged other general news, catching up on the year since they'd last seen one another, trying to piece together some sense of what had happened. By the time the fog dissipated Calvino made his apologies and headed back into the city. Portelli turned his attention to the ragged hoard encamped around him, a veritable city come to lay their protests at Carmelo's feet. He gave orders to the trusted team he'd assembled along the way, essentially councilmen and leaders who had left their homes in an overwhelming act of civil disobedience. They would assemble at the Temple of Nerezza and see what accounting Sylvio would force upon his prince.

By the time Aletta reached the Castello the annual peregrination to the Temple of Nerezza had begun, and were it not for the fact she knew this city and knew these rituals she would have failed to recognize Reena. It laid a ruin around her, nearly brought her to tears. There wasn't a litter to be had, not a horse to be hired. People starved, livestock all butchered. They were working their way through the dogs, cats and rats now, watching with hard faces as she passed with an armed escort from Almarè. Violina had turned her face to her several times, outrage there for anyone to see. Passerapina clung to Aletta's hand, beside her Ó Leannáin who pushed Violina's wheelchair.

Aletta felt obscene walking through these desperate streets, she with her fine silks and gold embellishments.

"There are so many ancestors here!" Passerapina whispered. "So many!"

"I know," Ó Leannáin answered. "Hush now, child."

There were no pedlars when they finally entered the Via de Dios. No puppet shows. No noise and clamour. Only the poor begging for alms, the starving staring from alleys while Carmelo led a painted and perfumed entourage along the avenue, songs and gongs marking his passage. And then they came upon people better fed and the crowds became denser, accusations rising with the dust of their passage.

And something else there, a quivering, a shifting of the light that made you think there were heat devils or mirages, and something so oppressive in the air it was like a weight upon the body, a pressure on the brain.

"He's here!" Passerapina cried. "He's here, Madonna, he's here!"

"Basta, pupetta," Aletta said, glanced down at this enigmatic child, back up to the crowds who now pressed upon them.

"Traditore!" they cried. "Feccio traditore!"

Aletta glanced over to Ó Leannáin. "Can you hear him?" she asked.

He nodded, his face, usually so mobile and beguiling, was a mask of concentration, his gaze darting about. "Him and the dead who are legion. Gods, what has he done?"

She tried to see ahead to Carmelo but could not, tried to take a reading but was overwhelmed. By the time they reached the red steps of the temple it was as if the world were poised to scream. Behind Carmelo she mounted the steps, her hand tight around Passerapina's. Others assisted Violina up the stairs in her chair. A path cleared for them. From within the temple plainsong spilled, achingly pure, out of place in this moment of madness. She stepped inside the coolness of the temple, blinded for a moment by the contrast between the bright day and this dim interior. The fragrance of myrrh washed over her. The tiny hairs on her arms stood out. She shivered.

Just as Carmelo raised his arms to undress before the goddess, acolytes arrayed around him, a voice called from the recesses of that gargantuan effigy of Nerezza.

"You are not fit to present yourself. You are called into judgement."

Sylvio's voice was as good as a brake. Everything stilled. No one breathed. Fear was palpable. He felt it from all of them. And there were the dead here with him, cries in his head, shimmers at the periphery of vision like eddies of smoke from the censers swooping overhead.

"Who dares judge me?" Carmelo asked, his arms still up-raised, a figure of mythology where he stood in a shaft of light. The acolytes hung back, looking into the dimness where Sylvio stood. And there, beyond him, ranged the red-cloaked figures of Simare's cucullati, silent and waiting.

"The ancestors of Simare judge you," Sylvio answered, and stepped out from the shadow of Nerezza. He heard the assemblage gasp, but his attention was only for Carmelo, beautiful creature, twisted boy. Carmelo's face was unreadable in the dimness, kohl around his dark eyes, the ivory and gold plaques of the bone crown utterly still where they framed his cheeks and jaw. Slowly Carmelo lowered his arms, the heavy folds of embroidered silk falling down over his arms to rest against hands that glittered with rings.

Sylvio took a few slow steps toward Carmelo, halted in a shaft of light from the clerestory windows of the dome. It didn't matter to him that he was blinded by the light. Nothing Carmelo could do now would harm him. The ancestors assured him of his safety, and of Carmelo's peril. Still, he kept the hood of his cloak drawn around his face, brought Aldo's staff before him, set both hands upon the elegantly carved head.

"We have travelled long and far to bring you here," Sylvio said. "And now, before these witnesses, we shall pass our judgement."

He watched as Carmelo recognized the staff, watched as the Prince turned his attention to Aldo, watched as suspicion and then fear washed over his features.

"Sylvio," he whispered, looking back at him. "You were exiled."

"And now I'm returned." Gods how he wanted this moment to pass by, how he wanted to step off the path of necessity and duty and let someone else bring about this terrible justice he was about to mete. "And with me the ancestors."

Carmelo's fingers trembled when he touched the bone of the crown on his head, his mouth working. "But, I –"

"Cannot hear them? I know. They've abandoned you. Or didn't you realize?" He gathered a deep breath, let it go, swept his attention over the room, trying to pierce the dimness and find faces he knew, to no avail. He was alone, as alone he knew he would have to be. "But they will speak to you now as they pass judgement." And with a rush like air filling a vacuum he heard the ancestors descend upon Carmelo, who staggered, his mouth open, his eyes wide with horror.

Betrayer! Traitor! Destroyer!

"Because it was out of love." Sylvio said, "that you attempted to raise up your mother from the dead, the dead mitigate your sentence. Because it was out of love that you succeeded in raising your father from the dead, the dead mitigate your sentence. Because it was out of love that you exiled me, the dead mitigate your sentence."

Those veils of smoke gathered now around Carmelo, sweeping around his legs, his arms, around his head and body, their calls like the chittering of dry leaves, stuttering, insidious. *Dopo di noi. Dopo di noi. Follow us.*

"No! Please!" Carmelo batted at the air, his face twisted. People in the temple backed away, their silence complete, a counterpoint to the hoard that howled in the heads of those who could hear, and remained a susurration to those who couldn't.

With all his heart, despite everything Carmelo had done, Sylvio wanted to spare the boy what was about to happen, this ugly, terrible fate. "And so," he continued, "to ensure no one will again disrupt the balance we keep here in Simare, the ancestors have decreed that no longer will the country be ruled by you and you alone, nor by any crowned head of state. Simare shall become a republic of the living and the dead, so that the living will keep the balance of hope and optimism, create the current that carries us forward, while the dead shall offer guidance and the wisdom of the ages. Simare will be able to rule in the present by looking to our past, and ahead to our future."

Carmelo sank to his knees, weeping, pleading, begging forgiveness, his gaze darting about him at the veils that swept around him. Still the censers swung ponderously, spilling sweetness into the horror of the temple, and impossibly that clear, young voice still sang the call to the Goddess that was their patron, Pie Nerezza rising with the incense.

Relentlessly, Sylvio continued, his heart aching, now pacing forward to stand over Carmelo. "And so for the living there shall be a senate elected by the people, a representative from each district, to convene daily in the Sala de Pubblico where the good governance of our country will be deliberated and legislated. It is within the Senate, this elected body, that the governance and order of Simare shall be kept. And for the dead," and he turned his attention out into the room, blinded as he was by the light falling around him, "there shall be a triumvirate of the living-dead who shall act as conduits and advisors. Abomination as we have known them. Legend come to life. But, hear me, Simari, the living dead are abomination only to themselves, walking as they do in the middle-world, the verge between life and death. They are our living link to the ancestors, to their wisdom and guidance. You all know this to be true. It is why we carry our ancestors' icons with us when we travel, why we light incense to them in the altars in our homes. " A murmur of ascent through the assemblage, a sense of calm. Good. Yes. This spoke to the very heart of what it meant to be Simari.

"And so," he continued, "to this end, to keep with us the wisdom of the ancestors, the former Principe Aldo Valerio shall be named to the triumvirate." And at that Aldo crossed the floor and stood beside Sylvio, cloaked and hooded in like fashion, a figure in red, a staff which Sylvio had come to realize during his long journey was fashioned from Aldo's beloved wife's bone, made to look like the one Sylvio carried.

"Papa!" Carmelo cried, reaching to his father. "Papa, please!"

"And as punishment," Sylvio said, again capturing Carmelo's attention, "to teach you to listen, to teach you the lessons and statesmanship you should have dispensed to your people, you, Carmelo Valerio, Il Principe di Simare, will join the triumvirate."

There was a moment of outrage among those assembled, cries of Carmelo's betrayal, of his inability to govern in life, and expected inability to advise in some half-life.

Sylvio raised his hand against their objections, brought them to quiet. Only the sound of Carmelo's weeping pervaded the temple. "Let us not forget it is an advisory triumvirate. Carmelo will learn, whether he likes it or not. Time and inevitability have ways of teaching us all."

Another murmur ran through the crowd, seemingly lifting and falling with the cantor who still sang Nerezza's blessings.

Sylvio leaned down and touched the boy's shoulder, gently, with care, for he did not wish this, found this sentence harsh beyond reason. But Sylvio had drawn others this way, assisted them from life to death. This time the ancestors who were gathered would bar the way, prevent Carmelo from dying and hold him in thrall, cast him into the half-world of the living-dead as Carmelo had cast his father. Carmelo screamed then, a long, shattering cry that brought tears to Sylvio's eyes, and a hard thump to his heart. The cantor reached the climax of the invocation, one seemingly endless, clear note that pealed through the dome, beneath that what sounded like the chittering of leaves on stone. Sylvio let Carmelo go just as he felt the boy's spirit depart. The ancestors engulfed him.

If a man were honest, he would admit he wanted no part in this. If a man were honest, he'd admit to wanting to flee up to those mountains of ice that had changed his life forever. Gods, how the boy screamed! Would he never stop? And then he did, his thrashing frozen, a battered young man in the prime of his life, pale as bone in a pool of light, there at Sylvio's feet. The cantor fell silent. And still that dry rasping of leaves echoing through the chamber, the veils of grey slowing, stilling, rising up to the censers.

Sylvio heard a child cry then, a soft sound of heartache in this temple of death.

Movement from Carmelo, a twitch of the hand, then an arm stiffly raised, eyes opened and staring up into the dome where light flooded.

Come, Sylvio thought, and with effort Carmelo raised himself, one foot, another step, standing between his father and his mentor.

"And so," Sylvio said, for the benefit of the living, "That leaves but one seat on the triumvirate." If a man were honest. "Which the ancestors have decreed I, Sylvio di Danuto, am to fill."

At that the crowd erupted. *Not di Danuto! Not the Maestro! Not di Danuto!*

And a child was suddenly at his knee, her sobs bitter and wracking. "Please, no! No! Don't take him! Nonna! Nonna! Make them stop!" He bent to her, this small package of bravery and brightness.

"Passerapina, aspetta."

She flung her arms around him, pushing the hood from his face, which brought a gasp from the assembly, her tears hot upon his cheek. "Madonna Aletta and I have travelled so far to be with you! I want to live with you both! Don't leave me! Don't go now that I have found you! Please, please, please…."

And if a man were honest he would prefer to deny this terrible burden of responsibility and country and duty. If a man were honest with himself he would admit he wanted to take this child and his wife whom he loved more than breath, and find some solace somewhere in the world.

But if a man were honest with himself he'd acknowledge that to deny his responsibility to this country he loved and these people he served would haunt him forever so that he would deserve the painting of shame he wore.

"I have to go," he said, thumbing her cascade of tears. "And it's not like I won't be here. You can talk to me anytime, even if you're somewhere else, just like you can with your nonna."

She pulled away, hiccoughing sobs. "But it won't be the same." She looked over at Aldo, pointed an accusing finger at him. "He couldn't talk to me except like Nonna."

He put his hand over hers, balling her fingers into his palm. "He didn't ask to be cucullatus. I go willingly."

"No you don't!" another voice rang out. Sylvio rose from Passerapina, watching as a man approached through light and shadow, light and shadow and stood beside him, looking down first upon Passerapina, then up to Sylvio. This was a man he would have called comrade in another life, a familiar soul who shared a similar burden of the dead as he, who had risked everything for a country he'd not known as his own until recently. "I cannot let you do this," Ó Leannáin said. He raised his face to the dome, as if seeking out the dead. "I cannot let you do this. Do you hear me?"

Sylvio shook his head, feeling the pressure of the ancestors around him, listening to the siren call of his own father. "How can I deny them?"

"You're not. I'm offering myself in your stead."

"No!" Gods! How many to suffer for the things he had failed to address? "No! I will not allow it!"

"And who are you to allow or deny?" Ó Leannáin turned his face back up to the dome, raising his arms. "I offer myself. Let him live. Let him serve the living. Let me go to the ancestors I never knew." At that the shimmering mass of the host enfolded him, caressing this time. Aldo raised his arm, touched the man. Ó Leannáin gasped, his eyes wide for a moment, closed and then he staggered, doubled over, clutched Sylvio's shoulder, and he, Sylvio, let his tears fall for the noble man who had gone beyond, took him into his embrace and spoke of love, of gratitude, of a debt he would honour for this gift of the few years left to him. The host retreated.

"Yes," Ó Leannáin whispered. "Yes. I understand now." He straightened, that same unfocused look to his eyes as Aldo and now Carmelo, as though he saw into a place that had no horizon. He took the staff in Sylvio's hands into his own, leaned on it, shuffled a few tentative steps to stand beside Aldo and Carmelo. The triumvirate. The cucullati of Simare.

Sylvio couldn't find enough air to breathe, pulled Passerapina against him, his hand like a shield upon her tiny shoulder. He could feel her breath quick and sharp. Life there. He inhaled again. Life. Looked out into the crowd, trying to find Aletta. Life.

"And so the ancestors have passed judgement," he said, trying to keep his voice steady. "Nerezza is appeased."

To his astonishment the silence in the chamber exploded into cheers and he found himself a touchstone of joy.

That evening, as the sun descended, the lights for the dead filled the waterways and the evanescence of the host that had come to bring Carmelo to justice swept out into the harbour.

In the weeks and months that followed, Sylvio put into action all the decrees of the Cucullati. Ó Leannáin and Aldo worked around the clock, keeping Carmelo to a strict regimen, teaching him despite himself. There were problems. But they were overcome. Election results streamed into the Castello. New senators arrived, hammered out a system of government, among them Antonio Portelli, who with his booming voice and wry humour became somewhat of a counsellor and mentor to the men and women who were to govern with the three unsleeping Cucullati. And as government departments were revised and revamped, the Senate appointed Vincenze Mambelli as head of security, but not before he'd wed that sloe-eyed Pina who had lost Donato to the ravages of this past year. She kept the brewery, and hired a manager for when she travelled with Vincenze. And Vincenze himself was delirious with work and joy, a far cry from the ragged ranger who used to spy the Breenai Pass and gather spider's silk for angeli strings.

Relief aid came in from Almarè and elsewhere, and despite Sylvio's reluctance to bring an army into the country, peace-keepers were placed at the Breenai Pass and ships patrolled the international waters just outside Simare's. It would be some months yet before world pressure brought Breena's expansionist policies to heel, but they would be checked. That was a certainty.

In the capitol the air rang with the sound of hammers and industry – a city rebuilding itself – and there wasn't a major thoroughfare that didn't have crews sweating through repairs. It would all take time, but certainly by spring agriculture could again bloom across the land.

The assize courts once again dispensed justice. Roads were policed. At the close of winter the first tentative markets raised gaudy awnings and hawked pots and treen, butter and cheese, cloth and trinkets. All left for Sylvio to do was to make that long journey home, back to Danuto, and reclaim his ancestral estates for which Portelli had returned the deed.

"Go and retire," Portelli had said over wine and a fire in the hearth against winter rains.

But retire to what, he'd wondered. Certainly Aletta waited for him, Passerapina with her, and apparently now Ó Leannáin's niece they'd smuggled out of Breena, fulfillment of a promise Sylvio had made that fateful day. It would seem he was to raise a family after all. The Cucullati urged him to open a school with Aletta, to teach the arts of the stregare and the bone-speakers, so that Simare could harness what seemed to be gifts unique to this land.

So it was that Sylvio found himself on the road once more, riding this time in comfort and without consideration for time, pausing at inns where he was met with exuberance. The Painted Man come to stay at their humble hostelry. Everywhere he went he was known, now in celebration of what he had achieved and what he had endured, so that the tattoos with which he'd been branded now served as a record of history, even of honour, it would seem.

Nonsense, all of it. He'd done what he had to do, and although he accepted their accolades with as much grace as he could muster, their deference to him sat heavily on his conscience.

Vincenze insisted he travel with a small escort. Aldo had pressed upon him the physician Pisano, who had returned to

Simare specifically seeking out Sylvio. He was watered, fed, clothed and cosseted and near ready to explode in a fit of frustration. But, were he honest with himself, he'd admit he was grateful for their care. He was weary to the core, waking sluggishly in the mornings, a general malaise that increased as time progressed.

During that journey he'd dozed during an afternoon break more than once, rocked by the voices of the dead who sang to him, eased him into dreams in the fragrance of an olive grove, or the shade of cypress by a gurgling stream.

Rest now, my son, his father would say. *You have done your duty.*

But there's so much left to do.

Let others take that responsibility, Aldo said.

And again Sylvio would slide into slumber, too tired to argue, too relieved to struggle.

Then finally, in the gentle warmth of a spring evening, with insects floating like gold dust over the road, the mound that was Danuto rose before him, banners blowing from wooden ramparts now giving way to stone. The banners were his own. The people who waved from the heights and ran from the gates were familiar, bringing with them ribbons and tambourines, a jostling, laughing, singing crowd come to welcome home their lost son.

He found himself swallowing a lump in his throat, reaching down from his horse to touch a hand, accept a cup. They sang and danced him up the winding streets, past the village well, the bakery, the tavern run by Vincenze's wife; they climbed through crowds, through showers of petals to the gate of his home, one he'd not called his own for over a decade, and promised him a proper welcome once he was settled. As if that weren't proper welcome enough. Gods, a man could be embarrassed by all this attention. The gates closed behind him. Ostlers and servants rushed into the courtyard, commands and welcomes racketing in a confusion of homecoming.

It was all here, the courtyard well-swept, the cobbles repaired, the fig tree in the centre seated like bunched fingers into the earth. Off to this left the stables, to the right offices which fronted lodgings for servants, and in the middle the long loggia that led into a home that had been in his family for generations.

A voice cried, "Sylvio! Sylvio!" and he turned in the saddle to find a girl racing toward him with dark hair tied up in ribbons, a gown of good fustian on her small body. He grabbed Passerapina's hand and hauled her up into the saddle with him, accepting her kisses and laughter, finding laughter himself, something he hadn't done for so long it felt strange and like a bark in his throat.

There across the courtyard a woman he assumed was Passerapina's governess, her look stern but belied by the crinkles around her eyes and she strode the cobbles and gathered the girl back to some form of decorum. He slid from the saddle, allowing people to take care of matters for him, and just stood there, looking across to the fig tree where Aletta stood – the wife, not the strega – her hair a tumble around her shoulders, the lines at her mouth and eyes a little deeper but lifted in joy.

He allowed the hood of his cloak to slide from his bald, painted head, closed the distance between them and stood there, unsure if he should hold her as he longed to, if he should speak, as he found himself incapable. He remembered another time they stood beneath this fig tree, some three decades past, both of them young and passionate. There had been rain. And figs as a blessing to their union, sweet as her mouth, sweet as the rain, and the thunder which might have been his heart or might have been the sky.

"I'm not staying," he said. He watched her blink, her eyes widen. She gestured impatiently to the people in the courtyard and they disappeared into stables and doorways. The quiet that enveloped them revealed the painful thud of his heart. He could hear her breathing, the piping of birds. Somewhere in the stables someone cursed elegantly.

"Why ever not?" she said, her dark eyes scanning him, a frown drawing those black, arched brows together.

"I've come home to give you all this, Aletta." He gestured to their surroundings. Suddenly there wasn't enough air to breathe.

You're being a fool, his father said, Aldo offering an agreement and with him Ó Leannáin. Even Carmelo was there, tentatively, urging Sylvio to find peace where he had not.

Leave off! I will not do this to her!

"You're telling me you're divorcing me?" she said.

He nodded. Gods, how to do this?

Then don't!

"Don't make me break my promise to you," she said, her voice lower. "Don't make me be the strega with you."

He bowed his head then, unsure if he could say what he had to, could get through this without weeping like the child he felt. "I have a disease, Innamorata," he whispered.

"So we'll get a physician."

"I have a physician. The best, in fact. This is incurable."

She inhaled sharply. "What caused this?"

He looked up at her, touched her cheek, traced her lips. "Jewels I thought would make a beautiful adornment for you." She let out an exasperated cry. "Assassin beetles. They often feed on open wounds, and I had a few."

"So you're telling me you're going to die."

"Yes."

She laughed then, touched his face, laughed again, tears wet on her cheeks. "And this changes what, exactly?"

"I won't have you fretting over a dying man."

"Did it never occur to you this might have happened anyway? That we're all born to die? Sylvio, don't be foolish."

You see, your wife agrees!

And then he felt her lips on his, his heart beating like a bird set free, and knew he'd come home at last.

Afterword

This is the first new novel I've written since *Shadow Song*, which makes it easily 16 years since I last put fingers to keyboard to create a work of fiction. It wasn't so much that I had writer's block, more that the recession of the Nasty Nineties desiccated all my efforts and resources, so that it was difficult to justify funds spent on paper and postage for submissions when Gary and I were trying to keep a roof over our heads and food on the table for two wonderful adolescent children.

Then the turn of the Millennium and with it dramatic changes in the publishing world and publishing technologies. The publishing world closed ranks. Legacy houses weren't considering new authors, and especially not authors sans agent. Agencies weren't considering new authors, especially not authors without a track record.

Publishing technologies developed methods to address fast, inexpensive printing methods that would allow publishers to escape from the financial burden of offset print runs, warehousing and distribution. Digital printing made an entry, and with it global distribution made possible because of the miracle of the Internet.

Legacy houses were, and still are, slow to respond. Independents, however, like me, saw an opportunity to circumnavigate the fortress that had become publishing, and find a direct route to the marketplace and readers.

What does all this have to do with the fact I hadn't written a new novel in 16 years? Everything. Now, with the ability to reach the marketplace in a meaningful way, and thereby readers, there was no reason to put off writing. *And the Angels Sang* and *Shadow Song* both were doing very well because of my venture into publishing and print on demand technologies, and so I launched into writing *From Mountains of Ice* in the fall of 2008.

The novel greatly changed from the original outline drafted in the '90s, and took on this Italianate milieu (perhaps a return to my own roots), with an overriding theme of a reverence for the dead. The inclusion of the cucullati in the novel was a serendipitous discovery, sparked by a comment from an acquaintance, Catherine Crowe, who is a gifted enamellist (http://www.imagocorvi.com/), that she had just created her own cucullati. What I discovered as a result of her comment fit the mourning and death rituals of my novel so well it was as though a muse had dropped this into my world.

For archery and other cultural aspects of the novel, I drew heavily from the following books:

Toxophilus -the School Of Shooting, Roger Ascham
Longbow: A Social and Military History, Robert Hardy
Roman Cultural and Society: the Collected Papers of Elizabeth Rawson, Elizabeth Rawson
The Medieval Archer, Jim Bradbury
Book of Archery 1840, Agar Hansard George Agar Hansard
The Merchant of Prato, Iris Origo
The Travels of Marco Polo, Marco Polo

Ishi in Three Centuries, Karl Kroeber

Pirate Skulls and Crossbones Tattoos, Jeff A Menges

Tattoo: Bodies, Art and Exchange in the Pacific and the West, Nicholas Thomas

There were, of course, musical influences that helped me create mood and tension. You may find this compilation of interest:

The Serpent's Egg, Dead Can Dance

Spiritchaser, Dead Can Dance

Karma, Delirium

Totemic Flute Chants, Johnny Whitehorse

Gladiator (Soundtrack from the Motion Picture), Hans Zimmer

Pan's Labyrinth (Soundtrack from the Motion Picture) Javier Navarrete

Russian Easter, St. Petersburg Chamber Choir

Canto Gregoriano, Benedictine Monks of Santo Domingo

Throughout this journey I have to thank my family for their indefatigable support, most especially my daughter, Kelly, who listened to every character shift, plot change, cultural inclusion gave valuable, impartial feedback and encouraged me through every difficult moment.

I'd be remiss if I didn't thank my proof-readers: Mike Aragona, and most especially Robert Runte whose insight and perspicacity are a treasure to me, as is his friendship.

What's next? I'm outlining another novel, to be called *The Rose Guardian*. All I can tell you is it a dark, modern fairytale in the tradition of the Brothers Grimm and Pan's Labyrinth. I'll be working on it over the course of the next year. We'll see where that journey takes us all.

Lorina Stephens

June 2009

Other Books by Lorina Stephens

Touring the Giant's Rib: A Guide to the Niagara Escarpment, Boston Mills Press
Recipes of a Dumb Housewife, Lulu Publishing
Shadow Song, Five Rivers Chapmanry
And the Angels Sang, Five Rivers Chapmanry

Coming 2010
The Rose Guardian, Five Rivers Chapmanry

Visit Lorina Stephens & Five Rivers Chapmanry at:
http://www.5rivers.org